THE BELTANE MASSACRE

THE BELTANE MASSACRE

RAY CRITCH

BREAKWATER
P.O. Box 2188, St. John's, NL Canada A1C 6E6
WWW.BREAKWATERBOOKS.COM

ISBN 9781778530531
9781778530548 (ePUB)
a CIP catalogue record for this book is available from Library and Archives Canada
COVER IMAGES: Shutterstock AI image / Yogesh Pedamkar
IMAGE PAGE 261 : Rook (Berserker), Lewis Chess Piece, National Museums of Scotland, Edinburgh
AUTHOR PHOTO: Jason Drake
PAGE LAYOUT: Nadine Hodder

We acknowledge the support of the Canada Council for the Arts. We acknowledge the financial support of the Government of Canada through the Department of Heritage and the Government of Newfoundland and Labrador through the Department of Tourism, Culture, Arts and Recreation for our publishing activities.

PRINTED AND BOUND IN CANADA.

Breakwater Books is committed to choosing papers and materials for our books that help to protect our environment. To this end, this book is printed on recycled paper that is certified by the Forest Stewardship Council®.

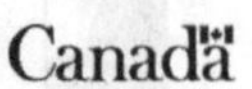

"For a while now he'd known the truth—
that it wasn't so much the underworld you had to fear
but the overworld."

—Ian Rankin

PROLOGUE

Even on the first of May, when the days are beginning to stretch toward summer, Edinburgh celebrates with fire. Just as with Hogmanay in the darkest part of winter, on the evening of Beltane, everyone in the crowd gathered outside St. Giles' Cathedral carried torches and followed two volunteers dressed as the May Queen and the Green Man, whose arrival signals the beginning of summer. Smoke from a thousand small fires stretched out to the east, pushed by a gentle wind, obscuring the stars and filling the square with the smell of melting wax.

The throng that stretched out behind them included a wider variety of costumes than any Halloween ever could. Thousands of people, all carrying fire, and yet it was the most orderly mob you'd ever see. Among the loincloth-wearing dancers with bodies painted in red, the college kids in medieval armour, and dozens of women in white dresses crowned by elm, oak, and poplar wreaths, no one noticed the man dressed as a monk, doing his best to repress a scowl until he realized that no one was watching. With everyone in costume, everyone is hidden.

The monk's thoughts were dark: St. Giles'; hardly a cathedral. This church, built in the style of the One True Faith from before discord and division, had been shrouded in darkness for hundreds of years. Now it focused more on Scottish power and independence and little on the unity that would be brought by submission to the One.

He hated everything about this. There was no real history to it; Beltane as it was being celebrated here was a debauched shadow of the rite that had long been wiped from the face of the earth by the One True Church from when it reigned imperious over the world it was beginning to civilize. But here in Scotland, long a haven of heresy and spiritual confusion, paganism was once again returning to the earth. Now, as before, it must be fought, even if his church no longer had the stomach for it.

He would fight.

Even through sulphur from the burning torches, Rowan McRae could smell change in the air. This was his third Beltane in Edinburgh, where he was in the final stages of his PhD. He hadn't even wanted to go to the first one. Never much for crowds, he nonetheless got dragged along by his wife, Lynn, and a few of their grad school friends. Admittedly, he was curious. While he'd read about the legends of Beltane in a few novels, he'd never expected to encounter it in the modern world.

Among the ancient Celts and Picts of Scotland, this was a fertility festival, marking the lengthening days and the coming of summer. It was believed to bring about abundance and growth, with cattle brought through a pair of bonfires to bless them with the sacred smoke. The modern version involved one bonfire and, in Edinburgh, a lot less cattle, but nonetheless the fire was key. It was the centrepiece of Beltane, just like the burning log was to the midwinter Yule festival. In the Edinburgh tradition, the modern Beltane celebrated the rebirth of the Green Man and the May Queen who, together, light the bonfire, bringing a blessed summer.

For Lynn, Beltane was a spiritual experience. Two generations removed from Glasgow, which her granddad had left for the colder but drier winters of Toronto, she gravitated to the pagan side of Beltane with a fervour only a member of the diaspora could bring. Rowan couldn't blame her. While some of his ancestors had emigrated from here to Ulster, and then on to eastern Canada a couple of hundred years before hers, he still felt an inexplicable and immediate sense of being at home among the ancient grey stone buildings and colourfully named alleys in a place he had not known until a few years ago.

If their first year was an exploration, by the second both of them were joyful participants. Rowan marched and Lynn danced in the parade until they met up at a spot on the far side of the unfinished National Monument to the Scottish nation and made love on a small patch of grass mere metres away from other revellers. Their son, Harris, was born nine months later in early 2018, further convincing Lynn of Beltane's potent force as a fertility festival.

With their three-month-old, Scottish-born son, they prepared to walk in the parade once again, but this time as a family. They met with friends at the Heart of Midlothian, an arrangement of cobblestones meant to mark both the centre of Edinburgh and to remember those who died in the gallows that once stood near the spot. Lynn told Rowan it was particularly important for the local pagan community that they start near here, since many of their spiritual ancestors would have been executed for their faith in the same place, or in nearby Grassmarket, centuries before. For Rowan, it was a welcome return to such an important part of their time in the city, which was now coming to a close. He had defended his dissertation only a week before, and with a position lined up in London, he was far from certain when they'd next be back.

One of the first things Rowan realized about Edinburgh was that the city will celebrate anything and everything with a festival. Established book, film, jazz, fringe, international, and multicultural festivals stood alongside more informal celebrations of Samhain, Hogmanay, and, of course, Beltane.

It was always remarkable to him that there was so little trouble when there was so much fire around. A couple of thousand people carrying torches was worrisome at first, but every year the parade made its way down the Mound and across to Princes Street without incident. From there, it was a mere ten-minute walk to Calton Hill, but the front of the parade was already reaching the three-storey-high effigy of a stag when Rowan, with Harris on his chest, came past the National Gallery, several blocks away. When pushed by the crowd up to the steps of the Balmoral Hotel, he could see the telltale smoke rising from the pathway and beginning to collect around the monuments atop the hill.

By the time they reached the top of the hill, the fire was well in progress. The lower reaches were in a full roar, while the flames were beginning to spread, forming a second set of antlers for the burning stag.

"My turn," Lynn said. Up to that point, Harris had been sound asleep in a carrier on Rowan's chest. "I want to introduce him to the fire."

The sound of his mother's voice seemed to stir him, so Rowan reached down, lifted his son gently, and passed the squirming bundle to Lynn.

She gave Rowan a raised-eyebrows glance to ask if he wanted to come too, though she knew he found the heat of the bonfire uncomfortable. "I'll stay here," he replied. "I want a few minutes to soak all this in."

She kissed him gently and quickly before turning with Harris and bouncing their way toward the bonfire, while Rowan let his focus broaden to take in as much of the scene as he could. Hundreds of revellers, fewer than at the start but almost all in costume, danced around the burning stag.

The three years they had spent in this city had been the best years of Rowan's life. When they came from Canada, he was still only a few years out from his time in the military and was only beginning to process what he'd been through in Afghanistan. As a military intelligence officer, he was responsible for liaising between Canadian, British, and American forces, assessing threats and risks, finding ways to keep as many as possible of their side alive, doing as little damage to the civilians as they could, while also eliminating threats before they happened.

When his time ended, he took advantage of the promised college tuition and turned to history. His knack for interpreting evidence and understanding the forces that once made people tick caught his professors' attention. Coming from a former British colony and spending his wartime in another country on the borders of the Empire also gave him a keen interest in the effects of colonization on different parts of the world. His writing, however, needed a lot of work. His professors referred him to the Writing Centre where he met the stunning redhead who would become his wife.

Before their sessions, Lynn was wary of him purely on spec. She had worked before with plenty of former servicemen trying their hand at college—and college girls. But this one was different. While he was interested in her, he was also genuinely trying to become a stronger writer and put in the work. Between sessions, he worked on his papers, and his writing improved quickly. By the end of their second semester working together, they'd developed a good rapport and had gotten to know each other enough to be genuine friends. When he invited her for a drink at the end of the term, she decided to give him a chance.

The next year, when he got into the master's program, they went out for dinner to celebrate. With a ring inherited from his late mother, he proposed. He was an only child, and his parents had died when he was in high school in Newfoundland, so Rowan and Lynn were married in a small ceremony attended by his aunt and uncle, Lynn's family, and their friends.

Their life together would be an adventure, they said, and it was. In the second year of his program, a few months after their wedding, he got funding to do a PhD in history. She was in training to be a curator and was having difficulty finding meaningful work. So, between his course and her Scottish roots, Edinburgh seemed a perfect choice. While her granddad would probably have disagreed, there were more museums there than in Glasgow anyway.

Lost in his memories of the preceding years, celebrating all they had done, Rowan did not see when, on the far side of the fire, the solitary monk took a parcel from a backpack concealed beneath his robe and threw it as hard as he could into the centre of the fire and ran. The monk was halfway down the steps to Leith Walk when his package burst with a hellfire Rowan knew only from his time in the military.

It was soon known as the Beltane Massacre. Dozens were killed in the blast or from burns sustained in the aftermath. Harris died instantly, from the force of the explosion. Lynn, holding the charred body of her son, died in Rowan's arms moments later. Oblivious to the screams around him, he held her. The heat from her body burned marks into his arms and dried his tears as he cried them.

1

It had been years since McRae had changed the morning alarm on his phone. He was driving down the remote back roads of central Alberta when "Elephant," the opening song of Hannah Georgas' second album, came on the indie station from the city. It started so softly, with a gentle pulse, that Rowan wasn't sure for a second if the station had cut out, as it often did when the wind was blowing the wrong way. It was only when the pulsing continued, then grew, and Georgas' ethereal voice slid in on top that Rowan realized this was the song. When he got home, he downloaded the album and on second listen, made it his alarm. When he was home, he woke most every morning to the gentle pulsing, followed by the near whisper "you are off-kilter with me."

Things were different on deployment. Mornings in Afghanistan, even on base, were much more abrupt, when they had any definition at all. As the attaché and unofficial intelligence adviser to the Canadian liaison to the International Security Assistance Force in Afghanistan, uninterrupted sleep was rare. When he was woken by reveille in the morning, it was a good night; it meant no one had died and there were no serious fires to put out.

His training had prepared him for the odd hours, but he had little chance to use his field ops kit. Shortly after his arrival, he had committed that most grievous of sins—he had spoken his mind. On the upside, he had been right and made himself indispensable to Major McTavish, the Canadian liaison and his commanding officer.

McRae and his squad had been patrolling a neighbourhood on the edge of the large town through which his superiors suspected the Taliban were resupplying themselves. The goal was to find out whether this was right and, if it was, to stop it. His orders were to patrol the town and see what was happening at night, noting in particular any convoys.

After one circuit of the town, McRae realized that nothing was going to happen while he and his men were there. He could only accomplish his mission by making himself and his troop inconspicuous and tracking the movements of any large vehicles leaving town. Choosing forgiveness over permission, on the second night he ordered his platoon to the rooftops of three large buildings in the town, from which they would be able to see anything happening. On the third night, they saw two trucks leaving town, heading northward into the mountainous region; the trucks returned an hour later. They followed the vehicles to a garage on the western edge of the town and created a distraction while the nimble Corporal Sanders, barely five foot six in combat boots, snuck in and placed a tracker under one of the trucks. When McRae finally informed his superiors what he had done, he had GPS coordinates of the Taliban base in hand, as a penance offering. Instead of getting dressed down, he got pulled inside and began helping to plan the Canadian side of operations.

At first, McRae hated being inside. He was a "house cat" now, and his former patrol took to meowing when they saw him. But when he stopped command from launching a mission that would have gotten many men killed in favour of an ambush that resulted in the capture of a dozen or so insurgents and almost no casualties, he knew he was where he needed to be. He also appreciated that he had a CO who listened to reason and didn't treat respectful dissent as worthy of court-martial. Not all commanders, Canadian or allied, were so enlightened.

The major himself was nearing the end of his career. What McRae didn't know until after he was back home was that McTavish had been in Rowan's shoes in Bosnia, and not being listened to led to many more deaths than necessary—both civilian and Canadian forces.

The allies—Americans and Brits, by and large—weren't so bad on individual levels but worked within a far more regimented system than McTavish and McRae had built between themselves. Still, McTavish was happy to go toe to toe with his counterparts in support of a plan he preferred, notwithstanding the other countries' constant treatment of Canada as the junior partner in the ISAF. Once in a while, when they had some leave, McRae and his British and American colleagues would find themselves in the base canteen, comparing the various merits of each country's beers, while all acknowledging that none of them could hold a candle to the Belgian, Czech, and German ones that would, from time to time, end up on offer due to a delightful mix-up in the supply order. Once they'd finished talking beer, the conversations would often turn to sports. While McRae and the American attaché, a young Pennsylvanian they called Fitz, debated the nuances of baseball, the NFL, and ice hockey, Martin Smalls, the British attaché, couldn't understand a word. But he was happy to wax poetic about Thierry Henry and the increasingly remote glory days of his beloved Arsenal Football Club, which made almost no sense to the two North Americans, who insisted on calling the game soccer. It was mostly out of spite when, years later, after watching football in Doctors pub in Edinburgh, McRae deemed himself a Spurs fan.

The three stayed in loose touch after each man returned to his home country. Fitz was now following in the family profession and carrying a patrolman's shield in northeastern Pennsylvania, cheering for the Flyers, Eagles, and, for his grandfather, the Yankees. Smalls was back in London, working in some sort of security service position and enjoying his occasional trips to the Emirates less and less each year. But former servicemen don't post much on Facebook, so their messages to each other were sporadic and mostly consisted of rubbing various victories and defeats in each other's faces.

Now that McRae was in London, he occasionally thought to look up Smalls and see if they could grab a pint. Eventually the right moment would come, but it hadn't yet. Then again, Smalls hadn't reached out to him either. Not in almost a year now. Condolences after Beltane, but nothing since Rowan's move south later in the summer.

Another Monday came and, with it, the familiar pulsing, lulling McRae from another fitful night's sleep. The sun had already risen, it being early May, when London's latitude reveals itself with earlier and earlier mornings each day. The spring term, during which students write exams, was beginning to gear up, and McRae had a revision session today with the long-suffering students in his colonial history seminar. They had the disadvantage of having taken a course with a new professor. For most of the history professors, there were well-worn sets of notes circulating, but McRae was an unknown quantity, leading to more meetings than usual while his students pieced together what was and wasn't important to him.

In a matter of minutes, McRae was out the door. He had put on his glasses, brushed his teeth, and pulled on sweats, but that was as far as his morning routine went at home. He wore sweats on his three-block walk to the gym, his clothes for the day packed in his knapsack. In Edinburgh and before, he and Lynn would run together—up to her seventh month of pregnancy—leaving their flat in the Old Town and running to and around The Meadows and back. Their runs would always end with them in a better mood than when they started. Now, however, he found any time he tried to run, he felt alone and angry. Instead, he turned to swimming, which he'd loved as a child but hadn't done in years until he learned there was a pool at the gym near his flat. It was as good as running for exercise, better meditation than yoga, and woke him up more effectively than coffee ever could, not that he'd ever developed a taste for the stuff. And it was something he had never done with Lynn, so he somehow didn't feel quite so alone while swimming. His counsellor said he needed to reclaim things he used to do with Lynn, make new memories doing them, and encouraged him to try running again. But McRae found that thinking about Lynn and Harris, and their deaths, was inevitable no matter what he did, especially now, around the anniversary. There had been commemorations in Edinburgh last week, but he couldn't bring himself to go back, even though the counsellor said it would bring closure. Rowan didn't feel like he was ready for closure yet.

His flat on Brown Street was small even by London standards, but it was enough for McRae. It was somewhere to sleep and store the few possessions he hadn't given away when Lynn and Harris died. The aunt and uncle in Ontario who'd raised him after his parents' deaths didn't have a lot of storage in their condo, so he didn't have anywhere to keep anything even if he had wanted to. It's not that he wasn't sentimental about certain things, it's that he had moved so many times in his life that he was selective about the things he was sentimental over, holding on to only a few keepsakes from his time in Edinburgh: his wedding ring, a few photos divided between his flat and his office, and a rook from a chess set Lynn had intended to give him as a graduation present. From the time he left for his morning swim, he was seldom home again before eight or nine at night anyway, preferring the office, the pub, or one of the many free museums and galleries that could be found throughout the city. Breakfast was a croissant from the nearby bakery. By now, after a full academic year of this, they knew him well enough not to mind that he kept his bike with him in the queue, though they never did inquire as to his name.

Rowan had learned early in his time in London to avoid the main thoroughfares while on his bike, so he twisted his way through the centre of the city to the main campus of the London School of Economics, near the Strand, typically arriving between eight and eight thirty. The first students of the day were lined up for coffee, but he was always the only faculty in that early. His nine a.m. seminar was a deliberate choice; it suited him and few others, so only serious students stuck with it beyond the second week. It was a gamble that paid off—while his numbers dropped off, the remaining cohort of slightly less than twenty students was ideal for an upper-year course. He took his turn during the faculty's introductory courses—as a new faculty member, still well on the far side of tenure, he had to do somewhat more than his share—but his real focus was on the seminar and the students there.

His office was a small, awkwardly shaped cell. Its only redeeming feature was a window overlooking the Strand, and even that had its drawback: as it faced south, the sunshine flooded in directly during the winter months, making it uninhabitably warm. He had done his best with the space, filling the shelves with his books and two sentimental pieces: a photograph of the Narrows of St. John's Harbour, showing his family's fishing boats before the collapse of the cod fishery, and one of his few remaining printed photographs of Lynn and Harris, taken in The Meadows on a beautiful April day, a little over a year ago. Despite being a prairie girl, Lynn's hair always looked especially good in the wind, and the falling pink of the apple blossoms only accentuated her porcelain skin.

While he usually preferred to write in the morning, when expecting students McRae found it hard to concentrate. He also knew he wouldn't be able to read, so instead he took the opportunity to do some printing. He needed to have a look at some articles in various journals read by no one but specialists, so he printed these for the afternoon part of his routine. In grad school he would work in the university office or at home on a desk he and Lynn had set aside for his use. Now, however, he found it almost impossible to concentrate on whatever he was reading in a quiet place. Instead, he'd begun to read in the pub. He found the din of the patrons let him focus on his work, and when he felt like company, the bartenders were usually amenable to an ex-serviceman looking for a chat, even a Canadian one.

Once his session was over and his student meetings wrapped up around lunchtime, McRae hopped on his bike and wound his way north to the more conventionally academic surroundings of Bloomsbury. Tucked behind the Russell Square station was his regular pub: the Friend at Hand. It was well-hidden enough that the throngs of tourists didn't tend to notice it, and being at the heart of the university district, a thirty-something man reading there wasn't out of place. So by one o'clock, McRae had ordered his light lunch and taken up his usual spot: a table to the left of the bar that allowed him a clear line of sight to both entrances and of any match that happened to be playing should he stick around long enough to watch the evening kickoff. More than his flat, this was McRae's home.

Monday in May was not usually a good evening for football, so after a long afternoon of reading, McRae gathered his things and settled his tab, planning to make his way home. Occasionally, he'd turn right up Gower Street, to the four-storey Waterstones that served as a university bookstore for the area. Sometimes, especially if he'd finished up a bit early, he'd head down to the British Museum or follow Shaftesbury and Charing Cross to Trafalgar for some sightseeing. Today, however, his decision-making was interrupted by a message from Smalls, inviting him for a drink. McRae rested his bike against the stand outside the Friend and thought for a moment. He tried but couldn't remember the last time he'd heard from Smalls, so he scrolled down through Messenger to see. Other than a brief consolation message when Lynn and Harris had died, there was nothing there from him. Nothing at all, which was disappointing given how close they had been when deployed together. Still, his curiosity—always a strong motivator—got the better of his doubts, so he replied in his typical perfunctory tone:

— Sure. When? Where?

While he could keep it brief, punctuation still mattered.

— How about now. I'll come 2U

This message told McRae two things: Smalls, a more typical millennial, did not share his discomfort with "text speak"; and whatever it was, it was urgent.

McRae wrote back,

— Friend at Hand: you familiar?

He only had to wait a few seconds for a reply.

— I will be. There in 20

In typical regimental fashion, McRae stood when he saw Smalls enter the pub through the alley-side door. McRae waved him over to where his own and a second pint of lager were waiting.

"I was wondering when I would hear from you," he said. "Didn't figure I'd have to wait most of a year for it either."

"I am truly sorry for that," Smalls said meekly, the foam now sticking to the moustache of his beard, grown since their days in Khandahar. "No doubt you've had it worse in so many ways, but it's been a hell of a year for me as well."

"What have you been up to anyway?"

"Oh, you know, a little bit of counterintelligence here, a little bit of espionage there. The usual." Smalls was trying to seem nonchalant, but McRae picked up an undertone that told him this wasn't a casual social call. And Smalls, himself no slouch, picked up on McRae's insight.

"There's really no point beating around the bush with you, is there?" Smalls asked.

"Probably not."

"Then let's down our pints and go for a walk. Can you leave your bike here? The Brunswick Square Gardens aren't far."

Before they had passed Brunswick Square's tenements, Smalls, in full spymaster fashion, began his story. When his tour ended, MI5 scooped him up immediately. After Afghanistan, he expected this to be a more relaxed position, but it was one counterterrorism operation after another. Then, a year ago, Beltane happened. Smalls was on the task force that was looking into it, but he'd been experiencing some puzzling resistance from his superiors. Why, he couldn't tell, but something about the whole situation made him uneasy.

"I know this is all far too personal for you, and really, I felt like trying to work through this case and find the bastard who did it was the best thing I could do for an old mate. But now I need a second opinion and, maybe, some help."

"Hence the need to go for a walk?"

"Precisely."

"Fair enough, though I will say there is no place in London where I feel safer than the Friend."

"I'll keep that in mind, and once I do some checking I'll let you know whether we can use it for future meetings. As it is, dropping in to see an old army buddy doesn't raise many flags. Meeting up twice in a few days would."

"Are you under surveillance?"

"Hard to say, but I think I may be. I took the usual precautions here; the crowd at Holborn station is always quite helpful for getting lost in. But I don't want to take more chances than I have to."

They rounded the corner by Brunswick Gardens as Smalls began telling McRae how little they knew about the Beltane bomber.

"We don't really know anything at all about him yet. We noticed a suspicious actor on the footage from cameras at the Waverley train station a few minutes after the bombing, and we traced him back to Calton Hill, where he was running away just before the bomb went off. Footage from earlier showed him arriving, wearing monks' robes that he seems to have ditched around the time of the bombing."

Smalls' words echoed in McRae's head long after they'd passed through his ears. "After the bombing," he whispered to himself as he processed this news—the man who killed his wife and son was alive. He stopped walking, braced himself against the iron fence of the nearest building, and looked down, trying to find some stability at this news turned his world upside down.

Smalls stopped beside McRae and spoke quietly but urgently as he continued. "The suspect arrives in London the next morning and gets into a car at King's Cross. We track the car for a while, but then there's a gap in the security footage around Camden Town, and when it comes up again, he's not there. There's no sign of him after that. None whatsoever. We tried running the licence plate of the 'getaway car,' but it was a dead end; the car doesn't appear in any records. We think the suspect is in or near London, and we know he has help, but who, and why, no one knows."

For a year now, McRae had been doing his best to avoid anger. The media had generally reported the massacre as a suicide bombing, and he tried to take whatever comfort he could in the thought that the killer was also dead. Now, knowing he was alive, McRae was shaken.

He finally spoke. "I thought it was a suicide bombing."

"So did we, at first," Smalls said, a note of contrition in his voice. "It took forever to sort through all the CCTV footage in Edinburgh, and I only got a look at the King's Cross tapes months after the bombing—we'd been told the footage had been erased. I only managed to get decent images of the suspect and the driver last week. But for some godforsaken reason, my goddamn boss is blocking my access to the databases I need in order to run a thorough facial recognition check on either of them."

McRae felt a wave of nausea begin to grow in him, along with a soreness of the burns on his arms. They didn't usually trouble him these days, but right now they seemed almost like a fresh wound.

As he stood there, Smalls watching in silence, McRae also felt a bubbling anger. For a year now, he might as well have been paralyzed. But with this news, McRae knew he needed to act.

"What can I do?" he said, tamping down the building rage.

"For now, just consider yourself on notice. You're not officially seconded to MI5, because I don't even know how much I can trust my own people on this one, but I may need someone to do some fieldwork who is very clearly off the books."

"Marty," McRae said, remembering how much Smalls hated this Americanized version of his given name, "my tradecraft is more than a little rusty, but I assume your mobile isn't secure from your own people. How will you reach me, and how will I reach you?"

"Your flat is too residential—yes, I know where you live—but your office isn't so bad a spot. Easy enough to come and go on a campus without being noticed, even for a big ginger bloke like yourself. There's a phone booth on Aldwych by the crosswalk from the Kingsway. Last one down when you're coming from Covent Garden. I'll put a yellow Post-it in the top centre if we need to meet that day after work. For you, put one in your flat window, and I'll check it nightly."

"And if we need to meet sooner than that?"

"I'll send you a message suggesting we grab a Budweiser. You know I'd rather die than drink that pish again," Smalls said, and both men smiled for the first time since they had left the Friend.

Rather than return with him to the pub, Smalls turned north after the third leg around the gardens, heading off to Angel and his Tube ride home. McRae made his way back to the Friend and started to bike home. He realized as he rode down New Cavendish, cutting through the student flats of Fitzrovia, that this was the first time in months he'd spoken to someone who wasn't a student, a colleague, or one of the bartenders at the Friend. Was Smalls a friend now? Was he a handler? Either way, it was something different.

As was this anger. Sure, he had been angry when Lynn and Harris died, but it was a stage of grief he'd moved through fairly quickly. Now, knowing that the man who had killed his entire future was still out there and that he'd had help to disappear, fury returned. But not a general fury at the injustice of the universe. This fury had a focus, a target. In a man with McRae's skills, this fury could be dangerous.

2

Smalls first suspected something six months earlier when they reassigned Moss. Sandra Moss was the most experienced investigator at the counterterrorism unit. She'd cut her teeth on IRA bombings in the mid-nineties and taken the lead in the TIF (Total Intelligence Failure, the polite term for clusterfuck) that was the 7/7 attacks in 2005: an embarrassment for an organization focused on preventing attacks rather than responding to them. She was a hard worker, but in counterterrorism, who wasn't? What distinguished Moss was her efficiency; she had an uncanny ability to cut through the noise and find the signal. She was the one who managed to get the King's Cross CCTV backup footage from the Department for Transport when Scotland Yard claimed theirs had been deleted. She suspected that the cameras going down in Camden was not a coincidence, and soon after she voiced that, she was removed from the case. Technically reassigned, to the investigation into an attack on an MP that could have been handled by someone much more junior. The fact that the victim was a politician provided convenient cover to whomever wanted Moss off the Beltane Massacre case.

When she was reassigned, the department's official policy was still to investigate every lead in the Beltane case. In practice, however, the resources went with Moss, and the department was back to investigating every mosque east of Liverpool Street station for radicalizing elements. A colossal waste of time and counterproductive, really, since it just further marginalized already isolated communities. But good soldiers follow orders. Smalls wondered whether he was one anymore.

He didn't want to discuss this with McRae—didn't think he needed to, and their relationship wasn't like that anyway—but in the quiet of the night, when he was unable to sleep and the images of the charred victims returned unbidden, Smalls realized that this was personal to him too. He and McRae hadn't kept in close contact since their deployment ended, but this was still his brother in arms. Trauma bonding, the counselling literature called it, but it didn't feel any less real for the impersonal, clinical name. His brother was hurting, and his sister-in-law and nephew were dead. Yeah, it was personal.

When he woke from his fitful sleep the morning after his meeting with McRae, Smalls, professional demeanour restored, was able to focus on the parts of the job and not just his growing rage at the sidelining of the investigation. Nevertheless, he resolved to find out why such an important investigation was being actively blocked by the man charged with leading it.

Denis Walterson was about ten years younger than Moss and twenty years older than Smalls. Through his political and family connections—his stay-at-home wife was related to some major Tory donors—he had risen to head of counterterrorism much faster than his experience warranted. He was a top-down manager. He did not make recommendations up the chain; rather, he ensured that whatever came down from the political masters was acted upon by the rank and file. He didn't really have any sense of what their work was and, helpfully, preferred to stay away from the day-to-day operations.

Smalls knew better than to ask Walterson for an explanation. For months now, whenever he had asked for resources or assistance, he'd been stonewalled. Now, however, with McRae's reaction lingering in his mind, Smalls went looking for an explanation with renewed urgency. He knew he didn't have the skills or the contacts for a hacking attempt, so this had to be lower tech. His one piece of good fortune was that Walterson himself wasn't terribly technically savvy either. He kept a small leather-bound, dark blue notebook in his jacket pocket, which he consulted frequently, including whenever he was accessing the computer system. Ideally, his email password would be there, but if not it should still have other information that could give a hint as to what Walterson's problem was with the investigation. It would be a risk, but there should be some payoff, and it wasn't like the job could get much worse.

Trouble was, Walterson never took his jacket off at work and made sure the AC was kept high enough that he never got warm enough to need to wear anything less than his full three-piece suit. Most of the female staff had taken to bringing fleece-lined leggings to work; when the only person who complained was quickly transferred to the Belfast field office—no longer the hotbed it was in Moss' early days—everyone got the point.

Smalls figured the best chance he had was to make sure the air went out on some sweltering day and then have a fire alarm to separate Walterson from his jacket and the notebook in his pocket. The AC system was simple enough; it shut down for diagnostics for an hour at night anyway, so when he was working late one evening, Smalls used his position as floor fire marshal to examine the inner workings of the system. He realized that it had been a very long time since the filter had been changed. It wouldn't take much for him to block the filter entirely, leading to a backup of the system. A few hours later, it would be hot enough that a small spark would cause it to light. Smalls used some old paper caps—the kind children played with—to rig a very small IED set with a telephone-activated trigger. When the building was hot enough, he simply had to call a burner number, which would spark the caps and light the dust-filled filter on fire. It wouldn't spread to any of the system's mechanical parts, but it would heat the office up and force everyone out of the building for at least five to ten minutes while emergency response came.

His opportunity came more quickly than expected. When Thursday's forecast called for a high of over thirty degrees, Smalls decided the time was right. It was already in the low twenties when Smalls awoke at his North London flat Thursday morning, and it was forecast to reach thirty-one by the afternoon. He packed the device—contained in the case of an old Nokia he had lying around—in his jacket pocket and headed off on his usual seven thirty a.m. trip on the Northern line, alighting at Charing Cross and walking the last few blocks past Trafalgar Square to headquarters. This early, it was more pigeons than tourists; the birds were no longer scared by the hawk statuettes that a former mayor, now prime minister, had installed to deter them. Another superficial solution that doesn't actually solve an imaginary problem. There are worse things than pigeons.

By the time he reached the office, just after eight, Smalls' undershirt was soaked. The blast of cold air as he walked through the twelve-foot double doors of number 24 Whitehall was a wall of relief. He passed through security and the metal detectors without incident; while his old Nokia was an unusual sight, it wasn't sufficiently bizarre to attract any attention at the busiest point of the day. As he approached the lift, Walterson came up beside him and attempted to make small talk. Smalls thought it would be quite some time before the older man ever figured out how, and given how his boss was blocking his investigation, Smalls would really rather not have to make chit-chat with him.

"My, that is a sweltering one out there today, isn't it, Smalls."

"Yes indeed, sir. Good thing we don't have to be out in the field today."

"Good indeed. I want to have a word with you on where we go from here with regard to the Edinburgh incident." Walterson never called it what everyone else called it. Couldn't bring himself to say Beltane without grimacing.

"Understood, sir. When would you like?"

"Let me consult my schedule and get back to you on that. I never know what kind of day I'm going to have until it's gotten away from me."

"I know how that goes, sir." It was painful to be so obsequious to such a naff twit, Smalls thought, but it was necessary to appease the boss's ego. Still, when the lift arrived, Smalls entered first, pushed the button for the sixth floor, their common destination, and held the door open for Walterson to enter. The older man turned to face the door. Small talk over.

The rest of the day must go as normally as possible, Smalls knew, so he kept to his morning routine of sorting through footage of the suspect leaving King's Cross, looking for identifying details of those who might have been with him on the train, or anyone interacting with the suspect or giving any indication that they knew him, people he could try to track down and question. After months of poring through CCTV footage from every conceivable angle by himself, he finally had a half-decent image of the suspect (Caucasian, likely in his twenties, wearing fairly generic clothing and a hat that obscured his hair) and one of the driver (middle-aged Caucasian male with no remarkable features), but when he asked Walterson for permission to access the confidential databases (passports, drivers' licences, other forms of basic ID beyond what was available to him in the criminal databases), his request was denied. Last month, Smalls had managed to identify a number of people to question as possible witnesses (though tenuous at best), but the agent in Edinburgh who'd been assisting him was taken off the case, and there were simply too many people for Smalls to contact them all himself, especially from London. Whatever he tried, Walterson was there to block him, leaving Smalls grasping at straws.

Walterson didn't speak to him for the balance of the morning. As usual, Smalls headed down to the in-house gym for a lunchtime run and then ate his chicken salad—he was a bit of a cook, and this featured some extra-blackened chicken he'd put together over the weekend—before deciding it was time to plant his device.

To ensure the in-house cameras were offline, Smalls used the terminal of a junior officer who had just gone to a late lunch and was sloppy about logging off. He then slipped inside the unlocked machine room. He opened the filter and sprayed it with a spray-on adhesive he'd picked up once when trying to fix some shelving in his flat, just enough to turn the dust already on the filter into a solid, flammable film. He planted the device at the bottom of the filter to ensure that it was most likely to catch. He'd need to wait an hour before triggering, so he returned the filter to its proper slot and removed himself, all within about forty seconds. He was quick enough that the junior's computer was still alive, so Smalls could turn the cameras back on without anyone noticing they were out.

Another uneventful hour passed, and the plan began to work. The AC was no longer effective, and the temperature of the room had spiked from the usual seventeen degrees to a balmy twenty-six. More importantly, Walterson began to feel the effects. He removed his jacket and hung it on the coat rack just outside his corner office. Smalls waited until Walterson was as far as possible from his jacket before igniting the device, triggering it only when it was least likely for the boss to go back for his coat. His chance came when a low-level signals officer at the far end of the open room noticed something on a video feed from outside one of the Southend-on-Sea mosques they'd been surveilling. With the boss called over, Smalls dialled the number, and in about thirty seconds the alarm went off.

This was not an institution to panic, so when the alarm sounded, everyone remained orderly. Walterson adopted an air of authority and called to the troops, "All right, everyone out, who knows whether this is a drill or not" and led his charges to the stairs. Smalls pulled his orange warden's vest out of his desk and began checking room to room, closing the doors of the offices and meeting rooms that surrounded the open area of computer terminals where most worked. He started at the office next to the boss's and made sure to end at the chief's. No one was left when he reached the final door. He threw the door closed then reached into the boss's jacket pocket with one hand and his own pants pocket for his phone with the other. Walterson's little book included a day-planner and a section of blank pages for general notes. He took photos of every page with writing on it but without paying more than cursory attention to what was on any of them. He'd work that out later. He was in the stairs on his way out when the fire department arrived.

For the fifteen minutes they were all outside, Smalls did what so many of his colleagues did—scrolled on his phone. However, instead of looking at Instagram or swiping for opportunities on Tinder, he was poring through the details of Walterson's notebook. His email password was easy to find; it was, as expected, a random series of numbers, letters, and symbols on the last page of the notebook. But other more promising details began to emerge as he scrolled, making Smalls think he might not have to access Walterson's computer at all. The phrase "Cornwallis" kept popping up, along with the note "L.R." or "Mjr. H." and various numbers—1930, 2000, 2015—that appeared to be times, always in the evening. A Google search of "Cornwallis" led Smalls to the Cornwallis Club, a conservative members-only club in Mayfair, the toniest and most staunchly

Tory part of London. Smalls, whose mother came from a military family and whose father's family were working-class from Sheffield, was never even close to such a place, but he was well aware of the role these clubs played at the upper levels of Britain's political establishment. To belong to one was a necessary first step in any successful career in business, law, politics, or the upper levels of the officer corps. Someone who was born to membership, of course, had a tremendous advantage over someone, like Smalls, who was working his way up from the outside.

That Walterson was a member of such a club wasn't a surprise, nor was having meetings there with people who could be trusted to advance his career. "Mjr" was clearly a major of some kind, and while "L" could be an initial, it could also stand for lord. But Smalls had no idea what the "H" or "R" signified. The Cornwallis, like so many clubs, did not make its members list publicly available. If you knew, you knew, and if you didn't, then it wasn't any of your business. What he did notice, however, was that the dates of the meetings seemed to coincide with times when there were significant developments in the investigation, and with Walterson's interference. Of particular interest was a notation for a meeting tomorrow, May 10, with both contacts.

The rest of the day passed without incident. Once home, Smalls continued his online searching but without getting any closer to identifying the owners of the encrypted initials. The only way to figure out who Walterson was meeting was to follow him.

Smalls took a long lunch the next day in order to do a first pass of the Cornwallis Club. Unless he knew a member, which he did not, there was no way for him to get in the room, but that would have blown his cover anyway. As with so many of these gentlemen's clubs, the building was a Victorian-era townhouse built for a landed family as their London residence. The ground floor included the dining room and meeting room. Based on his walk-past, it appeared to Smalls that the meeting room was facing the street and the dining room was likely at the back of the property, probably for increased privacy and because it would have been where the original family had it. Based on the timing of the meeting, coming right at the end of the workday at six thirty, Smalls presumed this was a drinks meeting, to be held in the front room.

The club itself was in the middle of the north block of Grosvenor Square, a private park to which Smalls could not get access. There was plenty of parking on the street and a café down the block at which Smalls could appear inconspicuous if only it were open late enough, which it wasn't. What Smalls needed was a car, but he didn't have one and couldn't drive.

He did, however, know a cabbie he trusted. An old friend from the regiment Smalls had trained with had been working in a black cab for a few years now, and whenever Smalls needed a ride, he would reach out. Simon Blackburn had been exactly what the British Army looks for in its foot soldiers. He came from a working-class family fallen on hard times but with enough ambition to want its best members to find a way out. He was not academic enough for the universities but was smart enough not to ask the kind of questions that got Smalls in trouble. Blackburn was loyal, dependable, and a Sheffield United fan, so you couldn't help but feel bad for him. Smalls knew that if he asked Simon to help him out and to keep it to himself, he would.

Smalls arranged to meet Blackburn at a taxi rank on Charing Cross, outside one of the ubiquitous theatres in the area. Blackburn had timed it well and was a few cars back from the front and the waiting tourists when Smalls climbed into the back seat.

"How're you today, Marty?" Blackburn called back from his perch in the driver's seat once Smalls had closed the door. He was one of the few people who persisted in calling him this, largely because he knew it bugged him. They'd come a long way from their early days, and Smalls had been much more successful in climbing the social ladder than Blackburn, so he figured it was to keep him humble. Smalls didn't object. He had too much respect for Blackburn, so if Blackburn wanted him humble, then humble he would be.

"In the thick of it, Simon," he said, being as vague as he could for now. Much as he relied on Blackburn, he didn't want to expose him to more than necessary, and he had to avoid breaking the Official Secrets Act. He changed the topic. "How's business?"

One of Blackburn's chief virtues as a cabbie, in addition to his keen sense of direction and willingness to drive in a manner that would get lesser men killed, was that he could talk. And there was nothing more he liked to talk about than his work. It took him the length of Pall Mall to tell Smalls the story of the honeymooning couple he picked up at Paddington—"Heathrow Express, waste of money only tourists use"—and brought to the Dorchester. He mentioned a very attractive young woman he'd brought from there to a flat in Soho—"an out-call if I ever saw one"—before, when turning the corner to St. James's Street, he brought things back to Smalls' work.

"So, what kind of mission we on today, Chief?"

"Reconnaissance, Simon. Do you know the Cornwallis?"

"Aye. You up for membership?"

Smalls snorted at the prospect. It was flattering that Blackburn would have considered this a possibility, but he was nowhere near wealthy enough, successful enough, or well-born enough to be on the radar of a club like the Cornwallis. "Not in this lifetime, no, but my target has a meeting there, and I want to see who it's with."

"Anyone I know?"

"I wouldn't assume so, but here's the picture," he said, holding up his phone to show a screenshot of Walterson's face, taken from his LinkedIn profile. A second set of eyes was usually helpful, and Blackburn's were better than most.

"Looks like a toff," Blackburn said, and Smalls couldn't disagree.

"Yeah, and despite being a civil servant, hasn't done a day of service in his life," Smalls replied, as Blackburn fronted the cab into one of the angled parking spots facing the gardens and pulled his copy of the *Daily Gleaner* from the empty seat beside him. The meter kept running, while Smalls switched to the rear-facing seats, allowing him a view of the front entrance of the Cornwallis Club through the cab's oversized rear window.

It was 6:13, nicely before Walterson was due to arrive, but Smalls wasn't sure if it was before his companions would arrive. Smalls knew he may not recognize them and so took photos of everyone heading into the club. A few solitary men arrived on foot, but then a chauffeured car drove up bearing a House of Lords licence plate. Smalls began taking picture after picture, trying to get every detail of whoever emerged. First out was an older man, clearly former military based on his haircut, posture, stance, and the way he held the door for the second man. The younger man was definitely not military. He had the matted mop of hair more commonly found in academia or business; he wouldn't have looked out of place at a city investment firm. He was clearly the one in charge, even if he was the younger and less polished of the two.

"A lord if I've ever seen one," Smalls muttered, half to himself but loud enough that Blackburn heard and started to look in his rear-view mirror.

"Marty, sure you know who that is, right? I mean, I gave him a pound fifty this morning just for this paper," said Blackburn, lifting his copy of the *Daily Gleaner* as punctuation.

"I haven't a clue, Simon. Who is it?"

"The older bloke, I don't know. An officer, sure, I can recognize one of them without him screaming at me, but the younger, he's the publisher. Lord Rutherford, I think." Blackburn flipped to the masthead on the fifth page to confirm. "Yup, that's him right there."

He pointed to the name under the word *Publisher*.

Smalls' mind raced. Lord Rutherford. Was this the L.R. from the notebook? The older man looked like he could be a major. So what was their connection with Walterson? And did they have anything to do with Walterson stonewalling his attempts to identify the Edinburgh bomber?

All he could say was "Well, fuck."

3

In the days that passed after his meeting with Smalls at the Friend, McRae barely slept. The spring term was always more flexible with its classes and appointments, so he had a modicum of flexibility and could lie in until the late-for-him hour of eight thirty before forcing himself from bed. As a junior academic, McRae's schedule was now more or less exactly as it had been in grad school: writing in the morning at his office, meetings at lunch, and reading in the afternoon, usually at the pub unless he needed to get something from one of the libraries or do some archival work. Each night, he found himself tossing and turning with memories masquerading as nightmares, both better and worse than the real thing. At least when asleep he didn't dream of the smell. It was a rough week, and the weekend was no better.

McRae's ride into work was more tense than usual, following his encounter with Smalls. Once again, like in training, he was noticing all the movements around him, which on the abysmally chaotic streets of central London at rush hour was a lot of movement. Cabs were always dangerous for cyclists, but now he was watching out not just for accidents but for deliberate attacks. When he reached his building overlooking Aldwych, he checked the telephone booth. No signal. While he usually left his bike chained to a bike rack outside, after his meeting with Smalls he'd decided to take the unusual, and annoying, step of bringing it into his office. If anyone was watching, he hoped this deviation from routine wouldn't be enough to raise any alarms but decided it was better than taking the chance of leaving his bike unsupervised outside on a busy campus. Beside the Friend was one thing; there was such light foot traffic that anyone tampering with his bike would be noticed. On Houghton, in the bustle of campus, there was no way to prevent bugging, slashing of tires, tracking, or even a well-made, small, homemade explosive. He knew that was a little extreme—he wasn't in Kandahar anymore—and it dawned on him that the fact he'd been catastrophizing meant the conversation with Smalls had triggered him more than he'd been willing to admit. Still, even though it was probably unnecessary, he dragged the bike through the entrance and into the lift, up to the fifth floor, and squeezed it into the side of his awkwardly shaped office.

Concentration was hard to come by this morning, so rather than try and write anything new, McRae focused on revising projects he'd already worked on. His specialization was colonial history, mostly the effects of the British Empire on the various colonies. This was a field that had underseen a seismic shift in the last two generations and was now split into two camps. The apologists claimed that the good done by Britain in all, some, or particular colonies outweighed the harm, while the critical realists focused on recounting, in increasing detail and specificity, the harms done, including noting new harms that would not have been thought bad at the time. Although he was a junior scholar, the apologists found McRae appealing because, as a Canadian, he was believed to be sympathetic. But while he, a white man born in Canada, owed his existence to colonization, McRae was from a part of the country where one Indigenous population had been entirely wiped out, so he knew that the sins of empire were so pervasive and enduring as to be incalculable. The way forward was the task of leaders; understanding the past was his.

A signal is only useful if someone is there to see it, so as time ticked away in McRae's morning, he felt annoyed that his plans with Smalls meant he was unable to leave campus as freely as usual. Instead, he had to make plans for lunch in the neighbourhood, which was more of a nuisance than anything. There were few places to eat, and most of them were overcrowded with students or tourists, or students who were basically tourists. As with many British schools, the London School of Economics was attractive to a certain class of international student. A few were the brightest of their homelands, but more often they were the outrageously affluent children of privilege. So the students were not only more than happy to fork out fifteen pounds for a sandwich, they were usually content to double that with a couple of pints as well. Assuming they came to campus at all. Parking was much harder to find on campus than at their Kensington or Chelsea flats, purchased as investment properties by their parents.

Still, since he couldn't really leave today, McRae forced himself to one of the chain cafés on Kingsway and bought a sandwich and a smoothie. It wasn't lunch at the Friend, or the mosque kitchen of his time in Edinburgh, but it would have to do. He decided the least he could do was to enjoy his turkey-and-bacon wrap outdoors instead of squeezed between two different conversations at the lone empty seat in the café, so McRae turned north, away from the river, and walked around campus to Lincoln's Inn Fields. They were only a few blocks away, so were also well occupied by students, but being able to sit on half a bench and eat in the shade of a centuries-old tree was still the better option.

He scanned the field for familiar faces and, finding none, breathed deeply. It was spring in London, and the pollen from the ancient poplars filled his nose. These sorts of public squares, small refuges of fresher air, were so important in a city like London. Even in these days of congestion charges, the Kingsway was still blocked with cabs full of of tourists slinking their way toward Covent Garden or, farther south, Trafalgar and Westminster.

Sitting in the square, McRae remembered his first time in London at the beginning of his time in grad school; Lynn was still finishing her curatorial program and hadn't joined him yet. A friend from his undergrad days was at the Institute of Education, a year or so into his PhD. McRae was living as cheaply as possible, but with his student card, the rail fare to London was reasonable. He could stay in the dorm for free and see this city he'd only read about.

He loved every impoverished minute of it. If anything, the cheapness of the city when you have somewhere to stay was a big part of its draw for him, almost making up for the surprise of having to pay three months' rent for their damage deposit in Edinburgh, leaving him with twenty pounds per week for food until his second scholarship payment came in December. But in London, he walked from free museum to free museum, eating only when necessary and from Sainsbury's and Tesco. The tenner he put on a round at the pub to thank his host was the most expensive part of his stay.

That was his first time learning the value of free museums and seeing the effects of empire up close. He felt awe seeing the Lewis chess pieces, a thousand-year-old set that washed, almost intact, onto the beach of an Outer Hebrides island in the twentieth century, or the Sutton Hoo trove of Anglo-Saxon gold and arms. But there were very few things in the British Museum that were actually British. Most of the contents were the spoils of empire: marbles from Greece, whole temple facades from Iraq, mummies from Egypt. The famed Rosetta Stone was stolen from the French as Napoleon retreated from North Africa. Still, McRae spent most of a day at the museum, eventually retreating from the overwhelming collections to the sweet embrace of the Friend at Hand for the first time.

On day two the size of London was his main discovery, as he walked from Bloomsbury across the city to Kensington and the V&A and Natural History Museums. The Victoria and Albert was charming, but the Natural History Museum quickly became one of his favourite places in the city. The building alone was remarkable, but the decor ensured that every corner of the building had something new to see. There were tiny statuettes and sculptures of various flora and fauna tucked everywhere, and paintings or murals of others throughout the ceiling of the grand hall. He spent an hour just sitting on the stairs, a few metres from the statue of Darwin presiding over it all, just soaking up each panel of the ceiling. Later, on another visit, he and Lynn had done the same, and when Harris was born, they talked of bringing him regularly, once they moved to the city. It wasn't just his wife and son that were killed that day—his dreams of the life he could have had also died.

McRae decided he'd been gone from campus long enough. He gave the grounds a thorough look, seeing if there were any of the telltale signs of someone watching him. Most of the people here didn't look out of place. Plenty of students, a handful of barristers wandering on their lunch break, but no one who looked like they didn't belong or didn't clearly look like a tourist. Most importantly, very few people on their own, which would always heighten suspicion. So he rose from the bench, turned to the southeast corner, and walked the five minutes back to his Houghton Street office.

Working in the office in the afternoon was unusual for McRae. He decided to take the opportunity to brush up some of the notes from his lectures for the year. It was likely he'd have to teach some modules in the modern history course again in the fall and that he'd get to offer his colonial history seminar again, maybe at the graduate level, and it never hurt to go through what did and didn't work. In particular, his challenge was teaching an audience composed of students who idealized Britain's role in the nineteenth and twentieth centuries, as well as students who loathed empire and all it stood for. To McRae there were two genuinely interesting features of this: international students were found in equal numbers in both groups, and neither group considered the fact that a history of the last two hundred years was not only the history of Britain. It was only his most engaged students that looked to Japan, Ethiopia, or the Ottoman world for their papers, and not just in the context of "British engagement in." If he had to read any more papers on the opium wars, for instance, that entirely ignored non-mainland China or Hong Kong, he might just resign.

It was sufficiently absorbing work that McRae didn't notice the time until it was 5:15. He looked and saw a Post-it in the window of the phone booth, with something marked on it. He made a mental note to bring his old stargazing binoculars to the office—wouldn't get much use in London anyway—and headed down to find out what it said, once again awkwardly manoeuvring his bicycle through the halls and into the lift, drawing a dirty look from the aging politics professor who wanted to get in on four but thought better of it. Wouldn't want to muck up his grey suit on the grease of McRae's chains.

In the days of mobile phones, telephone booths were more of a tourist draw than the practical necessity they had been only a decade or two earlier. When McRae reached it, he took the note and saw it was a circle with two lines, one short and one long, pointing from the centre to the bottom. Six thirty. Plenty of time to make it to the Friend on bike; still, he decided to take the direct route, riding north in the bus lane until it turned into Southampton Row, then a right onto Guilford before a quick left onto Herbrand. He saw Smalls there waiting for him, pint in hand, on one of the Hand's outside tables.

"I'd have thought Afghanistan was dangerous enough for you; cycling in London is a suicide mission," Smalls quipped.

"Enough talk of suicide missions, thanks. What have you found?" McRae blurted out, not even bothering to pop inside to place an order until he knew whether he was staying or going.

Smalls gestured at the pub. "It's pretty crowded inside today. Mind standing?"

"Not at all. Should I get a pint?"

"No need," Smalls said, just as the waitress popped out with a pint of Leffe, McRae's preferred lager, and set it on the tall barrel that doubled as a table.

"Then, cheers." McRae smiled, raising his glass to Smalls and then to his mouth for a long drink. The waitress left and they were again alone outside the pub. Smalls began to debrief McRae.

"What I know is this. Those cameras in Camden didn't go out by accident. The placement and timing were too perfect. There was no general power outage and no evidence of tampering from the outside. Which tells me it was someone in either the Metropolitan Police, my branch, or the Transit Commission who shut them down. I've run the logs in my shop, and I'm fairly confident it wasn't anyone in there. So there had to be someone in the Transit Commission or the Met who was involved."

"Great, so we only have to worry about the main police force and the supervisors of all the transit in London."

"It's worse than that. There is definitely something foul in my office too. You know I've been working on this for a year, but it's only me now. At first, it was all hands on deck, led by the best people in the office, but once we worked out that the prime suspect had survived the bombing, instead of asking us to double down and giving us the resources we needed, they started reallocating people elsewhere. Now, it's just me.

"My supervisor now is a by-the-book, old Etonian named Walterson. His dad was an MP for the Tories in the sixties and got pushed out by the Thatcherites once she took over in the seventies. Son is as traditionalist as they come. While he knows he has to keep someone on this—wouldn't want the *Guardian* to find out that no one was investigating the biggest mass murder in our country since '05—he is doing whatever he can get away with to make sure it doesn't go anywhere."

"How do you do that, slow down an investigation, I mean?" McRae asked, focused on the practical and leaving aside, for the moment, the ethics of it.

"Lack of resources, first off. But now the big thing is that although we have a great facial recognition system, in order to access non-criminal databases—like passports and drivers' licences—we need special authorization. Walterson won't give me that. I have footage of the driver of the car from King's Cross and of the suspect from both Waverley and King's Cross. When I finally got usable images of each of them, just recently, I was able to confirm that neither is in the criminal system, but without authorization, I can't go further. I should already know who these people are, but I can't get access. This is not a resources question, he's deliberately stalling me."

McRae agreed. "So what do you have, and what do you want me to do?"

Smalls looked almost sheepish for a second. "Well, fact is, I started my own internal investigation, so to speak."

McRae nearly spat out his beer. "Damn, Marty. Looks like you grew some serious balls when you got back from Kandyland," he said, using the colloquial for Kandahar adopted by British and Canadian soldiers.

"What can I say? Maybe something of your colonial cockiness brushed off on me." Smalls smiled. "Trouble is, I'm pretty sure I've found something, and I don't like it one bit."

Smalls explained what he had managed to do, bit by bit, without embellishment or unnecessary details. It was a briefing report between soldiers, but the reaction was something different. McRae, initially bemused and impressed by the plan, became more and more concerned as Smalls got deeper into the results of his investigation. When Smalls revealed Walterson's contacts, McRae almost knocked over his lager.

This was a name McRae knew. The Lords Rutherford—Halisbury was the family name, Rutherford the title—were legends in his part of Canada. They were a family of publishing barons established in the early twentieth century. In colonial times, they built pulp and paper mills in order to supply their need for newsprint and made their fortune developing all the worst parts of British journalism. They were pro-Nazi until Britain was at war with Germany, when they decided they were pro-war and then, after, rabidly anti-Communist. Thatcher was a wet dream for them, and the family prospered even as the rest of Britain declined in the 1980s.

"Rutherford? *The* Lord Rutherford? Seriously?"

"Certainly not who I expected to be at the end of this particular string, Rowan, but yeah, William Halisbury, the Fourth Viscount Rutherford, and his uncle, Major Hilary Halisbury, retired, chairman of the family trust."

"You do realize my connection with the Rutherfords, right?" McRae said, wondering if Smalls had dug that far into things.

"Connection? What connection?"

"They paid for my PhD, basically. I mean, not directly, but the Canadian university I went to had a scholarship for a student to study in the UK. I won that in my year, and it funded my time in Edinburgh. Jesus, man, I'm a 'Rutherford Fellow,' which might mean nothing around here, but the Rutherfords are why I'm here in the first place."

Smalls took the kind of long, slow pull of his pint that people do when they're deep in thought and stalling for time. After he swallowed, he looked McRae directly in the eye and asked with the seriousness of an officer about to assign a suicide mission, "Will that be a problem?"

McRae almost smiled through the smouldering anger. "Oh hell no. If they're involved in this, fuck 'em where they live." He raised his glass to Smalls.

"Seriously, though," Smalls said, raising his glass but not clinking, "this is the tippity top of the British establishment we're messing with. They run everything and control enough of the media to make sure most never know that they're the ones pulling the strings. Are you up for this?"

McRae raised his left hand, palm facing front, exposing the underside of his arm. It was the first time Smalls had seen McRae's scarring, a permanent reminder, as if one were necessary, of the brutal manner in which his family had been taken from him, more forceful than any tattoo could ever be.

Smalls tipped his glass toward McRae, and the clink resonated through the empty alley.

4

"Cheers" is a start, but now that McRae and Smalls had a target, they had work to do. Both men took long drinks and finished their remaining lager in one go each. Rather than leave their glasses, McRae picked up both and nodded toward the door to the Friend. Without waiting for a response, he started to walk in to the bar, with a nervous Smalls trailing behind.

With the quiet confidence of a regular, McRae laid the two empty glasses on the bar and caught the attention of the man tending it. The Friend at Hand was an old pub that had come under new management about fifteen years ago. Back then, Phil Owens was the lowest employee on the ladder, the new kid just moved to London from some small, post-industrial Wearside town whose name he never spoke, bringing with him only his Sunderland kit and his northern accent. Now, he was the day manager of the Friend, opening the place up at eleven thirty and working until the evening staff took over around seven thirty. Even still, he rarely went home after that. If there was a match on, particularly a Newcastle or a Sunderland match, he'd stick around for it, or if there was someone around he was having a chat with, he could be found at the Friend until near on close, when he would stagger to his flat in the formerly dodgy area behind King's Cross, only a dozen or so blocks north.

Today, the pub was sparsely occupied, as it was between the lunchtime rush and the after-work crowd. McRae took a moment to handle introductions.

"Phil, you might've seen this guy around a few times now, so I figured you should meet. Martin Smalls, meet Phil Owens, Phil, meet Smalls. We're working on something together, and so if you see him around, try not to throw him out. Unless he's in his Arsenal kit, and then do what you will with him."

"What are you doing making friends with a feckin' Gooner?" Phil laughed as he reached across the bar to shake Smalls' hand.

"We served together in Afghanistan, him for you folks, me for mine, but all on the same side."

This note served to shake Owens' usually jovial demeanour. McRae didn't typically speak to him of his time in the military, and the bartender was an astute enough judge of character not to bring it up. "Aye, well, I guess that makes up for terrible taste in football teams," he said, his light smile firming and his nod signalling appreciation for Smalls' service.

"Pleased to meet you," Smalls said, before McRae once again took over the conversation.

"Phil, we'll be over in the corner by the screen. Any way you can give us some space as new folks come in?"

"Aye, no worry. I'll put reserved signs on the next tables. Until we get full up around seven, you should be okay."

"That'd be brilliant, cheers. And two pints of Leffe as well. My turn," he said, turning to Smalls, who was beginning to reach into his pocket but stopped at McRae's word.

"You got it, Chief. I'll bring 'em over once they're ready." McRae and Phil had known each other for several months now, and McRae had never walked out on his tab. And McRae had done what he could to be helpful to Phil. He was never any trouble, even when he'd had an extra pint or two. Never got in fights, didn't hit on the waitresses, even when one of them was giving him the eye, tipped well enough, and was good for a chat. There were no bouncers at the Friend, and not much call for one—it wasn't that kind of pub or that part of town—but McRae made sure Phil knew that if he was ever backed into a corner, McRae would be there to help him out.

The main seating area at the Friend was off to the left of the bar, shaped like a long triangle. At the far end of the area, at the narrowest point of the triangle, was a round table located underneath the projection screen used on match days. Right now, it had two comfortable armchairs positioned at either side. McRae and Smalls pulled the table out from the wall and moved the armchairs behind it, so that neither man faced the other and both faced out. They might have looked like a youngish Statler and Waldorf to any incoming customers, but there were few of those, and the two men weren't really noticed anyway.

Owens brought over two pints of Leffe and two reserved signs for the nearest tables, then left the old comrades to their business. Both held off on beginning discussions until Phil had come and gone, out of respect for his listening skills and a desire not to involve him any further than needed.

Once Owens had safely turned the corner of the bar, Smalls spoke up. "So, what do you know of the Rutherfords then?"

"A bit of the history and a bit of the present. The first lord was a press baron, and the family still owns the *Daily Gleaner*, but the real money came from bringing back paper from Canada and printing everything possible on it back in the early twentieth century. Wood, labour, and electricity were all cheap in Newfoundland in those days, as it had no other industry to speak of. A job at the mill was more reliable than fishing and sealing and somewhat less dangerous, or someone who fished in the summer might go logging in the winter. The Rutherfords became typical colonial benefactors, founding libraries in the towns that sprang up to service the mill, and taking patronage posts at universities and benevolent societies. My fellowship is a remnant of that legacy." He closed by taking a long swig of his pint.

"Impressive, Rowan, you're as good as Wikipedia," Smalls joked, and McRae chuckled under his breath. As an academic he had mixed feelings about The Wiki. "What about their politics?" Smalls asked.

"Historically, there were too many rumours about their connections to the Nazis for there not to have been some truth there. Otherwise, these days I know the *Gleaner* is considered a right-wing paper, pro-Brexit, anti-immigrant, but that's about it. The *Guardian* fits more with my Canadian sensibilities."

"Figures you'd end up a lefty, but you're generally right. I don't have much to add. The Rutherfords are no Murdochs; while they run the newspaper and move in some very, very posh circles, including lesser royals, they're notoriously private. Most of the papers—the *Guardian* and the *Independent* aside—are owned by a handful of families, and they have a bit of a gentleman's agreement not to print too much gossip about each other. So the papers that would publish the salacious bits don't, and the other papers don't tend to publish that kind of stuff anyway. As little as there is out there about the viscount, there's even less on the major. Corporate records show him as the director of the family trust, but that's about it.

"Are you up for some surveillance?" Smalls asked, knowing he couldn't do it and risk exposure.

"Sure, but why don't we try a more direct route?" McRae said. "Remember I said I was a Rutherford Fellow? I wonder if there is some way we could use that to get me a meeting with either or both."

"How would you go about doing that?"

"There was a contact with the family trust that I was told to reach out to if I needed anything, and she seemed pleasant to deal with. I wonder if, now that I'm finished, she'd put me in touch with the family so I could meet them and say thanks." McRae smiled, delighting in the irony of using the family's benevolence against them. "Her name was Ellie Fullerton. She officially worked in the bursar's office of one of the University of London colleges, but she also handled the purse strings for the trust. If there was someone who could put me in contact with the family without raising suspicions, it would be her."

"Have you met her before? Would she know you from Adam?"

"No, but she'd know enough about me to be able to verify that I am who I say I am. No need to develop a legend here; I've already lived it."

Smalls agreed that this was a better plan than simple surveillance, but McRae could tell he was apprehensive.

"Listen," McRae said, "I don't have any reason to believe that anyone suspects me of having anything to do with you, let alone with your investigation. That said, if it makes you more comfortable, I won't reach out to you in the meantime. When I have something to share, I'll let you know the usual way."

"An X in your window?"

"Aye, just like you said."

Plans resolved, Smalls finished his pint and made to leave. McRae stood as he did and reached out a hand. "Thank you," he said. "I haven't felt this alive in, well, over a year now. Feels good to be actually doing something now. The teaching and the research are fine, as far as they go, but this is something I didn't know I needed to be doing."

"Don't mention it. And be careful. You're not a field agent anymore."

When he got back to his flat that evening, McRae pulled his laptop from his pouch and opened his personal email folder. He still had access to his Edinburgh address, and he used his LSE one for the day-to-day, but any records from when he started school would be on his Gmail account if they were anywhere. A search showed a few emails from Elinor Fullerton from four years ago, his earliest days in Edinburgh.

Back then, when it was just the two of them, life in Edinburgh was one adventure after another. The first few months were very tight, but once Lynn got work at the Writers' Museum and they had two incomes, they were living quite comfortably. Cheap airfare got them to Paris and Stockholm, and conference funding helped them visit Budapest shortly before they got pregnant. In Scotland they hiked in the Pentlands and the Cairngorms, and they had a lovely anniversary week in Skye.

McRae started to write.

Dear Ellie,

Don't know if you'll remember me, but I was a Rutherford Fellow at Edinburgh from 2015 to 2018. I've now finished my PhD and am working as a Lecturer at LSE, based in London. I was wondering if there was any way you could connect me with the Halisbury family so I could say thanks.

Hope all's well with you. Feel free to reach me at 0131 220 2659.

Cheers,
Rowan McRae

The call came the next morning, shortly after McRae had arrived at the office.

"Is that Dr. McRae?"

"Yes, although almost no one calls me that. Is this Ms. Fullerton?"

"And almost no one calls me that either. Ellie is fine, thanks."

"As is Rowan. I take it you got my message then."

"I did indeed, it was good to hear from you." She asked about his time in Edinburgh, and he responded with all the fond memories he could muster and without letting on any hint of the pain that now veiled them all.

Finally, she got to the point. "I've reached out to Nadine Flaggs. She's the personal assistant to Lord Rutherford and tends to coordinate any activities involving the trust. She said there was a special event this evening at the Grande Dame Gallery on Old Brompton Road. Are you familiar?"

"I know where Brompton Road is, but not that gallery in particular."

"Can't say I know it myself, but it shouldn't be hard to find. Anyway, the viscount is hosting a charity auction there, and you've been added to the guest list. I know it's last minute, but if you're available, you would be welcome to attend. It's business dress."

"That's grand. Thank you so much, Ellie. I can't tell you how much I appreciate this. What time?"

"Drinks reception starts at six, auction starts at eight. I'd recommend being there no earlier than seven and no later than seven thirty if you actually want a word with the family."

"That'll work. Thanks again."

"Glad to be able to help. Cheers, Rowan." With that, she hung up. Her voice was the happiest thing Rowan had heard in a long time, and by the end of the call he was in a better mood.

Rowan McRae didn't think of himself as a suit guy. He owned exactly two. One was his military dress uniform, which he hadn't worn since he left the forces and really only kept because he couldn't fathom giving it away. Part of him thought it might be the right thing to wear on an occasion like this. It would be a certain conversation starter and would get him noticed. But therein lay the primary drawback to the dress uniform; it was too memorable in a situation where he would quite likely be the only person wearing one. If he were called to meet the Queen, perhaps, he'd pull it out and see if it still fit. Until then, it would stay put in the garment bag in which he brought it over from Canada, four years and a lifetime ago.

Instead, he'd wear his one business suit for the fourth time. He had bought it for their wedding, under explicit instructions from Lynn, who didn't want him in his uniform. Grey, with a waistcoat, single pocket, two button. On sale at Moores but still the most expensive thing he owned apart from his laptop. He wore it for their wedding, his graduation, his job interview with LSE, and now he would wear it again.

Despite, or perhaps because of, how rarely he wore it, the suit featured prominently in his memories. It was in exactly half of the photos on his apartment's sparsely decorated walls: it is in the wedding photo, it's not in the family photo with Harris. But it was also always associated with Lynn. She loved him in it, and he loved the way her delicate hands subtly adjusted his tie every time he wore it, pulling the tail down ever so gently with her left while nudging the knot higher with her right, leaving it looking immeasurably better than it did when he had stumbled his way through a half Windsor. He could still feel her hands there now, just as they were immediately before their first dance and when he went off to the interview that was to be the start of their next adventure.

Tonight, though, he thought best to dress it down somewhat. Leave the waistcoat and don't bother with a tie. Wear instead a pink or cream shirt underneath that would provide some contrast with the grey linen. It wasn't going to look like a Saville Row masterpiece anyway, which he had no doubt was what the viscount and the major would be wearing. He'd encountered a few among the older professors who insisted on properly tailored suits and looked down on those, of their own generation or younger, who were complicit in the declining cultural standards of dress in the twenty-first century.

These days the three-piece old guard stood out as elitist among the khaki- and polo shirt-wearing young professors and students alike. On days when he knew there was a match, McRae would even opt for jeans instead, knowing they'd work better at the pub than light khakis. One particular professor emeritus stopped him one day in the halls, assuming he was a vagrant or a lost undergraduate exchange student. It took a faculty ID to convince him otherwise.

Flipping through his small closet, McRae settled on a fairly formal white shirt with small but noticeable blue pin dots. Lynn said they brought out his eyes. As he looked in the mirror, he could feel her gaze, smiling at him, proud of her choice of a partner. Subconsciously, he began turning the solid gold band he still wore on his left hand. He realized he didn't want to have that conversation tonight and took it off, placing it on his dresser as he did every night before bed. He felt like something was missing, though, an uncomfortable sort of weightlessness that made him momentarily disoriented.

He went through the contents of his jeans, taking the wallet from his rear pocket and his mobile from the front. He also pulled from his pocket a small replica of a warder, the rook from the Lewis chess pieces, part of the graduation gift Lynn had never been able to give him. He rolled the piece around in his hands and thought about the son he never got to watch grow. The memory of their nightly bedtime routine filled his mind: taking a sleeping Harris from Lynn after he'd nursed and trying to gently place him in the bassinet. Usually he didn't wake, but sometimes his bright blue eyes would startle open as his head touched down, and he seemed to recognize

Rowan before calmly drifting back to sleep. Caring for Lynn and for Harris had brought out the best in him. Rowan squeezed the piece tight before placing it in the front pocket of his suit trousers. He might have to leave the ring, but he could take this with him.

He knew, in the rational part of his mind, that Lynn would not want him to wall himself off, to isolate. But he wasn't ready yet for someone else to come into his life. His heart still had mending to do, if indeed it ever could. Broken bones were stronger once healed; the heart wasn't a bone but muscle, which when torn was never as strong again.

In the meantime, he had a job to do. The suit was a different sort of uniform, but he was once again at war. In this environment, his suit was camouflage, and the ring stood out, inviting questions that, if he tried to answer, might break his cover. Better to play the part of the single young professor, looking to thank his benefactors, and let them meet the man they helped make.

5

Despite living in London for most of a year now, McRae had only taken the bus or the Tube a handful of times; it took a heavy downpour to interfere with his daily commute by bike. When it was really raining, the bus stops on Edgware Road had a route that got him to Charing Cross, where he could transfer to any number of eastbound buses for a couple more stops, staying dry under his umbrella the whole way.

Today, however, in a suit and in the rain, he didn't really have any easy way other than the Underground or a cab to get himself to Brompton Road. As he wasn't exactly on the MI5 payroll here, when it came to a choice between an extra five quid or getting a bit of walk, he would always choose the walk. Especially as he now had a decent umbrella and was living in a place that wasn't too windy to use it.

The umbrella was a novelty for McRae. He'd been raised on the far-eastern extreme of Canada's east coast, where it was so notoriously windy that there were only three or four days a year where the rain wasn't so horizontal as to make an umbrella useless. When he'd arrived in Edinburgh, it took him a month to realize that the rain was falling straight down and that he could actually get away with using an umbrella to keep his face, if not his feet, dry. From then on, he was a convert. Any day that was too wet to bike was made slightly better by getting to use his umbrella.

Never one for idle purchases, he had two umbrellas. He kept the small one tucked into his knapsack so that, should he be trapped at work or the pub in a downpour, he wasn't unarmed. But his preference was for the long, wide, walking stick–style umbrella he'd picked up at Fraser's in Edinburgh. It wasn't cheap, but it was built to be used and to last. What he hadn't known at the time was that it also worked well with his suit.

As he made his way down Edgware Road toward the station, McRae reran his briefing with Smalls. This was an intelligence gathering trip, but they had very little to go on and weren't even really sure what they were looking for. Smalls was certain the Halisburys were behind the stifling of the Beltane investigation but had no real sense of their relationship with Walterson and even less idea of the agenda that would lead them to involve themselves in protecting a bomber.

It helped that they were expecting him and that there would be a reason for them all to engage in conversation. Smalls speculated that Walterson might be there but was more interested in who else might be around. An event like this, a charity art auction, brought all sorts of connections into play. Whose pockets could the viscount, or the major, count on to support them in something like this? Politicians, bankers, lawyers, players in a variety of fields might be involved, but none of them would seem out of place in such a gathering. If anything, McRae was the odd one out, likely one of the few in the room with neither money, status, nor power.

His goal, then, was to ingratiate himself to his hosts, see who else was there and who they connected with, and ideally make sure there would be some way for him to encounter the family again. He needed to make a good impression but had no idea how that would work.

As he walked down the few steps to the station and was putting his umbrella away, he wished, more pointedly than usual, that Lynn was here. She was always more comfortable at parties than he was and made him more comfortable just with her presence. Her hand, resting on the small of his lower back, as if propping him up, let him know that he was loved and made him able to talk to strangers. He remembered the sensation and felt his spine tingle as he tapped his Oyster card on the reader. While it made him sad to remember it, it also fortified him, straightening his posture. It made him once again feel like he wasn't alone and would be okay.

Knightsbridge was a section of London McRae seldom visited. Too rich for his blood, as they say. Plenty of the students at LSE spoke of it as their home stop. This was a very popular area for inter-national money—those who had benefited from colonization, usually at the expense of their fellow countrymen, to purchase real estate in London. It was close enough to Hyde Park to allow easy access to London's largest expanse of green space but also had enough amenities like grocery stores, cafés, restaurants, galleries, and so on. All the essentials of contemporary city life, but you paid through the nose for it. At £1,200 a month, McRae's one-bedroom flat in Marylebone was already too expensive; it would be twice as much in Knightsbridge, just the other side of the park. It was not a surprising place for some extraordinarily wealthy and powerful people to hold a charity art auction.

The rain had intensified when McRae reached the station exit, so he flicked open his umbrella. He'd have a couple of blocks to walk in the rain, but the umbrella did its job and kept all but his feet dry. His tightly laced oxfords, bought for the LSE interview a little over a year earlier, likewise did their job and kept his socks dry.

As he approached the gallery, he noticed a bit of commotion on the street outside, which distracted him from the nervous throbbing of his heart. Cabs were pulling up to the curb in quick succession, with men and women in gender-appropriate suits quickly exiting and making for the door of the gallery in haste. Not a lot of umbrellas in this crowd, apparently. McRae arrived at the entrance just as an older man and a younger woman of South Asian descent entered quickly, the latter holding the door just long enough for McRae to grab it. She did not look back but rather focused her attention on the older man in front of her, trying to keep up, as McRae himself held the door for an incoming middle-aged couple; the wife was one of the few people wearing something other than a dark suit.

The registration desk was set up directly across from the main entrance, with a queue bending through the entrance room to the left. McRae joined it, tapping the water off his umbrella and scanning the room quickly. There seemed to be a small cloakroom behind the reception area, and it was likely any umbrella stand would be there as well. There were a dozen people before him in the queue. Most were couples, judging by age and body language, but from what he could tell, the younger woman and older man who had entered immediately before him were not together in any romantic sense. If anything, he appeared to be her boss. He was discussing with her his connections with the Halisbury family, while she seemed to take it all in. Lawyers, perhaps, based on the conversation, but it was hard to hear over the chimes from the front door and voices from the back rooms. This would not be a small, intimate event.

McRae reached the desk and gave his name. While the clerk was issuing his name tag, he noticed a small asterisk next to his name on the list. The clerk waved over a woman waiting nearby, who immediately approached him.

"Dr. McRae, I presume."

"I am indeed," he responded, his throat dry.

"I'm Nadine Flaggs, personal secretary to Lord Rutherford. Would you like me to check your coat and umbrella for you? It is really coming down out there, isn't it." With a surplus of efficiency, she helped him with his coat, took his umbrella, and disappeared into the cloakroom, then returned, empty-handed, a mere second later. "I have your ticket with me; when you're ready to head out, just let me know and I'll retrieve your items for you."

"Thank you very much, Ms. Flaggs."

"Oh, Nadine, please. And Lord Rutherford will likely ask you to call him William, but Major Halisbury, well, he stays the major." She chuckled in a way that sounded almost schoolgirlish.

"Then I'm definitely Rowan."

"Lovely, then. We don't get a lot of academics at these events. In the four years I've worked with the viscount, I don't believe I've met one of the Fellows before, so this is a real treat. Thank you indeed for reaching out," she said, half over her shoulder as she led McRae through the crowd toward a large room in the rear of the building, guiding him swiftly past the real bottleneck—the open bar in the gallery's anteroom—and toward the man around ten years older than McRae who was holding court in the main chamber.

On first glance, William Halisbury, the Viscount Rutherford, was far more handsome than indicated by the few photographs McRae had seen online. His hair remained a dirty blond with only a few rare points of grey visible and was consistent enough with his eyebrows to suggest that it probably wasn't dyed. Clean-shaven, as were most British men of his class and generation, his skin was the slight bronze of a man who spent time in the sun but who also knew how to take care of himself. He had the bearing of someone who played rugby in school but who didn't put in the intense training required to be professional, and the posture of someone who had been trained in the military. He was, by all appearances, a man's man, in the upper-class British sense. Someone who looked like he could swing a hammer but whose soft hands betrayed the fact that he definitely never had.

Nadine demonstrated that one of the main skills required of her job was to interrupt people as gently and unobtrusively as possible, in a way one couldn't help but forgive. "Excuse me, my lord. Please allow me to introduce Dr. Rowan McRae."

"Ah yes, the Fellow. A pleasure to meet you, Dr. McRae."

"The pleasure is mine, Lord Rutherford," said McRae, with a firm handshake and a nod of the head that would serve for a bow if, indeed, one were required. "And please, Rowan will do just fine."

"Lovely then. I'm William, please. We are among friends here," the viscount said. "First, allow me to introduce my uncle, Major Halisbury." The major looked like a time-warped version of King George V, down to the bushy, military moustache, the ruddy cheeks, and the total lack of emotion crossing his face. Still, he reached out a hand, and McRae met his military firmness. For a second, a brief flash of a smile crossed the major's face, almost hidden beneath the moustache. A smile of recognition from one military man meeting another, or perhaps a smile of relief that this academic his family had taken in at least had the grip of someone who'd not spent his entire life in an archive or a library.

"A pleasure, young man," the major said.

"Lovely to meet you, sir," McRae responded, looking the elder man firmly in the eye, with the neutral expression he knew senior officers usually expect from their juniors.

"This is my wife," the viscount continued. "Officially she's Lady Rutherford, but in practice we all call her Emmie."

The lady, as McRae had resolved to think of her, was a classic beauty. He knew that she was the viscount's second wife; they were married only a couple of years ago. His divorce had been entirely without scandal, which, given the tabloid press in Britain, made it remarkable. Must be the gentleman's agreement Smalls talked about. After all, divorces among this class of British society were no longer unusual, and most of the publishers had one or two ex-wives to support. The current Lady Rutherford was a shade younger than McRae but not so young as to raise eyebrows in high society.

She too took McRae's hand, but gently, as she'd been taught by a governess or at one of the finishing schools that women of her upbringing would have been sent to on weekends, rather than full-time as their mothers had been. "Charmed," she said.

"Likewise," McRae responded, matching the gentleness of her hand, watching her eyes rise from his broad shoulders—more than a match for her husband's—to meet his gaze. She blushed slightly upon realizing that he'd noticed her admiration, but he flashed what Lynn called his "disarming" smile, which seemed to do the trick.

The viscount went on to introduce McRae to his fellow peer Lady Walderhome and her husband, Richard, known as Ricky, the "leading thoracic surgeon in London," otherwise known as Dr. Heathridge and his wife, Clara. At that point, the group was approached by the gentleman who'd arrived the same time as McRae, accompanied by his young companion.

"And this, Rowan, is the only barrister worth knowing in London, Charles Garson, QC."

"I wouldn't go that far, William," said the older man, as he reached for the viscount's hand to shake before turning to McRae. "I can think of at least one more, but you haven't met Miss Jamil yet, have you."

He introduced the young woman who'd accompanied him. "This, William, is Diksha Jamil, a recent pupil of mine who's just been admitted to the chambers as our latest junior tenant."

"Congratulations, Ms. Jamil, that's quite an achievement. Gladstone Chambers only admits the best. I should know. It's why I keep hiring them." The viscount chuckled.

"And for you, my good Mr. Garson, this is Dr. Rowan McRae, a recent Rutherford Fellow and now a faculty member of the London

School of Economics, Department of Economic History." So the viscount had also done his homework, thought McRae, or Ms. Flaggs had prepared good briefing notes.

"Pleasure to meet you, sir," Rowan said, as he forced himself to look at the older man and not be distracted by Ms. Jamil.

"Ah, then congratulations are in order to you as well, Dr. McRae," said Garson.

"Thank you, that's too kind, and please, call me Rowan," McRae added, before allowing himself to turn his attention to the junior barrister. "And congratulations to you as well, Ms. Jamil," he said, reaching out his hand once again.

In the year since Lynn's death, McRae had had little desire to date. He had briefly, on the encouragement of an old friend and with the support of his counsellor, gotten Tinder but found the vapid conversations with London's young, single set entirely uninteresting. Diksha Jamil, however, was the type of person he had not encountered in quite some time. She was beautiful, yes, but she had something else. He didn't know what it was about her—maybe the intelligence in her eyes, or the poise with which she handled herself in a crowd where he was straining to appear comfortable—but something about her struck him. She was that rarest of persons, someone he found genuinely interesting. At this moment she was a very dangerous distraction, but in a year on his own McRae had been so rarely distracted he was almost tempted to indulge the thought for a moment.

"Thank you, Rowan," she said, meeting his gaze with her large, dark eyes. McRae thought he saw in them a glimpse of something other than the impermeable confidence she was showing to everyone else. He put the thought aside, filing it away for perhaps a later time when he could chat with her alone. For now, he had a job to do, so he shook her hand, smiled politely, and returned his attention to the viscount.

6

The introductions complete, conversation turned to the usual array of subjects at a gathering of people who perceive themselves and their business to be important. There was some discussion of Labour's new leader, largely derisive in such a Tory crowd, and some about England's recent capitulation to Australia's cricket team in the Ashes. One more sign of the country's decay, said Mrs. Heathridge to general assent before the group was again interrupted by Nadine, who had slipped back into the conversation as stealthily as she had previously slipped out. The viscount was needed to get proceedings started. Lord and Lady Rutherford bade them all adieu, and as they did, the Heathridges and the barristers moved off to new conversations, leaving McRae in the company of Major Halisbury.

"If I'm not mistaken, you've some military in your background, do you not, Dr. McRae?"

"Yes, sir. I served in the Canadian Armed Forces."

"Branch and unit?"

"I was a captain with Canadian military intelligence, attached to what we called operation JTF2 but which my British counterparts called JTF6, in Khandahar."

"Ah, then you have seen a real mess over there, haven't you."

"Speaking candidly, Major, mess doesn't begin to describe what I saw there."

The major looked at McRae with respect. They were both military men, able to speak frankly with one another. While the major outranked him, they were both officers, and neither was in charge of the other. Far from being put off by McRae's bluntness, it led the major to a sense of camaraderie and the respect that came with it.

"I'll take your word for it. I saw action in Yugoslavia, of course, so I'm at least somewhat familiar with what can happen when things go from bad to worse."

McRae then spoke of his CO in Afghanistan, adopting the habit of his homeland to see if there was any sort of personal connection between the two men, which of course there wasn't. Major Halisbury's service in Yugoslavia wasn't in the infantry but in communications, which was a polite way of saying he was a press officer, not a soldier. Nonetheless, he had carried himself with the bearing of a pre-First World War officer for so long now that it was not affectation but persona, and one McRae was not going to interfere with.

"What do you make of this sort of thing, then, Captain McRae?"

"Sir, it's odd. While on the one hand it's a party like any other party, on the other hand it's something the likes of which I've never experienced. Not a lot of charity art auctions in the military."

The major laughed now, a full-bellied chortle. He was relaxing. "No, certainly not. They are far more my nephew's province than mine. But one must support the family."

"Which, as someone who has benefited from the support of your family, I can appreciate," McRae said, raising his glass to offer a toast to the major, establishing him as the benefactor of this young military man, making his way upward in the world.

"Indeed," the major replied. "We don't have a lot of contact with the Fellows these days. We had a bit of a reunion there a few years back, and it was pleasant to see the breadth of the impact the fellowship has had, but to have one among us here is a rare treat."

"The pleasure is mine, sir."

As their glasses clinked, McRae noticed a new man entering the room whom he recognized from a photo shown to him by Smalls. Walterson was making his way toward the major, and toward him.

"Major," Walterson said, abruptly, reaching out a quivering hand. McRae looked quickly at the older man's face and saw a sharp note of disdain cross it as he nonetheless took the younger man's hand out of politeness. "Might I have a private word with you?" asked Walterson.

"Here? Is it really necessary?" the major asked, before noting the concern on Walterson's face. "Very well. Excuse my rudeness, Captain. I hope we talk again soon."

Walterson and the major headed to the corner to ascend the staircase to the nominally off-limits mezzanine just as Lord Rutherford began to tap a glass, calling everyone to attention. The noise dimmed but not enough for McRae to overhear what Walterson and the major were discussing. McRae had never been that good at lip-reading, and reading through accents was even harder. He had no chance of finding out from here what the two men were saying up there. Still, Walterson's apparent panic and the major's disdain told him quite a lot. Something had gone wrong. The major was definitely senior to Walterson in whatever common business they had, and his patience was running out. McRae may not be able to read lips, but he could read faces, and the major was mad.

Two minutes later, as the viscount was calling the first of the auction lots—a minor work by a major twentieth-century British landscape painter—the major returned to the crowd while Walterson mingled with a few other guests. McRae watched as the major immediately approached Garson, the senior barrister, and pulled him aside for a quiet word. The barrister, as per his training, showed nothing as the major spoke with him. Instead, he took out his phone and entered something on it. A note? A text? No way for McRae to see from here, but once Garson was done and had put the phone back in the pocket of his jacket, the major's demeanour relaxed. Whatever problem he had was now with the lawyers. And McRae had his first hint of a lead.

McRae took a moment and gave half his attention to the auction. Lord Rutherford was a passable auctioneer. Mercifully slower than a professional, coaxing more money from the donors than McRae had ever seen in his life. The lowest item so far had gone for over eight thousand pounds, and most were well over twenty thousand. With about thirty items on the block, the auction could expect to generate a couple hundred thousand pounds for a new wing on the children's hospital in Chiswick, which would no doubt now also carry the Rutherford name. As the viscount announced the winning bidder of a small sketch—sold for fifteen hundred pounds to a lady in a floral dress—McRae noticed Walterson slip away from his earlier group and have a quiet word with Garson. Walterson initially seemed anxious, but whatever the barrister said seemed to set him at ease.

McRae was generally good with details—faces, appearance, dress, the minute differences of body language that are often far more revealing than an individual's words or even actions—but he found this crowd fairly uniform. Most of the men were older than the viscount, and most of the women around ten years younger. The notable exceptions were himself, Ms. Jamil, and members of the catering or gallery staff who were conspicuous for their dress as well as their age. The women who were here to bid were among the few in longer dresses, the ones working were in suits or shorter cocktail dresses. The men of the staff were largely in cheap suits, off the rack from Marks & Spencer or Selfridges, rather than the bespoke attire of the guests.

While the auction was ongoing, Rowan decided to head over to the bar for a refreshment; if anything, the lack of a drink in his hand was conspicuous. When he arrived, he found Ms. Jamil was already there. She was about to order when she noticed him coming toward her.

"I'll have a G and T," she said, in a voice soft enough not to interfere with proceedings but loud enough that Rowan, now standing beside her, could hear, "and you can put my friend's order on my tab as well," she added, with a nod at Rowan and a slight smile.

"At an open bar, Ms. Jamil. I'm touched," he said lightly before ordering a Peroni.

"Please, while I'll always be Ms. Jamil to most of this crowd, my mates call me Dee." She raised her glass, waiting to clink glasses with him while the bartender passed him the bottle of Italian lager.

"Then by all means, I'm Rowan," he said, returning her cheers with a gentle clink of glass on glass.

He turned his back to the bar, and she repositioned herself beside him, so they were both looking on the assembled guests as outsiders.

"So what do you make of all this?" she asked, after taking a healthy sip of her drink.

"Definitely not something you see every day in my line of work. You?"

"Unfortunately often," she said. "Life of a barrister, I suppose. Though there aren't many barristers that look like me."

"Referring to your age, gender, or ethnicity?" Rowan asked as the crowd broke into a polite applause; it seemed another round had ended with another artwork being sold for far more than its worth to someone with more money than they knew what to do with. Once that died down, the crowd stayed more or less static as the viscount introduced the next lot.

"All of the above," she said. "That explains why I'm out of place. You? You at least look like you could fit in."

Rowan felt himself getting drawn into the conversation but managed to keep his eyes on the crowd. "Maybe on spec, but in reality I'm about as far removed from this world as you are, if not further."

"You'll have to explain that to me sometime," she said.

Rowan now had a choice to make. Did he take the obvious bait? She was easily the most interesting woman he'd met in a long time, but something made him hesitate, a voice in the back of his head that said he wasn't ready for this. Still, with the apparent connection between her boss and his targets, there was some sense in it. Besides, he told himself in the split second before he answered, how could it hurt?

At the same time as she raised this prospect, he saw the major tap Garson on the back, then the two of them quickly left the circle of bidders and began a private conversation in the corner of the room.

"Drinks then?" he said, swiping his phone open and tapping on the messages icon without even looking before handing it to Dee. He remained fixed on Garson and the major; something had made Garson tense.

She put her number in and said, "Sure, maybe later this week."

"I'll check in with you, then," he said. Garson and the major began to return to the circle, so he took a moment and turned to look at her as he slipped his phone back into his pocket and raised his bottle.

"Please do," she said, then walked back to the side of the crowd where Garson was now bidding tentatively on a lot, as if he meant to drive up the price but didn't really want to win it.

McRae's attention followed Dee as she made her way back to Garson. Would it be possible for him to follow the elder man for a time? Odds are, he had driven here. Not many people in London even owned cars, let alone drove them in the city centre, but barristers were a notable exception to this rule. They might have a driver, but there would definitely be a car.

He decided it would be better to try and tail Garson with Smalls' aid, given the latter's access to a friendly cabbie. Instead, McRae focused on the original mission, which was so far a success. He'd ingratiated himself to the major, who seemed the tougher of the two men to crack, but had only a brief meeting with the viscount. McRae decided to stick around and see where the evening took him. It's possible that the viscount and his entourage would be going somewhere for dinner after this, and he might just be able to finagle an invitation. If nothing else, he'd get the opportunity to say thanks for the evening and to speak with Ms. Flaggs, and perhaps get himself on the guest list for some other future event.

The one thing McRae knew he didn't want to talk about was money. The idea of spending close to twenty thousand pounds on a painting boggled his mind. That was nearly half his annual salary, with the extra "London allowance," and almost double his living allowance on the fellowship. It was a shade more than the average Briton made in a year and would cover an exorbitant London rent for much longer than that. But for Garson or Dr. Heathridge it would be a morning's work, or investment income on their family holdings for a day or two. For the viscount, it was ten thousand copies of a daily newspaper with circulation figures more than one hundred times that.

That said, it would not do to point any of this out to his erstwhile patron. While McRae hadn't had a lot of exposure to the upper classes before now, he knew they did not talk about money, except in the most general and dismissive of terms. So he pushed down his shock and mild revulsion and focused on the job at hand: being a genial and intriguing guest, and getting himself on the viscount's radar.

As he scanned the crowd, looking for who was talking with whom, standing with whom, listening to whom, his gaze was briefly met by Lady Rutherford. It was a brief flash before she turned her attention once more to her husband, but the slight pinkness in her cheeks returned. She was watching him with interest, that much was certain. Perhaps her curiosity about him would be his in. If so, he'd have to make sure not to offend the viscount or the major; it would be a bad idea to become a problem in the marriage of someone you're trying to observe. If nothing else, it would make them observe you far more closely than you'd like.

The final item was up for bidding: an early work from Picasso's Blue Period, donated by the Halisbury family trust. The bidding opened at five thousand pounds and quickly shot up to twenty thou-sand when Lady Rutherford nodded at her husband. She was now bidding twenty-five thousand to buy back her own painting. At this point the bidding seemed to turn into a choreographed dance between the viscountess and Mrs. Heathridge. Lady Rutherford bid quickly, while her companion always hesitated before putting up her hand to once again raise the price. It was only when the viscountess hesitated before going to fifty-five thousand that Mrs. Heathridge finally shook her head, ending the dance and letting the Rutherfords off the hook for any larger donation. Lord Rutherford tapped a small gavel on the podium and it was over, to strong applause from the crowd.

Most of the guests did not disperse right away and instead availed themselves of the open bar one more time. McRae made his way to Garson, ostensibly to congratulate him on the Turner he'd got for twenty-one thousand pounds, but with the hope that he would get some clue as to what had passed between him and the major.

"Congratulations, sir, and well played. That's not a bad price for a Turner, I understand."

"Indeed, and given how important the Rutherford business is to my practice, it's definitely a worthwhile investment."

"You specialize in media law then?"

"I do. Usually defamation trials. Do you have an interest?"

"I can't say it's something I'm well versed in. I have an old friend who is a lawyer in Canada who once told me that defamation here is quite different from back home."

"Tremendously different. When it comes to freedom of speech, this country is far more like the Wild West than Canada; ironically, even America is less wild."

"Why is that, sir?"

Garson began to relax as he entered into his element, explaining how the law worked. "The Americans with their First Amendment have made it almost impossible to win a defamation suit. Canada is in between worlds but doesn't have the depth or breadth of media that we have. London is the media capital of the world and is a place where reputation is taken tremendously seriously. As such, we get more defamation actions than elsewhere, and with higher stakes."

"Then I can see why the Rutherfords would be important to that business."

"It is a very strong relationship. Otherwise, this Turner would be on someone else's wall tomorrow morning," Garson said, gesturing at the work now carefully wrapped and carried under his arm. "Though as I'm headed back to the office now, it's more likely it will end up there."

As Garson made his way to the line at the coat check, followed by Ms. Jamil, Rowan went looking for the viscount and found him in the midst of a crowd not far from the bar, glass of white wine in hand, with a touch of condensation on it. The wine was properly chilled, but the room was warm and humid.

Rowan approached their circle, bottle of Peroni in hand, and in a pause in the conversation raised his drink to the viscount. "A successful evening?" he asked.

"Indeed," William answered, with a polite smile. "I'm glad you were able to join us this evening, Dr. McRae," he said by way of introducing Rowan to the assembled guests.

"Rowan, please," McRae said, before adding, "I wouldn't be here if it weren't for the generosity of Lord Rutherford's family."

This drew confused looks. When one woman asked what he meant, McRae explained, "I did my PhD at Edinburgh as a Rutherford Fellow, a scholarship established by the current Lord Rutherford's grandfather when he was the chancellor of the university in my home province in Canada. So if anything, thank you for bringing me here, Your Lordship, not just tonight, but to London in general."

The viscount was momentarily taken aback by this public show of appreciation but quickly recovered his composure. This wasn't the first time he'd been thanked in public by someone who'd been helped by his family's largesse. "The honour is ours, I assure you," he replied. "We're just glad to be able to continue to help the best and brightest achieve their dreams. To meet one of the Fellows is a delight."

At which point Lady Rutherford appeared over her husband's shoulder, carrying two umbrellas. "Our driver, Willie," she said.

"I guess we're off then. A pleasure to meet you," he said to Rowan, shaking his hand again before bidding his farewells to the remaining guests. There would be no other opportunity to engage tonight, and Rowan felt a touch disappointed that he didn't get more out of the viscount. He caught a glimpse of Nadine Flaggs tidying up behind the registration desk and thought she might present his best chance to get a second invitation.

He made his way over and asked, "Anything I can help with?"

"That's far too kind, but we've got everything in hand here. Did you enjoy yourself, Rowan?" She had paused ever so slightly before using his first name.

"It has been a fascinating experience. I only wish I'd gotten a bit more time with the viscount himself."

"Don't feel bad there; he's a very busy man. It's my job to keep up, and he always keeps me on my toes."

"Do you have any other events planned that I could join in?"

With a practised noncommittal air, she said, "I'll have to check the schedule but will keep you in mind. Let me collect your things for you." She disappeared into the cloak room, then re-emerged with his coat and umbrella, the cue for McRae to make his way out into the rain.

As he stepped outdoors, feeling a sense of satisfaction at his first foray into espionage in many years, McRae saw Garson get into a car that had pulled up to collect him, and he quickly noted the barrister's plate number as his driver merged into the flow of traffic. *Even better*, he thought to himself as he wrote the number down in his phone.

7

When McRae woke the next morning he was surprised to find a text from Smalls, sent at 5:56 that morning. It was one word: *Guardian.*

While McRae was tempted to call him back, this would be a further violation of the protocols, on top of the one Smalls had committed by texting him. He assumed Smalls was referring to the newspaper and resolved to check for a copy on the way to the gym for his morning swim. He popped into the corner newsagent, and it didn't take more than a glance at the paper to see what Smalls meant.

The headline read: "MI5 stifling Beltane inquest."

McRae picked up a copy but knew it was imperative that he continue with his normal routine in the unlikely event that he was now under surveillance. He tucked it into his knapsack and continued on to the pool.

While swimming usually brought McRae a bit of mental quiet, this morning there was no end to the intruding thoughts. He wondered what the *Guardian* said, whether it implicated his and Smalls' work, who their source was (he was certain it wasn't Smalls), and what the fallout would be. He thought about the Rutherfords and their reaction. Was that the flurry of activity he saw at last night's event? It would make sense for them to contact a reliable lawyer and try and stop publication, or at least get an advance copy so they could check to see whether they were mentioned. As Garson worked for more than one media company, an inquiry by him could have been from any number of sources, but McRae now had a very good idea what urgent work brought the older barrister back to the office late last night.

He also had a few fleeting thoughts of Dee. He was more intrigued by her than he had been by anyone in the past year, though he hadn't been at that many social events. It was hard to meet new people who weren't students or colleagues at departmental mixers, and the Friend wasn't the kind of bar women went to looking for love. But he couldn't tell yet whether he was interested in her or in her connection to Garson. Either way, he wouldn't shut anything down just yet. He'd see where time and the investigation took him.

Twenty laps later, McRae emerged from the water, showered, and made his way across early-morning London, fuelled by a sense of purpose and his usual croissant. He again brought his bike up to the office, and before reviewing his lecture plans, he noted the presence of the Post-it with an *X* on it in the phone booth opposite. He expected as much. There would be no way he wouldn't meet with Smalls after a headline like this.

Much as he needed to prepare for his lectures, he needed to read the paper more.

> *Sources inside MI5 tell the* Guardian *that the investigation into the largest mass murder on British soil has stalled, and that the actions of the department are to blame.*
>
> *The bombing of the pagan celebration in Edinburgh last May killed 73 people and wounded hundreds as an incendiary device*

was exploded in a bonfire at the top of Calton Hill. There was also significant damage to several nearby historic buildings.

The Guardian *has learned that* MI5 *became aware that the bombing was not, as originally reported, a suicide attack, but when investigators were getting close to learning the identity of the suspect, the investigation was all but shelved. Senior investigators were reassigned to other, less pressing matters, and technical and staffing assistance that could have helped identify the suspect was diverted elsewhere. Our source reported that there were now only four investigators assigned to find the perpetrator of the worst mass murder on British soil since 2005.*

"The attack on Stephen Lethbridge, MP *for Southend, gave the department the cover it needed to once again shift its resources to surveilling the local Muslim population and to stop the investigation of a mass murderer."*

Our source also reported that security footage they were attempting to access appears to have been deliberately deleted. The source could not offer an explanation as to why the department would want to hamper the investigation.

Jane Salisbury, spokesperson for the Security Service, said that while the department does not comment on ongoing investigations, "we continue to investigate this tragedy with all available resources but cannot allow the present security of Great Britain to be compromised by our work on finding the culprit for one incident, no matter how serious."

So there was a source in the department, and suspicion would probably fall on Smalls. McRae's friend would now come under greater scrutiny, and his communications would be monitored. McRae hoped Smalls had deleted the text this morning, since his phone would likely be confiscated now. McRae would have to wait until this afternoon for more. In the meantime, he had students to attend to.

Indeed, the morning was very difficult for Smalls. He got a call at five a.m. from the office, ordering him in at the earliest possible opportunity. He got dressed in minutes and took a cab. On the ride, he began a quick perusal of the news apps. The *Guardian* was his third hit, and as soon as he saw the headline, he sent his text to McRae and then deleted the text and the contact from his phone. He also went into the system on the phone and deleted any reference to the text from his metadata. It was as much covering his tracks as he could do without raising suspicion.

After the text, he asked the driver to reroute to Aldwych and the last phone booth on the street. He left the customary Post-it and walked the rest of the way to Charing Cross and headquarters.

The MI5 building was already busy when Smalls arrived, and he was immediately met by Walterson and two agents from Internal Affairs. He was relieved of his ID and his phone and led by one of the IA agents to an interrogation room.

These small, windowless rooms looked different on this side of the table. Smalls was confident there would be nothing problematic on his work computer, and he'd erased the only evidence on his phone. There would still be some trace of his connection to McRae, but only the faintest one of being friends on Facebook, which these days was next to meaningless.

He'd been in the room for a half-hour, going over possible scenarios of what could happen at this point. He knew he'd been brought in for questioning and that his every move would be examined. He was the lead—really, the only—investigator on what remained of the inquest into the Beltane Massacre. He was an obvious possibility for the source of the leak. But while he had spoken about the events to someone else—McRae—he had never spoken about them to, or in the presence of, any reporters, let alone *Guardian* reporters. And whoever wrote that article had information Rowan didn't have, so Smalls eliminated him as a possible source.

The *Guardian*, after all, was the only truly "leftist" major newspaper still in operation in Britain. As voracious as the press were, when it came to issues like taxation, immigration, prisons, the social safety net, and even the royal family, the other papers largely toed the Thatcherite line they'd held now for the last three decades: brown-skinned people bad, taxes bad, cops good, public spending bad, and to hell with Europe.

In the security services, any other major newspaper was considered acceptable by at least some of the force. The brass pretended not to read the *Mail* but admitted to reading the *Times*. Staff pretended to read the *Mail* but really read the *Sun*. A few folks read the *Independent* but mostly only picked up the free *Metro* on the Tube in the morning to check the scores of the previous day's matches and to see which minor member of the royal family was now caught with their pants down.

The *Guardian* was the only newspaper willing to take on the Tory establishment at all, even after the move south from Manchester to London in the sixties. It was the paper that exposed *News of the World*'s use of phone hacking as a source. It was the paper that reported Edward Snowden's classified files. It was, in short, exactly the place one would expect to find a leak from MI5 and the last paper anyone in the services would admit to reading.

Smalls calmed himself partly by remembering his training and partly by remembering that he was, in fact, innocent of what he was likely being accused of.

The thick silence of the interrogation room was broken when Walterson and one of the IA agents, the one who had taken his phone, came in. Walterson, in his most patrician tone, began by saying, "I presume, Mr. Smalls, that you know something of why you're in here and not at your desk."

"Yes, sir. I saw the report on my way in this morning."

"And as the primary investigator, you are, of course, one of the primary suspects in leaking confidential and classified information to a reporter."

"Sir," Smalls said, then took a deep breath, "much as it isn't how I wanted to spend my morning, were I in your position, I'd have put me in here too. I have no doubt of my innocence, but I would be the first person I'd check."

This contrite and astute analysis surprised Walterson, who was no doubt expecting a bit more objection from Smalls. "Do you have your suspicions, then?"

He did, of course, but Smalls had no desire to start sharing those with Walterson. If he was wrong, it would look like misdirection. If he was right, then whoever had talked to the *Guardian* would be in trouble, and right now Smalls needed all the allies he could get, even if they were unwitting ones. "I'm hesitant to start throwing out theories at this stage, sir, as I have no idea whether they'd even make sense."

"Very well then. For the moment, Mr. Smalls, I believe you. An initial scan of your computer and phone indicate nothing problematic, but given where we work, these measures are far from conclusive. As such, I have no choice but to place you on administrative leave pending an investigation."

It was the best Smalls could have hoped for. He might lose access to his internal contacts, but as long as he wasn't under too strong a surveillance, he would actually be free to help McRae in what he now saw as the proper investigation. Still, he was impressed by Walterson's composure in the face of what must be a maelstrom of shit.

"I understand that, sir. I assume you'll be keeping my phone as evidence?"

"We'll have to, but we can provide you with a loaner phone for the time being. We've taken the liberty of cloning your device." Because he was an MI5 employee, they had the right to this invasion without his knowledge or consent. It's what he expected they'd do.

"That would be helpful, thanks." While he had already decided to get a burner for contact with McRae, it would help maintain the illusion that everything was normal if he kept his phone. He'd need to be careful about where he took it—it could track his location as well—but when he went places he usually frequented, that would do. That said, Smalls usually kept geolocation off, and since they had cloned his phone, it should be off on the burner too. He'd need to check before making contact.

He also needed to assume he would be followed. He'd have to find a way to inconspicuously lose his tail before meeting with McRae. He definitely couldn't risk bringing someone from MI5 to the Friend at Hand.

Once released, with his burner in hand, Smalls made his way across Trafalgar Square, through Leicester Square, to O'Neill's, the only Irish pub in Chinatown. It was close to the theatre district, and he'd been there on a couple of after-show dates over the years. This time of day it wouldn't be crowded, but it was also in a location that was hard to surveil, as the chaotic bustle of Chinatown made any interlopers conspicuous.

Once inside, he quickly approached the bartender and asked to make a local call. He punched in the number for the Friend at Hand and asked for Owens, the manager.

"Aye, you're speaking with him."

"Owens, this is Martin Smalls, Rowan McRae's friend. He's expecting to meet me there, but I'm going to be held up by work. Can you pass along a message for me?"

"For you, nae. But for Rowan, no problem," the manager said with a chuckle.

"Got a pen and paper? I need it to be exact."

"Aye, go ahead."

"I'm held up at work. We'll have to grab a Budweiser another time. And maybe a Marlboro too."

"He smokes? Didn't know that."

"He doesn't often, as I recall, but I might need one. Can you read it back to me?"

The message was exact. Budweiser was easy, their code word for an urgent need to meet. Smalls had to hope, however, that McRae would understand what he meant by Marlboro and that it wasn't really the cigarette.

Smalls left the pub after an hour or so, before the lunch rush began. To make sure no one was following him, he wandered the side streets of Soho for another hour, stopping in Soho Square Gardens and Bedford Gardens for a half-hour each, until making his way north, to Torrington Place and the Marlborough Arms.

The Marlborough Arms was exactly the kind of place that the Friend at Hand was not. It was near Gower Street, in the heart of the student district, and so was a favourite after-class local for students of University College London, Birkbeck, and the other colleges in Bloomsbury. Professors too, Smalls noted, as the crowd began to fill in after three. He decided to move himself to one of the tables outside, facing toward Gower and what he thought was McRae's likely route home.

A half-hour later, as expected, McRae came cycling up from Gower. Once he spotted Smalls, he let his pace relax and glided off to the side, parking his bike against the fence.

"Should I get a pint? Or perhaps a ciggy?" McRae smiled tensely.

"No, let's head on, shall we?"

"Fair enough," McRae said, as Smalls drained his third pint of the afternoon and rose to leave.

They began walking westward, through the student housing of Fitzrovia, toward the more middle-class Marylebone. Once, the Marylebone high street was the main commercial street of a village outside London. Now, it retained some of its own character but was squarely part of the city centre. With fewer students than Fitzrovia and fewer tourists than nearby Hyde Park, it housed a wide array of small businesses. As McRae lived on the western end of the district, he seldom visited the high street, but now as he and Smalls wandered their way through the area, he realized he had been missing out. It seemed quieter and quainter than the rest of London but lost none of the sophistication you'd expect to find in Mayfair to the south.

McRae had read the *Guardian* article several times by now. If anything, it made clear that the source of the leak couldn't have been Smalls. For starters, the article said someone had deleted the CCTV footage, which, while true, was a problem Moss had overcome some time ago when she tracked down the DfT backup footage. It also said that there were still four officers assigned, which was no longer true as the other three members of Smalls' team had recently been reassigned elsewhere. While the source was someone familiar with the investigation, it was likely someone who had been taken off it months ago.

"So if it wasn't you, who was it?" McRae asked.

"If I had to guess, I'd say one of the reassigned agents. They weren't happy about our little squad being broken up. But I'd rather not know, quite frankly."

"Still, I'm pretty sure it confirms the one good lead I got out of last night."

Smalls shot him a confused look, but McRae began his debrief without breaking his stride. Smalls was particularly interested in Walterson's appearance and in the apparent connection between him and the major, and between the major and his lawyer, Garson.

"Given what's happened since," said Rowan, "I expect Walterson got word of the story yesterday evening from the *Guardian* desk looking for a comment. He tracked down the major, who tried to see if Garson could do something to stop publication or at least figure out whether the story mentioned any connection to the Rutherfords. Which, of course, it does not."

"No, it doesn't. Which is a relief."

"To them even more than to us, I'd say. They're bound to be a bit more cautious, as there will be other reporters sniffing around now, but they shouldn't entirely shut down whatever it is they're doing that has anything to do with the investigation."

"We need to get access to the major. But how?"

"Would it make sense to try and go through the lawyer?" Rowan asked.

"Perhaps, though I don't see any reason to suspect his involvement is anything other than professional. And I don't have any real way to tap Garson's phone."

"Don't you secret agent types have some sort of gadget we can use for that?"

"Does this seem like a movie to you? I mean, we do have tech that can pick up mobile numbers or signals, and if we're close enough we can even hack into a laptop, but I can't get to it now, and even if I could, I don't know how that stuff works."

"Then perhaps his home computer would be the way. I managed to get the licence plate number of his driver's car. Any way you can get your cabbie friend to track him to his home?"

"I'll reach out once I get a burner."

"Why don't you give me his number and I'll reach out?"

"Better yet, give me your mobile," Smalls said, and McRae obliged. Smalls swiped the screen and held it up to McRae's face to unlock it. "Why do you need my gadgets when you've got this kind of kit?" he said as he punched in a number.

"Simon, this is Martin. No, it's not my phone, but I'm calling from my good mate Rowan's phone. Got a job for you. I've got a couple of business addresses and names but need home addresses. Target one is Major Hilary Halisbury," he paused, "yes, that Halisbury, the one we saw the other day. Good? Okay, second target is Charles Garson, barrister with Gladstone Chambers." Smalls paused for a second. "Do you really want to ask that question? I didn't think so. I'll text you the plate number for the barrister's driver. Bill me when you're done. Oh, and if you get any calls from this number, treat them as if they're coming from me. Rowan and I served together, so he knows his business."

He ended the call then turned to McRae. "There," Smalls said, smiling for the first time all afternoon, "you now have access to my entire surveillance network."

"When do you expect we'll hear from him?"

"Likely tomorrow night."

By this point the tonier parts of Marylebone were behind them and the more commercial Edgware Road lay ahead. McRae and his bike accompanied Smalls to a discount phone shop where the latter acquired a cheap flip phone and a new number. He put the number in McRae's phone and then tucked his new device in his pocket.

"Call me on this. Don't text. And I'll be deleting your number each time, just in case I get taken in for questioning again."

"Sounds good. Should we make a plan to meet day after tomorrow?"

"Aye. Go to the Friend as usual. I'll call if I need to leave a message. If I'm clear, I'll meet you there."

"That'll work," McRae said, and the two men went their separate ways. Smalls headed south, toward Marble Arch, to get the Tube home. McRae went north, to the local Tesco, to pick up some supper. He'd missed his lunch at the Friend and was famished.

As he browsed for something edible for supper—the stock at these city centre grocers always got pretty slim by the end of the day—McRae's thoughts turned to tomorrow. Thursday was usually a research day, but he knew he wasn't going to be getting much archival work done, leastways not on early twentieth-century shipping routes. Most of his mind was focused on the Rutherfords and how to make sure he stayed on their radar. So along with his take-home chicken tikka masala and small bottle of ginger ale, he picked up a thank-you card to send to the Rutherfords.

That wasn't all that was on his mind. Thoughts of Dee and her intelligent, dark eyes intruded as well. So once he was done supper and was settling in for a night of music and reading—Ian Rankin with Amy Winehouse on vocals—he sent her a text.

— Hope you've had a good day. Still up for drinks?

That was enough for now. Anything more would be too pushy, but he didn't want to send nothing. For now, he'd read his book, listen to his music, and let his mind turn off as best as he could.

8

When McRae woke in the morning, with the Spotify playlist now on the obscure Joni Mitchell track "In France They Kiss On Main Street" and his copy of Fleshmarket Close on the bed beside him, he saw the notification.

> — It was a long day in court that I can't possibly tell you about over text. How's tonight for you? 😉

McRae wasn't used to getting a text first thing in the morning, so his usual routine was a bit thrown off at first. Even more, though, the substance of the text and the sight of the simple gold band sitting on his dresser made him realize that he hadn't put on his wedding ring since taking it off for the auction two days before. It was the longest he'd gone without wearing it since Lynn had put it on his finger, now four and a half years ago.

He picked up the ring and rolled it between his thumb and forefinger thoughtfully. They had talked about this, what should happen if either of them died. Each of them expected the other to try and move on should something happen, but neither one of them wanted to have to deal with that prospect for long, and so the conversations were fleeting. As the edges of the plain gold band pressed against his fingers, he could feel her presence. He knew his wife well enough to know that she'd approve.

By the end of his first session with Lynn, she working through a relatively basic history paper with him, explaining when to use commas and when not to use semicolons, he was smitten. It wasn't just her ginger hair or porcelain skin. It wasn't even just her obvious intelligence. It was the kindness that got straight to the core of him. Something about her reminded some unconscious part of him of being a child, when everything was safe because his mother, a kindergarten teacher, was there. Whatever differences there were between Lynn and his mother, the kindness at her core was what drew him in and made him want to get to know more of her.

Nonetheless, he kept their relationship professional for two terms, only broaching the possibility of a date in their last session, before the April exam break. By then they could banter like old friends, but given what he felt—and was pretty sure she was starting to feel too—he decided it was worth the risk.

Now, six years later, her memory filled his mind again. He looked up at the morning sunlight streaming through his east-facing window. He knew she would want this for him. She couldn't be with him anymore, but that didn't mean he should be alone.

Still, he couldn't quite bear to leave the ring home again today. When he wasn't wearing it, he felt as if something was missing. As, indeed, something was. But right now he felt like he needed that reminder, whether it was a chess piece in his pocket or the ring he once wore on his finger.

For now he put the ring in his trouser pocket before folding his pants and placing them in his knapsack. It would be safe there until he got to work. He knew there would be some string in the departmental supply cabinet he could use to let the ring hang around his neck and against his chest exactly where Lynn liked to rest her head after a long day. He then pulled himself from his bed and made his way to the pool, only a few minutes late for his swim.

For Smalls, the day began with a phone call. It was Moss. "Smalls, had a good day off yesterday?" So she knew, then.

"Aye, delightful, Sandra. To what do I owe the pleasure at this hour in the morning?"

"You're back to active duty. A lot has happened in twenty-four hours. I'll see you at eight thirty."

Following a brief acknowledgement, Smalls ended the call on his regular phone and called McRae from his burner. There was no answer, but he didn't leave a message. Instead, McRae called him back, five minutes later.

"Was riding into work. What's up?"

"I'm back on active service. Moss seems to be in charge now. Meet at the Friend after work?"

"Briefly, sure. I've got plans tonight."

"Plans? All right, you can fill me in later."

"I'll be there by three. Come when you can," McRae said, and ended the call before Smalls could inquire further.

For the second day in a row, Smalls took a cab in to work. This time, however, he called Blackburn to come and get him. It would take a few extra minutes, but they could debrief en route.

It was twenty minutes before Blackburn arrived, giving Smalls enough time to dress and flip through the news. The *Guardian* had more follow-up coverage, focusing on a response from the Home Secretary, who said he would take a personal interest in the matter and make sure that the culprit or culprits were found, but most of the other dailies only mentioned it in their politics section. The *Gleaner* was conspicuously silent.

A quick toot of the horn alerted Smalls to Blackburn's arrival. He flicked his burner to silent and tucked it into his briefcase's inside pocket before slipping his office phone in his jacket pocket.

"Morning, Simon. How was your expedition yesterday?"

"Aye, expedition is the right word. I was all over town chasing down your targets."

"Then first things first, what do I owe you?"

"Total on the meter was two hundred."

"Ouch," Smalls feigned. He'd been expecting about that and passed a folded wad of twenties through the window. "Here's two forty for your trouble. So tell me everything."

"Started out straightforward enough. Picked up the barrister's driver's car in a lot near Chancery Road, as expected. I got myself parked and kept an eye on the car rather than on the building, and around six, he went to pick up the gentleman. They went to a place on Fulham Road for dinner, a curry spot, where he met with your other target, that military bloke from the other day. Was two other men with them there. Both posh. No military background to speak of, though."

"Did you get pictures?"

"You know it." Blackburn smiled as he handed Smalls his phone, with the picture already pulled up. Smalls reached into his briefcase, grabbed the burner, and took his own photos of Blackburn's work.

"Brilliant work, thanks. Where did they go from there?"

"Garson went back to his office for a while, then home for the day around nine. Lives in a white townhouse on Cadogan Place, Belgravia."

"That tracks."

"Once I had an address, I got back to regular work, if you don't mind."

"Not at all. I appreciate the help."

"One of these days you'll have to buy me a pint and explain to me what this is all about."

"You sure you want to know?"

Blackburn laughed. "Not in the slightest."

They finished the drive to Trafalgar in decent time, despite the rush, and Smalls arrived at HQ around ten minutes before his appointment with Moss.

It was a very different scene from the day before. No one was waiting for him other than the usual front desk security folks. They returned his credentials and waved him through the metal detectors, as if yesterday had never happened. He went to the lift and pushed six, just as he had hundreds of times before.

When he arrived, he noticed more of a bustle of activity than he'd seen in some time, with Moss at the centre of it. Despite her relatively short stature, she was a strong presence in any room, ordering around her troops with a commander's certainty.

"Smalls. Good. Welcome back. In the black room, please."

The black room was the secure central room at the heart of counterintelligence. It was lead- and god-knows-what-else-lined to ensure it stayed safe in the event of an attack, and no one attempting to listen in could hear anything. It was as secure a spot as possible.

Smalls made his way in and took a seat at the eight-person table, on the long side facing the door. There was a smattering of papers around the table, all relating to Beltane. In a moment Moss entered, alone, and closed the door.

"Correct me if I'm wrong, Smalls, but there was no love lost between you and Walterson, was there."

She had one of those expressionless faces at the moment, which it was usually harder for women to get away with than men. Nonetheless, in their position, it did its job. She seemed stern but also non-confrontational. Smalls, without exactly being put at ease, decided to trust her, to a point. "No, ma'am."

"And you were both personally and professionally aggrieved with the treatment of the Edinburgh investigation, correct?"

"Absolutely."

"You've been pretty thoroughly investigated, and I am confident you had nothing to do with leaking the story to the *Guardian*."

"You are correct."

"Now this part is more speculative on my part, but I think you may have been investigating Walterson. Is that right?"

"What gave you that impression?"

"For starters, the convenient lapse in the security cameras when we had that fire break out last week. You are the fire marshal for the floor. The kid whose terminal was used didn't do it. He was barely competent enough to review video and couldn't have pulled off something like that. So I think it was you. Am I right?"

"Not sure what you're talking about there."

"Well done. Good and evasive. We'll need that. You see, I'm sure you were investigating Walterson, and I've had my suspicions about him for a while too, which I was happy to share with the Home Secretary when I was questioned yesterday. Mad as he was about the leak, Walterson was even more furious that there might be any perception that the Edinburgh investigation had stalled, which, as we both know, was his doing. He's on administrative leave now, and I'm Acting Director. So I'm going to reassign you. I'm taking over the Edinburgh investigation, with most of the resources of the department. Special directive from the head of the General Communications HQ, following the instructions of the Home Office. You're officially tasked with taking over the Southend investigation from me, but in practice, you're going to be figuring out what the hell was up with Walterson. Not officially sanctioned, but that's what you're going to do, understood?"

Moss was going out on a limb for him here. Unofficial investigations like this happened all the time, but they always had to be off the books, and the officers involved had to trust one another.

"What resources do I have?"

"Departmental credit card. Standard five-hundred-pounds-a-day limit. Don't go over or it'll draw red flags. If you need something run—names, numbers, plates, faces—do it and don't tell me about it. We debrief each morning in here. Got it?"

"Understood."

"Now, back to work. And thanks, Martin."

Smalls' desire to get back to work, now that he was finally able to do so properly, overwhelmed his relief at the sudden change in tides. He bolted down the hall to his cubicle and logged in, using the new password provided to him by security—they'd changed his to search all his actions—and found that he now had access to the secure databases; Moss must have made it a priority. He immediately began running all the images he had of key players through any database he could. Then he took the memory card from his burner mobile and uploaded the photos he'd taken from Blackburn less than a half-hour earlier. About three minutes later, he had two hits, one for each of the men in Blackburn's photos. When they came through, Smalls' heart sank.

The major and Garson were meeting Samuel Banks, Special Assistant to the Prime Minister, and David Clegg, Deputy Commissioner of the Metropolitan Police. The search turned up home addresses for both, the former at a flat in Pimlico, the latter a townhouse in St. John's Wood. At least Smalls knew where the surveillance had to start.

Moments passed and there were no hits on the other images—nothing in any database on either the suspect or the driver. This was odd; surely the driver must have a licence, and it would be highly unusual if the suspect had no form of ID at all. Smalls had some theories of why this might be but wanted to discuss them with Moss before acting on them.

Smalls approached his boss and nodded for her to join him in the black room. She followed and again closed the door.

"Anything new on Walterson?" he asked her.

"His emails have come up clean, if that's what you're asking."

"It is. But that's not why I brought you in here."

"On with it then," she said, slightly peeved.

"If I have leads and need surveillance, where do I turn?"

"Any issue enlisting Metro?" she asked, referring to the police.

"Yes," he responded, looking her square in the eyes. She processed this quickly and sighed.

"Okay, anyone you trust?"

"Other than you, not particularly. Not right now."

"Fine then. I trust Eyre's squad. Will they work?"

Gareth Eyre led a small team of field operatives that usually did undercover work, when required. Five in total, they had spent much of the last few months knowingly wasting their time surveilling mosques. Smalls hadn't worked with them before, but evidently Moss had and knew their work.

"If you trust them, I'll trust them. Shall I bring them in?"

"No, we're using this room too much, and someone will notice. We don't know who's watching on this. Take them out in the field and give them their orders. I'll patch Eyre in. Give him a call in half an hour and set a meeting point outside the building. Do I want to know who?"

"I think you do. So far, we're up against the PMO, the Met, and the *Gleaner*."

Moss voiced a lesser expletive while she breathed out heavily.

"There's more," Smalls continued. "While I could get IDs on the men meeting with Walterson and a couple of his contacts, I couldn't get anything on the suspect or the driver. I can't imagine the driver didn't get a licence, so I think someone may have deleted his photo from the databases."

"I don't even know what would be involved in that," she said.

"Neither do I, but it strikes me as something Walterson could have handled, or maybe Clegg from the Met. He's one of the people Walterson's contacts met with."

"Clegg, bloody hell," she said with an exasperated sigh. "It's possible, but either way it doesn't get us any closer to the suspect, does it?"

"No, it doesn't."

"Let's get a move on the surveillance first. And keep it close, Smalls. If this goes sideways we're all fucked."

He again looked her in the eye, and with a deadly seriousness and emphasizing each syllable, he said, "Understood."

A phone call and an hour later, Smalls was waiting in a snug—a small room off to the left of the main bar—at the Lord Marlborough when Eyre and his four-person squad, two men and two women, walked in. They were all dressed in street clothes and could have passed as students or backpackers easily enough, except for the looks of determination and annoyance they all shared.

"Listen, I don't mind going where I'm told," Eyre began, with a strong current of Welsh in his accent, "but getting pulled around like this isn't for the best."

"I can appreciate that. What can I say? Moss is in charge now. She's given me a special assignment, and you're the only ones she trusts to help me with it." Smalls knew a little bit of flattery never hurt anyone, even in MI5.

"Fine. Who's the new target?"

Smalls laid two sets of photographs on the table, face down. "Have a seat. James, can we get a couple pots of tea in here?" he called to the bartender as the team took their seats and looked at the photographs.

No one spoke until James had come and gone, leaving behind him three pots of tea, half a dozen mugs, some milk and sugar, and taking a tenner from Smalls with a smile in exchange.

"Anyone know who this is?" Smalls asked, holding up the photo of the younger man. He was met only with blank stares. "This is Samuel Banks. Place of work, 10 Downing Street. Residence, Dolphin House, Pimlico. Age forty-one." He paused a moment, waiting for this to sink in. "And if that's not daunting enough, this," Smalls continued, lifting the picture of the out-of-uniform copper, "is David Clegg, Deputy Commissioner of the Metropolitan Police. Age fifty-three. Residence 31 Jamieson Street, St. John's Wood.

"Neither of these is a particularly easy target, but we need to know where they go and who they meet with when they're not at work. We know they're associated with these two men," Smalls showed a photo of the major and Garson, "but anyone else, we need photos of. We believe they're part of a network, and we need to know just how far this web goes."

Eyre spoke up. "That's not so bad, really, but how do you track someone like the deputy commissioner, when he can simply send Met coppers to do his work for him?"

"We have someone assigned to monitor the police band to keep tabs on whether there are any unusual requests coming from the deputy commissioner's office. So that's covered. For now, it's just surveillance. I'll leave you to sort out the details."

"How do these folks connect to Beltane?" one of Eyre's team asked, a particularly young man with the kind of cocky on him that new recruits usually had.

"You sure you want to ask that?" Smalls responded, which prompted Eyre to step in.

"No need, boss. We'll get to it."

"Overtime is covered. Receipts, run sheets, and reports come to me or Moss, no one else. Understood?"

"Loud and clear. Cheers," Eyre said. At which, Smalls gave him a small nod.

"I'll leave you to it then," he said. "Need more tea before I leave?"

"Naw, and it's too early for pints."

"Never," Smalls said, as he made his way from the snug and left the team to their work. The less he knew of their inner workings, or they of his, the better.

Smalls decided not to head back to the office. He had about four hours before he had to meet McRae and needed to clear his head in the meantime. He was now investigating his own boss, an assistant to the prime minister, the deputy head of Scotland Yard, a leading barrister, and the owners of the third-highest subscription newspaper in the country. This week he had gone from frustration to excitement, then to being on the edge of fired to basically promoted. All since he reached out to McRae.

He wondered how this was affecting Rowan. He'd been through something a year ago that breaks most people, and Smalls couldn't tell yet how it had affected him. McRae was always a closed book. The intervening decade between their time working together and now didn't seem to have changed him. Time hadn't softened him or opened him up any more. The violent deaths of his wife and child must have affected him, but how remained a mystery to Smalls.

9

When Rowan arrived at the Friend, he found Smalls already sitting in the corner with two pints of lager. Given that the one in front of Smalls was about a third gone, Rowan assumed he'd been waiting for a while.

"Cheers," Rowan said, sitting beside him, with both again facing the interior of the bar and both possible entrances. "You first. What the hell happened?"

Smalls took him on a brief tour of the last thirty-six hours: going from departmental pariah on administrative leave to having unofficial official support for their investigation with a small task force working with him. As for the investigation, it had gone from having a possible lead in the Halisburys to tendrils extending into Scotland Yard and the PMO. Things had certainly changed quickly, but McRae didn't trust it. If it could change for the good this quickly, how quickly could it get drastically worse?

"You trust Moss?" he asked.

"I do. Not with everything just yet; if she knew the extent of what we've already found, I think it highly likely she'd shut us down or at least bring us completely inside. But she does know I'm investigating Walterson and knows there was something fishy behind the way the Edinburgh investigation was handled, so she's at least on our side for now."

"And the team you've got, how discreet can they be?"

"My understanding is that they've got a couple of the department-issued black cabs. They blend in as well as anything in central London. They've done a lot of work together so they know each other's style. And Moss trusts them. Whatever her motives here, she is a good judge of competence."

"I don't know, didn't she make you her deputy?"

"Har har, delightful. Now, how was your day? Lectures go well? Find anything interesting in the archives?"

"I've been behaving entirely like a proper professor today. Got up, went for my swim, rode in to work, got your call, read a really shit paper on British influence in South Africa that totally ignores the role of Thatcher's commercial interests—or her son's, rather—in sustaining apartheid for an extra few years, then came to meet you here, to get the good news."

"All right then. Where do we go from here?"

"You'll be getting updates from your team in the morning, right? Would it make sense for us to meet after that to go over what's new and to plot the day out? I don't have classes tomorrow, so I'll be available for a bit of reconnaissance as well."

"The one thing that worries me right now, apart from everything, of course—"

"Of course."

"—is what Walterson will be up to now that he's on leave. Did he get much of a look at you at the auction?"

"I don't think so. We weren't introduced. The auction was on when he arrived. I saw him come in, take the major upstairs, and then mingle for a few minutes in the crowd before slipping out after a quick word with Garson. It's possible he'd recognize me but likely not if I'm in a hoodie and jeans."

"Then do you have any objection to tailing him tomorrow?" Smalls asked. "I can't very well put the team on him without giving away the link between the department and the targets."

"It's one target, really. Some sort of conspiracy," Rowan said. "Some of these folks have known each other for a long time, and I think there may be more pies that they've been sticking their fingers in over the years. I wonder how deep they go and how organized they are."

"For now, all we can do is keep following the leads we have and see where they go," Smalls said. "Walterson is an unsupervised lead. He, the viscount, the major, Banks, Clegg, and maybe Garson are the only ones we have reason to suspect right now, and tailing a barrister into his chambers seems almost impossible."

McRae felt a twinge in his stomach. He could try and use a relationship with Dee as a pretext to be coming around Chancery Road, but he really didn't want to. First, he didn't like being manipulative in that way; it felt dishonest and he wanted to still be able to look himself in the mirror—and her in the eyes—tomorrow. But even more, he doubted Dee was the kind of woman with whom clingy behaviour would work. Or, at least, he hoped she wasn't. He valued his independence and didn't want anything to do with a woman who didn't also value hers. So he let it go and decided not to tell Smalls about the connection unless it came up in some other way. Still, Smalls noticed him thinking and now needed an explanation.

"No, you're right. The chambers is a road block, but Walterson isn't. I'll do a preliminary circuit of his place now and see what I can do to keep tabs on him from there. Where does he live, anyway?" Rowan asked.

"He's got two places. There's a family country house in the Cotswolds where he could be, but if he's there then we don't have to worry about him meddling much. If he's in London, he'll be at 61 Chester Square, near Victoria."

"I'll look it up, but it shouldn't be a problem." Rowan finished off his pint and stood to leave.

"Why the rush?"

"Well, Martin, I have a date."

"Do you really?" Smalls said with an incredulous smile. "Well then, you'll need another pint," and he motioned toward Owens.

"No, definitely not. One will have to do for now. We're meeting for drinks at seven."

"Who is this mystery woman?"

McRae sat back down. "Met her at the auction. Diksha Jamil. A barrister who works at the same chambers as Garson."

"Mixing business with pleasure—well done. You sure you're Canadian and not Italian or Spanish or something?"

McRae had become accustomed to this sort of casual racism during his time in Britain. He would never forget when Lynn came home and told him about a conversation two of her coworkers were having over drinks at after work about how annoying they found all the foreigners. It never dawned on them that they were having this conversation with a foreigner. A Canadian, from halfway across the world, wasn't a problem, but the Polish guy at the chippy and the Romanian cab driver were concerning to them.

"No one suspects the Canadian, Marty. It's our secret weapon, the element of surprise. But I do have a few hours. I can get a bit of a swing by Walterson's in now and then make my way to the pub where I'm meeting her. But I'll need to head out. Do we have any other business?"

"Walterson drives, and if he decides to leave, there is no way you'll be able to follow him on foot. So take this." Smalls handed him a disk, magnetic on one side and black plastic on the other, about the size of a two-pound piece. "Put this on his car, and text me if he leaves. I'll give you a new location once he gets wherever he's going."

"No problem. Anything else?"

"Nothing pressing. Let's meet up again tomorrow, assuming you're not too tired," Smalls added, getting in a little dig.

"As a countryman of mine, pretending to be a countryman of yours, famously said, 'Oh, behave.'" With that, McRae took his leave.

McRae stashed his bike at his apartment and got changed. He needed to wear a hoodie for his surveillance task but didn't want to be wearing it for drinks with Dee, so under his hoodie he put on one of his dress shirts along with a pair of black jeans. When he headed out to get the bus to Victoria station, the sun was starting to descend, but it was still definitely daylight. He was enough of a newcomer to London to enjoy sitting upstairs on the bus when he had more than a couple of stops to go. He put himself in a window seat with a view of Hyde Park to the left.

Victoria station was always busy, and today, a Thursday night at the cusp of summer, was no exception. It was still too early for theatregoers, but the Market Halls were packed, and throngs of workers were heading toward the station to make their way home. Victoria was where several subway lines intersected, along with suburban trains to Dulwich and Croydon and larger trains to points south of London. It wasn't unheard of for people to commute from Portsmouth or Southampton several days a week. Even with the daily fare added on, the cost of living could still be cheaper at some remove from the city.

McRae joined the throng heading toward the station, taking comfort in the anonymity of being part of a crowd for as long as he could, until his route forced him to turn west, heading on Lower Belgrave Street toward Chester Square. After a block, the apartment complexes nearest the station gave way to the white plaster and brownstone row houses that were ubiquitous throughout London, occasionally with small shops on the ground floor. A few generations ago, these might have been family homes for relatively ordinary

Londoners, he thought to himself, but now they were either the preserve of the wealthy or listed as short-term lets on Airbnb, if not both. Still, there were a few signs that it was a real neighbourhood: he passed a grocer's and noticed a pub across the road, the Plumber's Arms. He wondered if this was Walterson's local but thought it nowhere near posh enough for him. Still, it could be a good place to escape to if he sensed trouble.

The shops thinned out when he turned the corner to Chester Square. Now it was all white plaster buildings, squeezed together tightly like hard enamel teeth in an overcrowded mouth. The cars parked in the spaces on the side were largely modest ones, indicating that while this was a "comfortable" area of London—affluent by the standards of anywhere else—it wasn't yet the province of the gentrifying super-rich. Not a place he would likely run into any irksome students who would blow his cover.

As with most of the tonier neighbourhoods of London, there was a park running along one side of the road, and the numbering continued all around it. As he got deeper into the block, and the numbers on the houses rose, the cars also improved. Vauxhalls and Skodas were replaced by Range Rovers and the odd Porsche. Across the road from the far south end of the park stood a small chapel—St. Michael's, it said on a plaque beside the door—but McRae walked past it and turned again. There was no sidewalk on the park side of the street, so he had to walk on the same side as the houses. Based on the numbers from the first side, he knew number 61 would be almost at the midpoint. Unless he could find a vantage in the park, there would be very little cover for him here. Worse, it was a two-way street, so he couldn't be sure that if he was at either end he would catch Walterson coming or going. The only saving grace was that there was a small gate in the park almost directly across from his target's house, with a bench not far back from it. That would be his perch tomorrow. For now, he merely observed.

The house looked quiet today, but it was still too bright outside to know if there were any lights on. He also didn't know what Walterson drove, but he made a mental note of the nearby vehicles and, once he turned the corner back toward Victoria station, jotted down the plate numbers in a small notebook. As the station came back into view he realized that his pulse was slowing down. Despite his training and the relative calm of the day, he'd been nervous without really realizing it. He gave Smalls a call.

"Any idea what Walterson's licence plate number is?"

"Let me look it up," Smalls said, followed by a few seconds of clicking and then a few more of muted silence. "LF 42 237."

"Received, thanks," and McRae ended the call. Checking his notes, he saw it was a black Audi.

That was it. One walk-past, taking about fifteen minutes. He hadn't learned much, but then again the point of this trip wasn't surveillance, it was to plan for surveillance. The park provided ideal cover, so as long as he could get here before Walterson left in the morning, he would be okay.

On his way back to the station, McRae came to a small archway leading to a parkade just off the main street. He ducked in quickly, tucked himself behind the columns and wall, and pulled off his hoodie. He stuffed it into his knapsack and gave himself thirty seconds to allow anyone passing to move on, then he returned to the street. No longer the unidentifiable vagrant wandering the well-to-do end of town, he looked like a young professional on his way out for the evening. Which he was. Reality was always the best cover.

10

On this bus ride, McRae was squarely focused on his destination. He was more aware of his nerves now than he had been on his reconnaissance trip. The point was still the same—getting to know more about your target—but it was a very different experience. With reconnaissance, the goal was to get to know them and to have them not know you. Dating requires you to be far more vulnerable, and it had been a while now since Rowan had been vulnerable with anyone.

The first thing he did to get himself in the right headspace was to remind himself that Dee was not a "target" or a "subject" or even a "focus." She was a woman, one in whom Rowan, despite himself, was interested. She was pretty, which helped. It helped more that she was a barrister, so there had to be a decent mind at work there. And from what he observed of her at the auction, she also had poise, a certain self-assuredness that he found compelling.

He arrived at the Clerk and found that he was there first. It was about quarter to seven, so this wasn't a surprise, but it was a welcome relief. From long before his time in the military, lateness made McRae uncomfortable. He felt it was rude to keep someone waiting and didn't like being kept waiting himself. Still, if one of them was going to be late, he was glad it wasn't him.

He walked up to the bar and realized there was a certain measure of strategy to ordering a drink on a first date, as what he ordered would say something about him to Dee. If he ordered a pint of lager, that would indicate that he was "ordinary." A fruity cider might indicate that he was comfortable enough in his masculinity to have a pink drink in front of him. But either of those would be gone within a half-hour or so, and he was fairly certain he wanted to be here longer than that. A cocktail would take longer to drink but did limit his options. He had no taste for rum and preferred whisky to gin or vodka, so an old-fashioned was reliable but also indicated that he was far more of a traditionalist than he really was.

In the end, McRae decided to stick with his policy of being himself. He was thirsty after his expedition to Victoria and so opted for a blackberry cider with a little ice, just enough that the glass didn't overflow when the can was poured in.

The Clerk was a little more polished than most of the pubs he frequented. Rather than simple wood, the chairs had leather seats. Also, there was no television; they probably didn't want football fans flocking in on match days. The bar itself was wood on the outside but had a polished granite top. There were no stools; it was a place to get your drink and get out of the way. The menu, handwritten in cursive on a chalkboard at the end of the bar, indicated far more ornate food options than the Friend. While he had nothing against harissa-smoked Scotch egg, or sea salt and rosemary thrice-fried chips, they weren't what he usually encountered.

When the bartender passed him a glass with two cubes of ice—just the right amount—and the can of Rekorderlig, McRae poured it at the bar and made his way to one of the tables to the left, beside the windows on Vine Hill, the small side street leading away from Clerkenwell Road.

At this point the pub was moderately crowded, but since it was a relatively warm spring day, many of the punters were gathered outside at the picnic tables or standing around them. The inside of the bar was well occupied, but more people were eating than drinking. Still, his table was clean and allowed him to watch the entrance for Dee's arrival.

He did not have to wait long. She slid breezily through the gathered drinkers and looked around the bar, smiling when she caught his eye. McRae was fairly certain she had changed, as you can't wear a green cocktail dress to court. He stood as she made her way over.

"You've ordered, I see," she said, as she leaned in to kiss his right cheek.

"I did, and I left my card, so feel free to add to my tab."

"You can buy this round. I'll get the next." She placed her mustard-yellow blazer on the back of her chair, then turned and made her way to the bar.

McRae almost missed the chair on his way back down—as lovely as her dress looked from the front, it was stunning from the back. At the auction, Dee's suit gave McRae no idea how beautiful her shoulders and back were, but this dress—fairly high in the front—swooped to her mid-back, revealing the mahogany skin of her toned shoulders. He knew she probably felt him staring, and he distracted himself with a sip of his cider, realizing in the process that this was likely exactly the effect she meant to have. As he returned the glass to the table, he thought to himself, "Well done, Ms. Jamil."

He looked back at her and caught her gaze. She smiled before returning her attention to the bar as she waited for her drink. It afforded him another moment to turn his attention to how she stood and moved. She was leaning against the bar, indicating comfort. As this was a first date, she must be comfortable with the surroundings and not just him, so she came here fairly often. She also seemed to have a rapport with the women behind the bar, confirming his theory. As she stood, though, she raised her right foot, resting the toe of her mustard-yellow shoes—brands of women's shoes were well outside his area of expertise—on the floor in a subtle gesture of anxiousness. She wanted to get back to the table, then, to him.

Aperol spritz in hand, she turned and made her way back to McRae, smile now firmly planted on her warm, kind face.

"Cheers." She raised her glass to his as she took her seat.

"Cheers," he responded, "and nice shoes."

Dee's smile at his compliment brightened. "Thanks, they were a present to myself on getting called to the bar. Needed something that would provide a bit of brightness after a day in court clothes."

"Entirely understandable. How was court yesterday?"

"Too early to say, unfortunately," she said with a sigh. "The Lord Justice reserved her decision."

"When will you find out?"

"On something like this, should only be a few days, a week at most."

"What were you arguing?"

"Oh, this was just a costs application. We already won the trial, so now it's a matter of trying to convince the court to make the other side pay for it all. I was the junior on the trial, but something like this is usually handled by the junior counsel. We're pretty sure we'll get something, so my job yesterday was to point out to the court just how wrong the claimant was to have brought the claim in the first place, and to point out all the delays they caused, while making ourselves look eminently reasonable."

"Makes sense to me. And it went well?"

"It did. You never really know, of course. I know I didn't do us wrong, but when it's a difference between getting what's normal and getting a great result, it's hard to tell. The other side was the one with more to lose anyway."

"Because for them it's the difference between paying some costs, no costs, and a lot of costs?"

"Pretty much. They can try and make the argument that their claim was reasonable, or novel, or that they acted in a way that was prudent, but even then, when something ends up in trial like this one did, it's unusual for there not to be a cost award. So they really had an uphill fight, and the judge didn't seem like she was buying it."

"Which is good for you."

"It is. So definitely not commiserating, if not exactly celebrating yet. How was your day?"

This was the question McRae had been dreading. He knew he couldn't embroil her in his work with Smalls, but he also didn't want to mislead her entirely.

"A pretty typical day in the old history factory," he said, and she politely chuckled at his weak joke. "More reading than writing today, which often happens toward this time of the year."

"Why is that?"

"The new terms has started, and students are working on their papers and preparing for exams, which means I am being interrupted by drafts and questions more often than at any other time of the year. It's harder to write when you're constantly being interrupted, so I end up reading more. Also, my papers for the summer conference season are pretty much locked in anyway, so now is more about revising them and making sure there aren't any important bits of scholarship I've missed."

"What is your field, anyway? I don't think it came up at the auction." This was the first time McRae detected any hint of the north in her accent. He made a mental note to ask where she was originally from if it didn't come up organically.

"Colonial history. I deal mostly with shipping and the late imperial period—1860s to the First World War."

"You should meet my father. His father moved here from the newly partitioned Pakistan but brought with him a lot of my great-grandfather's memorabilia. Great-Granddad was a clerk for the East India Company and a total anglophile. It's why we're here, after all."

"Interesting that we come from very different colonies. Most of my family had been in their part of Canada for a couple of centuries, since the 1750s at least, and I'm the first one to leave for any extended period of time since then. But then comparing the experiences of the different colonies is a big part of what I do."

"And how did you enjoy Edinburgh? I'd been as a kid but haven't been that far north in a long time."

Rowan thought for a moment. His last weeks in Edinburgh had been the worst of his life, but now, a year later, he could remember the times before that, all the good times from the three amazing years they had shared there. "It's a beautiful city, and I loved living there. It really had everything. Speaking of north, I thought I picked up a hint of the north in your accent. Am I mistaken?"

"Impressive, particularly for a Canadian," she said, laughing and taking a sip. "I was raised in Cumberland, on the western side of the Scottish Borders. A bit of brogue slips out now and then."

"How'd your family end up there?"

"My father was born and raised in Manchester, but he's a doctor and got an offer to work at the surgery in Carlisle. Far as he's concerned, though, he's still Manchester through and through. A red, if you're wondering."

"I was, in fact. Could be worse."

"Oh God, don't tell me you're into football."

"Only as much as the next Canadian," he joked. "But I've got nothing much against either of the Manchester clubs."

"Long as you're not a Liverpool or an Arsenal fan, you'll be allowed in the door."

"I'm meeting the parents now, am I? This is going well." He smiled and reached out to brush a strand of hair that had fallen into her face. She blushed, and he said, "So, what happens if I'm a Spurs fan?"

"Pity, mostly," she said with a laugh. "And your parents?"

"Well, you won't have to worry about them. They were killed by a drunk driver when I was in high school. I do have an aunt and uncle in Toronto I'm close with; they took me in for that last year before I graduated."

"I'm sorry to hear that," she said, reaching across the table and touching his elbow.

"It's okay, was a long time ago, but thanks," he said, smiling and changing the subject back to football.

The conversation continued, broken only by laughter and three trips to the bar for new rounds and a couple orders of rosemary sea salt thrice-cooked chips, before Dee declared that she needed to leave soon if she was to make her train north.

"Where do you live, anyway?" McRae asked.

"Cambridge," she said. "My sister, Riba, and I have a flat there. She's in her second year, so I do have to keep at least one eye on her most of the time."

"Is that where you went to uni?"

"Aye. Dad insisted. Manchester might have been good enough for him, but it was always going to be Oxbridge for his daughters. King's College, then Lincoln's Inn, with pupillage and now tenancy at Gladstone."

"Riba must love living up to those standards."

"Oh, she holds her own. Currently holding down a first in modern languages and starting a summer placement with the Foreign Office in a few weeks. She speaks Punjabi, Urdu, Hindi, English, and is working on her Arabic."

"I'm almost embarrassed to just have a PhD, a bit of French, and a few words of Pashto I picked up in Afghanistan."

Her head tilted in surprise. "Were you in the army?"

"Canadian Forces, yes. One tour," he said. "But I was in intelligence, so I picked up more of the language than most soldiers."

"Fair enough, and it's one she doesn't have—she'll love that," Dee said, as she stood and put on her blazer.

"How about I walk you to the station."

"That'd be lovely, thanks," she said, and they headed to the bar and split the rounds between their two cards.

"Ta, Deirdre, see you later," Dee said to the bartender.

"A good one then?" she responded.

"So far so good."

McRae smiled. He didn't realize the bartender had been evaluating him but was glad to have passed.

They made their way up Gray's Inn Road toward King's Cross. The last train would leave in an hour, so their pace was fairly leisurely, and they kept talking throughout. They spoke about her family and Cambridge, about his work and the upcoming conferences in Brighton and Cardiff, about Canada and India and Britain. Then, as they could see the lights of the station in the distance, Dee asked a question she seemed apprehensive to touch on.

"I noticed when we were at the bar that you're wearing a string around your neck. Can I ask what's on it?"

"Ah, this," he said, pulling out his ring.

"You're married?" She looked wary, almost aghast.

"I was. She died in Edinburgh."

A look of sadness with a touch of relief passed over Dee's face. "I'm sorry."

"It's okay. There's really no good way to bring that up in conversation, is there. We got married in Canada then came to Edinburgh. We had a child, but they were both killed in the bombing last year."

"Rowan, I'm so sorry to hear that."

"Thanks. It's been a little over a year now, and I'd be lying if I didn't say she was still a presence in my life, but it's also okay. She wouldn't have wanted me to stop living."

"What were their names?"

"Lynn was my wife, Harris was our son."

Dee reached out and took his arm, pulling herself close to him and resting her head against her shoulder. "I really don't know what to say."

"It's okay," he said again, as he squeezed her closer with his arm. This was the first truly human contact he'd had in over a year now. While it was tinged with a touch of sadness and the memory of Lynn doing the same thing, it also felt right somehow. Like he was meant to have Dee's head on his shoulder.

"So that's my deep, dark secret. Still fancy a second date?"

"Absolutely," she said, raising her head but keeping his arm.

"I'm glad. When works for you?"

"I've got plans tomorrow and with some girlfriends on Saturday, but maybe Sunday?"

"Sunday afternoon?"

"Aye, that would be lovely."

For the first time, they walked in silence, Dee holding his arm until they reached the crosswalk toward the station, when she let hers fall. McRae took her hand instead as they crossed the road.

"I guess this is where I leave you," he said. "Thanks. This has been the loveliest evening I've had in a very long time."

"For me as well," she said, still holding his hand and looking him in the eye.

"May I?" he said, with a soft, hopeful smile.

She nodded.

She was still holding his right hand, so he reached his left around her, pulling her close by the small of her back. He lowered his head to hers and they kissed, a long, slow kiss that neither wanted to end. When it did, both smiled.

"Guess I do still remember how to do that," he said.

"Definitely," she said, and she reached up to kiss him again.

A few minutes later she was on the train to Cambridge and McRae was off for a long, joyful walk home. Euston Road, connecting the three stations of North London, would eventually turn into Marylebone Road. After an hour or so on both, he'd be able to turn down Seymour, past his pool, and then down to his flat.

It was a warm spring night, and McRae walked as if in a dream, largely oblivious to everything around him.

Hours of nothing but talking; it had been a couple of years since that had happened. With a young child there were few occasions when he and Lynn had the time to just talk. He remembered one of their first trips after coming to Edinburgh, a train journey to Inverness for an overnight. They spent the entire time talking about things they'd seen since they'd arrived in Britain, things they still wanted to do, noting every "Highland coo" they passed, sharing dreams and plans and life. For the moment, given his joyful mood, the memory was more sweet than bitter, but it did come with a tinge of guilt.

He reminded himself as he passed Euston station that Lynn would be happy for him tonight. Her husband, whom she loved more than anything, was happy, and that was a good thing. He was less alone than he had been for a year, and she would have wanted that too.

The thought occurred to him, as he began to approach the southern tip of Regent's Park, that this had been the busiest and most complicated week he'd experienced in a long time. Yet he also felt more alive, more satisfied, and more energized than at any time in the past year. The world had regained some of its vibrancy.

Part of this was the glow of his evening with Dee. It was an unqualifiedly good date. She was smart, driven, but also able to not take herself too seriously, taking the piss out of her upbringing and her and her sister's achievements, and her father's ambitions for his children. Which is not to say she didn't respect her family, just that her respect didn't go beyond a healthy threshold into reverence. And she seemed interested in him, too, which was also a refreshing change for a man who'd been largely alone for a year.

But part of it, he realized, was that his work with Smalls was far more stimulating than his research. He enjoyed the academic life, but it didn't capture his attention in the way the investigation did. He looked forward to meeting with Smalls again tomorrow, to learning what the team had found and what new leads they would generate, if any.

As he thought this, his hand instinctively went to his pocket, and he held the rook, letting it turn over in his fingers. As alive as he was, he would never again get to hold his little boy, hear Lynn's laughter, or smell her hair. These sensations came back to him and refocused his mind on what he needed to do.

His own task for tomorrow was clear, and after a late night it would be a very early morning for him. He might have to forego the swim in order to make it down to Chester Square early enough to be sure he didn't miss Walterson leaving in the morning, if, indeed, he did leave the house. And even more so to make sure that the black Audi with plate number LF 42 237 was tagged in the event he did.

As he rounded the corner of Seymour Place, a text came through to his mobile.

— Made it to Cambridge safe and sound;
thanks again for a wonderful evening.

The smile that had faded from his face when he began plotting for tomorrow's surveillance returned. He responded:

— Glad to hear, on both counts.
Looking forward to Sunday.

— As am I. Send me a note that morning,
and we'll see what we feel like doing. xx

— Will do. Sweet dreams. 😊

11

Friday started with the soft pulse of his alarm waking him from a deep and dreamful sleep. Rowan awoke in a lighter, brighter mood than he'd been in for a long time. He had plans, both immediate and future, and that structure made him far more comfortable than the self-directed malaise of academia did.

There was no need for him to be in office today, and he'd already decided to forgo his swim, so it was onto his bike and then off quickly. He picked up his usual croissant but packed it to eat in the park once he arrived.

The route south was one of the easiest and most pleasant bike rides in London. He cut down Edgware Road and through the loop of Marble Arch, heading south past the west side of Mayfair toward Hyde Park Corner, where it met with Green Park. Instead of heading straight down Grosvenor, he turned west an extra block and went down the calmer side street of Upper Belgrave, past Eaton Square and then one extra block to Chester Square. He decided to do a preliminary lap of the park before heading in, partly to check whether there were any noticeable countermeasures in place. He didn't notice any oddly occupied cars, any out-of-place people on benches or steps, and saw as he passed that Walterson's Audi was still in its spot. Based on the pollen and other debris from the ancient overhead maples, he judged that the car hadn't been moved in more than a day.

McRae finished his lap and then entered the park on the far side, chaining his bike to a rack rather than keeping it with him. A man sitting on a bench with a bike is more noticeable than a man sitting on a bench without one. Carrying his croissant and a copy of the *Gleaner* he'd bought at the corner shop, he circled the park rather than walk through it, approaching Walterson's vehicle from the rear. When he reached the rear driver-side tire next to the park, he bent down to tie his shoes and slipped Smalls' tracker into the wheel well, out of way of any loose debris. He then stood up and walked through the gate, taking his place on the bench nearest Walterson's home, where he ate his croissant and opened the morning paper.

The *Gleaner*, it seemed, had decided to ramp up the Islamophobia in response to MI5's change in resources. The cover and three full pages inside were devoted to profiles of the Southend assassin, the mosques he might or might not have attended, interviews with alleged—and allegedly supportive—distant family members or family acquaintances in Pakistan from their foreign correspondent, and an editorial calling for a return to the death penalty for "Islamist terrorists, threatening our Christian and British way of life."

McRae was annoyed at having spent a pound fifty on this trash, but what made him nauseous was the thought that it was families like Diksha's that would face the worst of this. Like him, her grandfather had arrived in a country he'd worked with in another land. Rowan was more a foreigner than Dee was, but as far as *Gleaner* readers were concerned, he was more welcome in the country than she.

He thought back to their talks the night before. She had not mentioned any racism to him, but it was their first date, and it took him long enough to get around to sharing that he was widowed and had lost a child, so fair enough if she didn't want to bring up her experience with racism. The thought passed through McRae's mind, unbidden, that they'd have plenty of time for more conversations, but then he caught himself. More than anyone, he knew that you never know how long you're going to have with someone, so you should make the most of whatever time you do have. More than anything, he was looking forward to seeing Dee again, watching her dark, intelligent eyes looking intently at him while she explained her work or her family. Feeling her arm on his. And her lips. He hadn't been kissed in over a year, and the memory of their kisses in the station filled him with warmth.

He was so distracted by the force of these recent memories and the dreams they were spawning that he almost missed it when Walterson's door opened. Out from the house emerged a woman in professional attire—Mrs. Walterson, McRae presumed—and the man himself, looking more weasel-like now that he was dressed in a pullover and khakis, wearing an idiosyncratic tweed flat cap. They appeared close in age, but neither looked particularly happy. Walterson carried golf clubs, indicating his destination, while the woman carried only her oversized purse. While he finished locking up the house, she continued walking, without so much as a goodbye, turning in the direction of Victoria station. Walterson paused a moment, watched her walk away for a few paces, and then sighed visibly as he picked up his clubs and made his way toward the car. Guess he wouldn't be dropping her off, then.

Clearly Walterson's suspension had led to some tension at home. McRae decided to wait until the car had left and then follow the woman to see where she ended up. He would have to come back for his bike later.

Thirty seconds after Walterson's departure, McRae began his tailing of the woman he'd think of as Mrs. Walterson. He presumed she was heading to Victoria and figured that if he cut a diagonal through the park he would be able to make up some ground. He walked at a brisk pace and was dropping his croissant wrapper in the bin at the northern gate when he caught sight of her again, as expected, walking north toward Lower Belgrave Street.

He pulled his mobile from his pocket and sent a quick text to Smalls:

— W off to play golf. Now following Mrs. W.
Will call in 1h for update.

He then quickly angled the camera up and snapped a pic of Mrs. Walterson as she turned the corner on to Lower Belgrave. In profile, she looked every bit the upper-class wife: small, pointed nose, thin lips, flawless skin, and a scowl. He would try and get better images, but it would have to be done subtly; no point risking his cover for a photo of what he thought was probably a secondary actor in this particular drama.

Victoria station was busy with the arrival of morning commuters, but the escalators down to the Victoria line were only modestly crowded—enough space for Mrs. Walterson to walk down but enough people for McRae to be confident that he wouldn't be spotted tailing her. He'd need to be close enough to know when she left the train, so he stayed about fifteen metres away and made sure that when he was facing the direction of travel he would also be facing her.

They were not on the Victoria line for long; only two stops later, at Oxford Circus, she alighted. McRae ran through scenarios. Oxford Circus was at the heart of London's shopping district, with Regent Street to the south and New Oxford Street extending for a dozen blocks east and west. Alternatively, she could be heading to the Central line, which could take her to two different train stations—Liverpool Street in the east, Paddington in the west—either of which would take her farther afield than McRae could reasonably go today. Since she wasn't carrying any luggage, McRae assumed she wouldn't be leaving London, but he wanted to be sure. As she exited, he watched to see which way she would go. If she walked away from him, fine. If she came toward him, he would find a map and play the tourist for a few seconds, allowing her to pass and boosting his cover.

When they left the train, Mrs. Walterson immediately turned to the left and walked in McRae's direction. He did the same, pausing in front of the nearest map. He waited for a count of three, then followed. He was far closer to her now than he liked to be, so he slowed his pace and allowed her to get ahead of him. She took the escalator up one level and then turned down the hallway leading toward the Central line. A transfer it was.

Once he re-established a comfortable following distance in the busy station, it was just a question of whether she went to the eastbound or westbound tracks. Eastbound would lead to the heart of the city and could be going anywhere. Westbound was basically along the north side of Hyde Park to Paddington station. She turned left at the end of the path, indicating she was heading for the eastbound train. McRae blended himself into the crowd and made his way down the throng, knowing he would catch sight of her again once he got to the platform.

It was 8:15 on a Friday morning. People were sandwiched into the platform and pushing one another to make a path farther down, trying to find a couple of square feet of space that they'd be able to occupy while waiting. Mrs. Walterson was no exception. The trains here came from the far end of the platform and left from the end nearest the entryway, so, like most seasoned travellers, Mrs. Walterson was pushing her way to the far end, where the crowds were thinnest and the train most likely to have room on it. McRae set himself up a little behind her; when they got on the train he would be in front of her and would have to find a way to make sure he was facing backwards when they boarded.

The whoosh of the train began from the tunnel, and in seconds, it was beside them. Mrs. Walterson stopped and prepared herself to squeeze into whatever car entrance was closest to her. The train was crowded, but this was a popular stop, so there would be room for most of these passengers. McRae kept going, and in the twenty seconds it took the train to come to a stop and open its doors, he had managed to get one doorway past his quarry. They would be in different cars, but at least he'd be able to keep a lookout more easily.

The next stop was Holborn. As the nexus of the Piccadilly and Central lines this was one of the busiest in London, but, fortunately for McRae, this wasn't her stop. She stayed on, but once the doors closed made her way close to the exit. The next stop would be hers.

Chancery Lane. McRae's heart sank as he exited the train; this was much closer to Dee's workplace than he wanted to be while under cover. Still, he focused on the task at hand. Chancery Lane was much less busy than Holborn but still fairly well travelled at this time of day, providing enough cover. And he was behind Mrs. Walterson now anyway.

Chancery Lane had three exits: two on Holborn, one east and one west, and a third exit north onto the bottom of Gray's Inn Road. McRae realized it was about twelve hours ago that he and Dee were half a dozen blocks from here, ordering their third round of the evening, talking about his research, politics, her life as a barrister, how the law worked, teaching, and everything else that crossed their minds, while the Rekorderligs and Aperol spritzes worked their magic and softened the discomfort that usually came hand in hand with growing attraction.

He was once again in the neighbourhood but now trying not to be seen. He followed Mrs. Walterson to the station's main hall, and his heart began to race. If she went north, that would be heading toward Gladstone Chambers, and he would have a decision to make:

How far would he risk heading before the possibility of blowing his cover became too large?

On the one hand, he really only knew two people who worked at Gladstone, and from what he'd seen it wasn't a small chambers. It also wasn't exactly the only chambers on Gray's Inn Road. This was the heart of legal London, after all, with all four of the original Inns of Court within a square kilometre of this station. On the other hand, if he did run into Dee or Garson, he'd need some kind of explanation for what he was doing in the area.

As Mrs. Walterson confidently strode to the north staircase, he followed instinctively, allowing his body to make the decision for him. The crowds were mostly heading east or west and thinned out as he walked up the north stairs, so rather than take them two at a time to keep pace with her, he took them slowly, allowing the space between them to build before he emerged into daylight.

Mrs. Walterson was now a half-block ahead of him and showed no signs of slowing until she reached the intersection with Baldwin's Gardens, where she used the raised crosswalk and made her way to the east side of the street. McRae decided to stay on the west side and get a little closer; he was now only about thirty metres back, in full surveillance mode, looking deep into the block to see if there were any familiar faces or figures that he'd need to avoid and making note of his target's possible departure points. His biggest worry was the bus station he was approaching on his side of the street, which had a few people outside waiting for the number 17. None appeared to be dressed as barristers, so he decided not to cross the road.

As he approached the bus stop, he saw Gladstone Chambers was the next building on the east side of the street; he also saw Mrs. Walterson walk in through the public entrance at the corner of Gray's Inn and Verulam. So this was her destination. Now, instead of being an issue, the bus stop provided him with cover.

The route 17 bus was coming toward him, northbound on Gray's Inn. He pulled the Oyster card from his pocket and prepared to board, but more movement from the chambers caught his eye. Just before the bus pulled up in front of him he realized it was Dee, coming out of the building in full court clothes, rolling a briefcase behind her, heading south. She was apparently on her way to court and didn't look his way.

Once he'd tapped in and made his way up the stair to the second deck, Rowan allowed himself to breathe. His heart was still racing, but he deliberately slowed his breaths, knowing that would slow his heart rate soon enough too. Dee was off in the opposite direction, and he was now safe.

Smalls wasn't waiting for McRae's call. He had too much to do.

He began the morning with a call to Eyre on his walk to the Highgate station, to get an update on the team's work on their first day and overnight of surveillance. He knew he'd get Eyre at this time, as he'd taken the overnight shift sitting on Clegg's house. Eyre sounded tired, but fair enough. Smalls knew he'd worked four overnights so that each member of his team could get a full day off, which Smalls respected; it was a good leader—a rare one too—who took the burden on themself and made sure their team was okay.

"What's the word?"

"Not much activity yesterday. We picked up Banks when he arrived home late—23:15, arriving alone by cab—and he left this morning at 6:22. He was dressed for a run, so we didn't tail him, but he was back by seven, and then got dressed for work and walked to Downing Street. We tailed him on foot, and he arrived there at eight. We can't exactly set up a maintenance van outside there on Whitehall, but we'll do our best to tail him if he leaves the building—

regular foot patrols, playing tourist, you get the picture—and will see where he goes."

"And Clegg?"

"Nothing. Got home at seven. Wife got home before him at five twenty, and they didn't leave the house until this morning, when both headed out at eight. He got picked up in a squad car, which we tailed. She walked in the direction of Warwick Avenue. Our reports indicate that she works clerical for an HR company in Kensington, so that's our assumption for her. We're now sitting on the Met HQ, which I've got to tell you is a first for me."

"Understood, but that's the target. Stay on both men, and thanks again."

"No problem. Thanks for keeping it quick. Unless one or the other starts firing live rounds, we'll be in touch again tomorrow morning."

"Of course. Sleep well." With that, Smalls ended the call.

Smalls' ride in was usually a chance for him to plan his day, one he'd missed in the chaos of the last few. He had to update Moss, but he wanted a chance to connect with McRae first. A date. Well, it was probably about time. Smalls wasn't exactly cutting through the town, but there were a few women he went out with from time to time, keeping things casual for the most part. Every once in a while he met someone new and would give it a go, but things didn't usually click for one or another of them. Something small, typically, became an issue. And he wasn't exactly in a rush to settle down or anything. In McRae's case, given what he had been through, a date was a clear sign of progress.

The other thing Smalls couldn't get out of his mind was Garson. Every other lead they had on this was being followed, but the lawyer was still in the shadows, and they had no real way to shine any light on him. They couldn't exactly snoop on a QC, not without a warrant anyway, which would make things very public, very quickly. This left him uneasy. He planned to spend his day learning everything he could through legitimate means about the barrister. Taxes, family, travel—any database he had access to was fair game, but it needed to be done from the office. Preferably behind a closed door.

When Smalls reached Charing Cross he got the notification that McRae had called. It was 8:35, not far off his prediction.

"How was your date?"

"Fantastic," McRae said, without even a hint of enthusiasm or sarcasm. "Now listen. Walterson's wife went straight to Garson's chambers, and I can't think of any good reason for her to be there; if she wanted a divorce, she'd go to a solicitor. I tagged Walterson's car, but based on the clubs in the boot, I'm pretty sure he was heading for the links. But his wife got on the subway and headed straight to Gladstone Chambers, and she really didn't look happy about it. We need to know more about this lawyer."

"That's my plan for today. As for now, you can stand down. No need to risk getting any closer to Garson. I'll update you if you're right about Walterson. Friend at five?"

"Aye. Now what am I supposed to do for the rest of the day?"

"I don't know, what do academics do on Fridays? Flirt with undergrads? Is there a late game on?"

"I'll have to check. About the game, that is—I'm not daft enough to try anything with the undergrads. See you at five. Ta."

12

McRae hadn't said "ta" to anyone since Scotland. He was definitely getting more comfortable with Smalls than he had been. Or maybe he was just more at ease than he'd been in a long time. Who'd have thought espionage would be more relaxing than academia?

After such an eventful fourteen hours, McRae was ready for a normal day. He had to collect his bike, so he went once again into the Central line—moving against the thinning pedestrian traffic—to make his way back to Victoria. He was now quite certain the lawyer was involved, and this made him deeply uncomfortable. At some point his world and Garson's might collide; he hoped Dee didn't get hurt in the process.

As the carriage swayed, he replayed snippets of their conversations in his mind. Stressful as it was, she loved her work. Garson was one of her mentors, but when he came up, McRae had steered the conversation away from him, so he didn't really get a sense of what she thought of him. On the one hand, he felt a small twinge of guilt about this. For the sake of the investigation, he probably should have pushed a little harder. On balance, McRae didn't know whether the loss of Garson would be a blow to Dee's career or whether it might be a benefit. Either way, if Garson was involved in protecting the man who'd murdered his family, the barrister needed to be dealt with.

A half-hour later McRae found his bike exactly where he'd left it, chained to the rack outside the park at Chester Square. He rode a quick lap and had a brief look at Walterson's house again. Sure enough, there was a door camera, so a break-in would not be a straightforward task. Not without getting caught anyway.

He carried on and cycled his way through central London toward Aldwych and his office. He hated the traffic this time of day; it was partly why he always left so early in the morning. But today it couldn't be helped. It was made worse by the route. There were not a lot of side streets between Victoria and Aldwych. He'd have to cut through Soho or Westminster, and then past the mayhem of Trafalgar Square before he'd get to the western edge of the old City.

He dismounted his bike on Houghton Street and made his way up to the fifth floor. Today, he would be a professor again and respond to the backlog of student emails waiting impatiently for his reply.

While McRae was weaving his way back across London, Smalls was arriving at headquarters, preparing to brief Moss on the investigation. First, though, he needed to confirm that Walterson had gone golfing for the day and wasn't trying to mislead them. It's likely that Walterson thought he would be under surveillance, but whether that would make him lie low or prompt him to act depended on the character of the man. Was he wise or foolish? The wise man would go to ground; the fool would think he could misdirect his trackers.

A quick check of the tracking software indicated that his vehicle was parked at the Richmond Park Golf Course. Wise, it turned out, to Smalls' surprise. A call to the club indicated that Walterson had come alone and picked up a foursome on arrival, fitting in with a few other lone people out for a random round. So had he sent his wife on an errand, or did she have some business with Gladstone Chambers of her own? Based on McRae's report that she seemed unhappy this morning, it was likely that she was a reluctant messenger. It might be time to start tracking Garson's car as well.

He needed more information on both Garson and Mrs. Walterson. Smalls had one up on McRae—he at least knew that Mrs. Walterson's name was Sarah. He decided to run her through their databases and a quick Google search to see what came up. He knew from Walterson's small talk that she didn't work. Facebook showed photos of her at a few "ladies who lunch" type galas, and she was apparently on the board of a gardening charity. All perfectly respectable activities for the upper-class housewife. Their kids, a boy and a girl, were off at Eton and Cheltenham, so they weren't around this time of year. As McRae had said, if she was planning to divorce her husband—which would be fair, considering the circumstances—she wouldn't go to a barrister's chambers; she'd need a solicitor for that. In the end, Smalls was reasonably confident that her trip was on Walterson's behalf. He had sent his wife on some kind of errand. Did she know what she was getting into, or was she just a messenger? No way to know as yet.

He decided to brief Moss before looking into Garson, as that would occupy much of the rest of his day. He made his way into the black room, making sure she noticed, and took a seat, waiting for her to follow. He wasn't waiting long when she marched in and closed the door behind her. She stayed standing and looked at him, waiting for him to start.

"We now believe that Charles Garson, a high-profile senior barrister, is a part of this investigation. Walterson sent his wife to meet with him today. About what, we don't know, but she has no business that I can think of requiring a barrister. Surveillance is in place on targets Clegg and Banks. Given both targets' workplaces, surveillance is very difficult, but we'll know if they leave their buildings, and we think it unlikely that they'll initiate contact with other conspirators from their offices."

"How did you learn about Sarah?"

It was time to come clean about McRae, at least a little bit. "I have an additional source, someone I served with in Afghanistan. I'd trust him with my life. I already have."

"Okay, fair enough. I don't need to know more now, but if something goes sideways on that end, I didn't know or sanction anything. Is there more?"

"How do you feel about bugging a barrister's chambers?"

Moss let out a rare laugh. "Not without a lot more probable cause than you have right now."

"How about his home, then?"

"Definitely not."

"The only other prospect for now would be to look into Walterson's house and to add Major Halisbury to our surveillance. But I'd need more resources for that."

"Halisbury? Of the *Gleaner*? What's his involvement?"

Smalls grimaced, realizing he hadn't filled Moss in on these details. "He was the intermediary between Walterson and Garson. For now, we're not sure what his involvement is beyond that."

"Fair enough. I'll assign another two agents to Eyre's team. Will that do?"

It was better than he'd hoped. He nodded. "And Walterson's house?"

"Off the books, but do it. If you need a couple of clone drives, take them from storage," Moss added. Clone drives looked like ordinary memory sticks, but they were programmed with a virus that enabled them to copy a computer's entire memory when inserted into a standard USB port. A nasty but highly useful piece of tech in the right circumstances.

"Thanks," Smalls said, and Moss quickly made her way from the room, leaving the door open behind her. So this is what it's like to have departmental support, he thought as he stood and made his way down the hall to tech support, where he picked up a couple more magnetic trackers and half a dozen clone drives. He also grabbed an adapter to allow a connection to a mobile phone, should they get the chance to copy one of those too.

After that, it was back to the computer to search for anything he could find about Garson. No database would be left untapped, no detail would be too small. Smalls had no team for this job; he was on his own and would need to work through lunch to get as much done as possible before his meeting with McRae.

He started, like most people do, with Google. Quite often, people like Garson would have profiles that give a sense of their background. His QC announcement, for starters, confirmed his educational background (Eton, Jesus College at Oxford, Inner Temple) and, based on his dates of call and the lack of anything else, indicated that he was likely born in 1955 or 1956, putting him in his late sixties now. He was widowed—his wife, Mary, had died in 2013 of cancer, judging by the donation requests in the obituary—and had three daughters, Ruth, Margaret, and Sara, and a son, Joseph. The funeral was held at the Catholic Church of the Immaculate Conception in Mayfair, which, in addition to his children's names, told him that the family was fairly staunchly Catholic. Marriage records weren't online, but it wouldn't surprise him if the Garsons were married there too. The son wasn't on any social media platforms, but the daughters were, and there were a few family photos. The sisters all seemed tight, but there weren't many photos of their brother, and when he was there he seemed sullen, apart, like he didn't quite fit with the family. There were grandkids, at least three or four, and a couple of wedding photos—also at Immaculate Conception, based on the announcements—but again, there wasn't much on the son.

Smalls opened the records for border control to see what kind of activities the family had been up to. Travel records for Garson indicated that he basically stopped going anywhere about six months before his wife died. The daughters had family vacations in Spain, Italy, France, and Greece—nothing out of the ordinary. The son's travel records indicated that he went back and forth between Italy fairly often for most of a decade, but that he hadn't left the UK since March of the previous year.

He also found a few references to the Halisburys and Lord Rutherford; they were definitely invited to the daughters' weddings, but as members of high society, that would be expected. Garson was also regularly referenced in the *Daily Mail* archives, and from what Smalls could tell, always in a positive light.

While there was some connection between Garson and the Halisburys, it was unclear if or how the barrister was involved in hiding the bomber. He could provide legal counsel, sure, but the connection seemed too tenuous to Smalls. Still, if the lawyer could provide another point of access into what the viscount and the major were doing to prevent MI5 from finding the bomber, it would definitely help to keep an eye on him.

After a day of reviewing drafts and responding to emails, McRae was ready for a trip to the Friend, a decent meal, and a proper pint. Since lunchtime yesterday he'd had four ciders, a croissant, a mediocre sandwich, some thrice-cooked chips, and an awful lot of water. Tonight called for fish and chips, or maybe the chicken katsu burger.

He'd called ahead and Owens had reserved the usual table. Since it was Friday, there wouldn't be many people in to watch football, but there would still be plenty of the usual students that you always found in a pub at the heart of Bloomsbury. He and Smalls wouldn't get a quiet night, but they could also be fairly confident they wouldn't be overheard.

Standing at the bar, waiting for his drink, McRae checked his phone and saw a text had come in from Dee. This was a pleasant surprise.

— Hope your day has gone well and that you've not gone off me yet.

McRae smiled.

— It'll take a lot more than a busy day to go off you, Dee. I'm looking forward to seeing you Sunday. Any suggestions as to what we should do?

He put the phone back in his pocket but, in a departure from his norm, turned the ringer on. Just before his food arrived, he heard a muffled ping.

— Long as it doesn't involve drinks. After tomorrow night with the girls, I'm going to be pickled. 😉

— Entirely fair. Enjoy yourself. I'll come up with plans. Meet you at King's X. Let me know when you board your train and I'll make my way there.

— Lovely. See you then.

It was only when he was trying to contort his mouth around the massive burger, leaning over his plate to avoid splattering sauce on his shirt, that McRae realized he had no idea what people in London do on dates. Picnic in the park? Museum? The zoo? Did they go to a play or a movie? He sighed as he realized he'd probably have to ask Smalls.

Smalls came in just as McRae was finishing the last of his chips and mulling over the relative merits of London's different parks as picnic grounds. While Smalls was taking a seat, McRae decided to broach the topic.

"So what do people around here do on a second date anyway?"

"It went well then?" Smalls said, with a smile. "You're asking the wrong bloke. Most of mine are first dates, so what do I know? What were you thinking?"

"I was thinking a picnic, then maybe walking down to the V&A. If it goes well, there's a decent Thai place around there we could go."

"Sound like a reasonable plan to me. What's she like, anyway?"

"Beautiful, brilliant, and kind, in ascending order of importance."

"Well, who could resist that?"

"I know, right? Only complicating factor, as you know, is that she works at Gladstone."

"Which means you need to stay away from that side of the operation. That's okay, I have a new job for you."

"Oh, great. Something archival? Need some research on shipping routes?"

"No, I did my own research on this one. I agree that Garson appears to be involved somehow, but we're going to have to go at him from the side. For now, you're going to get a little closer to the Waltersons."

"Delightful people. What's the plan?"

Smalls reached into his pocket and pulled out three clone drives. He explained their workings to McRae.

"You'll need to break in, plug one of these into any device you find, wait between thirty seconds and ten minutes, and then take it out. The blinking green light will turn steady when it's done. If there are any phones around, use this adapter and get them too."

McRae took them and did a quick once over. They looked like ordinary memory sticks with red and green lights on them.

"A door, I can handle. Your border control failed to notice my old lock-pick tools from training. How do I get past the camera and any alarm system?"

"With this," said Smalls, reaching again into his bag of tricks. "Most basic home security systems, like those with doorbell cameras, use a particular set of frequencies. This will jam those frequencies. You'll still be on camera, but no one will be receiving the signal. Assuming you activate it before you're in the line of sight, no one will know you're there. Battery life should get you a couple hours, not that you'll need them."

"And here I was just thinking I'd put some gum on the camera and hope for the best. Anything else?"

"Not right now. And just so you know, this is the first of two of these ops. We also need to do Garson's house."

"I assume you want me far away from there."

"I do, not least because I don't have authorization for it. I'll handle that one myself."

"Okay then. When?"

"I'm thinking tomorrow."

"Why tomorrow?"

"The Waltersons have a place in the Cotswolds. If you're on administrative leave, wouldn't that be where you went for the weekend? Surveil their place in the morning and see whether they leave. Text me if they do, and I'll track their car. Once they're an hour out of town, you can go in."

"And if they don't?"

"Then that's even more interesting, and we'll want to know where they go and what they do, so either way, I want you on them tomorrow. If they go by car, text. I'll provide a location once they get where they're going."

"Okay, so that's my Saturday. Guess I won't be watching the Spurs match."

"Why would you want to do that to yourself anyway? Not like they're going to be in the Champions League places."

"Long as they're ahead of Arsenal, we'll make do."

"With any luck, we'll both be done long before the match. Though I think Garson may be a bit more likely not to leave the house on a Saturday than the Waltersons."

"Maybe. Seems to me like the kind of guy who'd spend weekends at the office anyway."

"That's my hope. Also hoping he gives the driver the day off so I can tag his car. Can't do it otherwise."

"If he's going to the office, he's going to keep the driver. Will give him Sunday off instead."

"That would make more sense, frankly."

"Why do you say that?" McRae asked, and Smalls filled him in on his research. McRae wondered aloud if Garson would still be going to Mass now that his wife was gone. "If the faith was hers, maybe not. If they shared it, then it would be even more likely he wouldn't miss a week," McRae said, and Smalls nodded.

By this point, the Friend was getting very crowded with all the usual participants on a Friday night. "Plans tonight?" Smalls asked.

"This is about it. You?"

"Pretty much."

"That typical for a Friday night? Don't tell me you're dating even less than I am."

"No, but I've got one lined up for tomorrow night."

"Someone new?"

"New to me, anyway. Someone from one of the apps."

"How do you find those?"

Smalls thought for a second before answering. "Effective," he said, and McRae gave him a questioning look. "Good for some company and a bit of physical contact, but I've yet to meet anyone on them who I'd like to spend more than a few hours with."

"Isn't that what the apps are for?" Rowan asked, before adding, "I mean, I'm pretty clueless about them, so I don't really know. That's just the reputation they seem to have among my students."

"It's hard to say, but you can usually tell from one meeting whether someone's really just looking for a good time or if they want something more substantial and just aren't admitting it yet. Including to themselves."

Rowan looked at Smalls with understanding; he knew that Smalls thought he was talking about the women he met, but Rowan was fairly certain Smalls was also talking about himself, even if he, too, wasn't prepared to admit it yet. Back when they had been deployed together, Smalls presented himself as a playboy, and it seemed to Rowan that he was still living that life now. But the stories of his adventures weren't offered as freely as they once were, and Rowan had sensed a touch of sadness when the adventures inevitably ended. As far as Rowan was concerned, Smalls was ready for more but wasn't quite ready to admit it to himself yet.

"How you doing, anyway?" Smalls asked, breaking the silence.

"You know what? I'm actually doing well. If you'd asked me that a week ago, the answer would have been completely different, if I was being honest. It's been over a year now. Not a day goes by that I don't miss Lynn or think about what Harris would be like now had he lived," he said, feeling the weight of the chess piece in his pocket. "Up to a week ago, I was just drifting through life, not really living it. Now, I don't know, for the first time since Edinburgh, I'm starting to dream again. Guess I owe you thanks for that."

"No need, mate. I'm glad to hear that, though. I can't imagine what you've been through. Frankly, I don't want to. But I'm glad I can help," Smalls said, then added, "But next time you meet a gorgeous woman while on assignment, give her my number instead of yours."

13

McRae didn't normally swim on Saturday. He slept in, walked to one or another of London's neighbourhoods, soaked up some atmosphere, and had lunch in a pub where he could watch the early match, having skipped breakfast. Since he missed yesterday's swim and had to get to Chester Square early anyway, he pulled himself from bed at six instead and took to the pool.

He knew his job today, and it was simple enough. No copy of the *Gleaner*, though. There would be a Saturday *Times* to pick up for the book reviews, and maybe a *Guardian* in case he was there for a while. He walked through the plan: switching on the jamming device, picking the lock, walking in, doing a circuit of the house from top to bottom, plugging in his cloners to any device he found, waiting till they'd done their thing, and then getting out. If he saw anything of particular interest in an office or study, he could take pictures but had to be careful not to leave any trace of his presence.

After which, his day could get back to normal, or to whatever normal looked like now. He decided to play out his date with Dee as well and see how he would work through that, though he was even less familiar with dating than with B and E. Meeting her at the station was easy enough, but from there, would they walk to Hyde Park? He'd get the picnic supplies before anyway—some strawberries, fresh bread, a bit of cheese, chocolate, and a bottle of sparkling wine for them to share, with two unbreakable glasses from his flat—but would she be up for biking, would she expect to get a cab, or would she be good with the Underground to the park? In the end, he decided to take the bus. Was it romantic? Certainly not conventionally, but it was what he was used to, and this was a chance for him to show her how he experienced London. Next time would be her call.

Next time. Was he getting ahead of himself? After their lovely first date, he didn't think so, but there was always a risk. Would he say the wrong thing? Would she tire of him? When you'd only known someone for five days it was impossible to predict what they'd do and how they'd respond. He knew he had to just be himself and couldn't help but feel the faint tinge of hope that things would keep working out between them.

If it rained, of course, things would have to change, but the V&A was a good backup anyway. A new exhibit on the politics of food had opened there recently, and he'd been wanting to check it out, but there were several wings of the museum that would be interesting to them, with their varied colonial backgrounds.

His twenty laps done, McRae showered, dressed, and got himself down to Victoria on his bike, following the same route as the day before. Once again, he looped the park before heading into the gardens at the far side. The Waltersons' car was in its spot, not much cleaner for having been driven yesterday. Only the windshield showed any evidence, and there only in the pattern of the wipers.

McRae took up his spot on the bench opposite the Walterson doorway and sorted through his reading material. *Guardian* first, he decided. There was some follow-up from Wednesday's story, but mostly the news had moved on. Which was for the best; when the issue was in the papers daily, the conspirators would be more likely to be lying low. If the coverage stopped, they'd eventually be more comfortable and get back to normal life. How long that would take, there was no way of knowing. For now, McRae was content to watch and wait.

He finished the *Guardian* cover to cover, including the supplementary magazine, and was beginning to wonder if he'd need to go get a coffee somewhere nearby, when the Waltersons finally emerged from the house. Mr. Walterson was carrying his clubs again and a duffel bag, while Mrs. Walterson rolled a suitcase behind her. McRae fired off a quick text to Smalls.

— Departure imminent: they have bags.

A few moments later, he received a response.

— Noted. Garson off to work. Give it half an hour. Unless you hear from me, green light.

Smalls, indeed, had an efficient morning. He checked in with Eyre. Banks had a bit of a night on the town—drinks at a posh place on the South Bank, followed by some kind of reception at a gallery near Borough Market—but no sign of any contact with anyone on their list. Clegg was living a life of domestic respectability for now; wife home at five thirty, him home at six thirty, both stayed in.

When he arrived at Garson's place at seven thirty, escorted by Blackburn in the unobtrusive black cab, the lawyer's car and driver were already waiting in the road for him. The lawyer emerged moments later, apparently in a bit of a hurry. Smalls asked Blackburn to follow them and make sure Garson was going to work. If he went somewhere else, text the destination. If they were coming back, call once and hang up.

Smalls did not wait. He had no reason to believe Garson would be coming back, so he seized the opportunity. He turned on his jammer, scanned the block while waiting the obligatory three seconds, and then made his way to the front door, hoping that it worked.

He'd spent the night before practising lock-picking, as it had been many years since his rudimentary course at the academy. It paid off. Garson's house had two locks, one a standard mechanism, the other a deadbolt. The tools alone took care of the former, but Smalls had brought a strong steel piece that did the job on the deadbolt as well. His gloves precluded any fingerprints.

The weight of the door pulled it open once the locks were released. Smalls stepped through and quietly closed it behind him. The alarm box to his left indicated red, meaning it had been tripped, so Smalls was reliant on the jamming to make sure no signal went out while he was in the house. For now, he would trust his tech. If it didn't work, he was screwed, but there was nothing he could do about that now.

Smalls had entered into a large hallway, typical of these sorts of Belgravia manor homes, with rooms off to the right and a staircase directly in front of him. A quick inspection indicated that the rooms on the main floor were meant for entertaining or for family gatherings. The front room appeared to be largely untouched. At the rear was a kitchen and dining room that the family would have used for ordinary meals. As with the front room, it was clear that it wasn't often used now. The kettle and toaster showed signs of use, but the fridge only contained the basics and a few condiments.

The first floor of this four-storey house was more revealing. With a family portrait from when the children were young in pride of place over the mantel, this would have been the family room at one point. Smalls took a photo of the portrait. In the centre of the room was a big, square, marble-topped coffee table with large couches positioned around three of its four sides, leaving only the side with the fireplace open, despite there being no evidence of its use in a long time. At the rear was Garson's study. The door was closed and the lock was not engaged. Clearly there was no one around these days to bother him.

Dark wood bookshelves with glass doors lined the back wall of the barrister's home office—so far the most lived-in and opulent room in the house. A large window overlooked the back garden at the left. In front of it were two leather wingback chairs, and to the right was a collage of certificates and commemorative photographs of Garson with notable individuals—prime ministers from both parties, several royals including Her Majesty, a justice or two, and one with Geoff Hurst. Garson was a football fan at some point but kept his politics ecumenical, thought Smalls. Facing the door was an oversized oak desk with a large ergonomic chair. The desk had two monitors on the top, but the tower was on the floor, against its back panel. Smalls knelt down, plugged in the clone drive, and watched tensely as it began to blink green.

He browsed the room for other leads. Garson's desk bore all the hallmarks of a brilliant mind, with papers, knick-knacks, and photographs spread throughout without any organizational scheme that would make sense to anyone but the man himself. Smalls noticed one prominently placed photo in particular, an old one of a youthful woman wearing a gold cross. His wife? She was quite pretty, with a look of piety. There were photos of each of the girls and their families, but none of the son. Smalls took photos of all the photos in the room. Clearly family was important to Garson, which made them important to Smalls.

Garson also left his office drawers unlocked. He had an address book, and most of the entries were fairly typical, but one listed under *G* only had the name Joseph. Smalls took a photo of the number—a UK mobile number, he knew—and kept looking. Under *H* he found both the major and the viscount. Sure enough, Clegg was under *C* and Banks under *B*.

Smalls checked but found no calendar. That would be on his phone then, and hopefully on the computer, too.

To the left of the desk, in an organizer, were a number of bills. Most were as expected, relating to the house, phone, and credit cards. Smalls decided to grab a photo of the credit card statement; if you have enough of someone's banking statements, you can know basically everything about their lives. He wouldn't have time to examine them now, though; he had a house to go through, and the drive had stopped blinking.

Smalls grabbed the memory stick and left the room, closing the door behind him as he did. He doubled up the stairs to the second floor where he found three small bedrooms, all of which were decorated in a very old-fashioned feminine style, with frilly, floral-print curtains and wallpaper trim depicting roses and ponies. They could easily have been turn-of-the-century recreations.

The top floor had one small bedroom, decorated sparsely but in a more stereotypically boyish style—blue curtains and knights instead of ponies on the wallpaper trim. The master bedroom was beside it, with the bed made on one side and unmade on the other. A phone charger, a Bible, a sleep mask, and a lamp were all that occupied the night table on Garson's side of the bed. A photograph of his wife was alone on the unused side.

All in all, Garson's appeared to be an ordinary family with a bit of a conservative streak. Smalls felt an unexpected welling of sympathy for the man. He had clearly adored his wife, and all he had now was his work and his children. But the daughters had families of their own, and there was no real sense of what had happened to the son.

Once Smalls had done everything he could in the house, he quickly made his way down the stairs and out the front door, leaving it unlocked. Once he was out of range, the alarm would be detected and someone would come. They would find the house open and no one there and would assume the burglar had been scared off by the alarm.

Smalls turned north on Cadogan Square and headed toward the Knightsbridge station. Sloane Square was closer, but the Piccadilly line didn't go through there, and Smalls had already decided that the best place to run things from today was the Friend at Hand.

He arrived just after nine. The pub wasn't open yet, but Owens was around nonetheless, cleaning, setting up, and letting the day cook in to begin prepping for a busy day. Saturdays were match days, and while the Friend was a "neutral pub" in the sense that no one particular team treated it as "theirs," it was nonetheless a very popular place for students in the area to watch matches. If Smalls and McRae were to get their usual table, one or the other of them would have to get there early.

"I don't let just anyone in this early," said Owens on seeing who was tapping at the door.

"I appreciate it. Rowan will be meeting me here in a while, but I'm not exactly sure when."

"It's all good. Can't offer you anything but tea this early, but the kettle is always on."

"That'd be brilliant, thanks," Smalls said, making his way to the corner table and rearranging it as usual. Until the matches started at twelve thirty, they'd be okay there. But once they started, he and McRae would be right where the projector screen was, and they'd have to move. Nothing comes between the drinking public and a football match.

In the meantime, he decided to call the number for Joseph Garson, but the automated voice told him it was no longer in service. Smalls then checked in with Blackburn, to see how the cabbie was making out with his tailing of Garson's car.

"Aye, straight to the office and no deviation. Wouldn't know but it was Tuesday."

"Thanks. You're free to go now. If you want, come by the Friend and I'll settle up."

Twenty minutes later, Smalls saw him coming and met him at the door so as not to bother Owens.

"Nothing unusual then?"

"Other than going to the office on a Saturday at eight in the morning, no." Blackburn took his cash before adding, "I got a picture of the driver as well, if you'd like."

"Brilliant," Smalls said, pulling out another tenner, "text it to me," which Blackburn did before closing up his window and heading off to find a fare.

Smalls was running out of reading material and was starting to worry—still no text from McRae. It was pointless to worry, but having brought his friend into the investigation, he couldn't help feeling responsible. Soon they'd debrief. For now, he turned on the tracking app on his phone and watched the Waltersons join the slow-moving throng of traffic driving out of the city and onto the M4, heading west.

After a half-hour of anticipation and the kind of silence that only exacerbates it, McRae made sure the coast was clear, turned on his jammer, and went to the front door of the Waltersons' home. He took out a Post-it note he'd brought just for this purpose and stuck it on the camera; even if the signal was jammed, he wanted as little evidence of his involvement as possible. The locks were not a problem. Two bolts, both on tumblers, took him about twenty seconds to crack. Once they were opened, he put his shoulder to the door and it opened without difficulty.

Inside there was no evidence of a private alarm system, which didn't mean there wasn't one, just that it was well enough hidden not to show. Either way, McRae had to trust Smalls' tech.

As he began his survey, Rowan's tension and inexperience began to affect him. He quickly walked a circuit around the front room, lined with bookshelves that held more tchotchkes than texts. There were phone chargers but no phones. The kitchen was well used, and there was a small office at the rear where it was evident that Mrs. Walterson handled her personal affairs and the household accounts. Her MacBook Air didn't have a USB port, but the adapter worked just fine and the clone drive turned solid green in a matter of seconds, though to McRae, it seemed like hours.

On the second floor were the two kids' bedrooms, each oversized beyond anything a child could possibly need. Other than flat-screen televisions and, in the boy's room, a PS4, there were no devices. They must have those at school, McRae figured, before making his way up the stairs to the top floor.

The stairs showed the age of the house; every one of them creaked under McRae's weight, no matter how delicately he attempted to walk. Given the stillness of the empty house, the sound of each footstep echoed throughout. He was sure the neighbours would be able to hear it, if they were home.

On the top floor was the master suite and Walterson's home office. This appeared to be seldom used and was well organized. Again, no books except leather-bound first editions posed for show. Many pictures of Walterson with political figures, but only on the conservative side of things, and a laptop left open on the table. McRae plugged in the clone drive and looked through the room for other hints as to Walterson's activities. In the top right-hand drawer he found what he was looking for—a second phone. McRae plugged in the adapter and his third and final clone drive and waited.

As he did, he heard sounds outside; he ventured over to look out the window to the street below and saw a couple walking up to the entranceway. He couldn't be sure if they were coming to this house or the next one, but given the close proximity of their doorways, it was possible they would notice it was still ajar.

The seconds that passed were an eternity to McRae, until he noticed the light on the memory stick in the laptop turn green, followed a moment later by the one in the phone. He grabbed both, then made his way down to the entrance of the house and paused to listen for voices coming from the landing. When he was sure that the only sound he could hear was the beating of his own heart, he made his way out, grabbing the Post-it as he passed.

As he walked down the street, away from the scene of this victimless crime, McRae realized just how fast his heart was beating. He could feel it through his chest, and at first it unnerved him. He had unwelcome memories of waiting on the rooftop in Kandahar for the Taliban convoy to return and lead them to the warehouse. He was now, as then, in enemy territory on a mission that, if successful, would lead to more conflict. Still, he had a job to do. Only now, it was finding the man who had killed his family and bringing to justice those who helped him, then and now.

14

McRae was sweating heavily when he locked up his bike outside the Friend. It was hot for May, closer to twenty-five than twenty, made worse by the ubiquitous London humidity. To top that, Saturday traffic in central London was just as bad as weekday traffic. Worse in some places, as there were more tourists and plenty of bankers, lawyers, and others who worked on Saturdays. So his journey from Victoria to Bloomsbury had been a difficult one today, weaving in and out of traffic, taking side streets, and eventually going full speed up Southampton Row to try to make up the time he'd lost in Trafalgar Square and on Charing Cross Road.

"Water, please, Phil," he said, quickly making his way to the bar. He grabbed a napkin to wipe off his forehead.

"Morning workout?" Owens said, filling up a pint glass with ice and running the tap to cool the water down.

"Something like that. Martin here?"

"Aye, got here not long after me. Going to have to put him to work next time."

McRae gratefully accepted the now full glass then went over to the table to meet Smalls. He passed over the three drives.

"Cheers. To a job well done," said Smalls.

"Aye, too well. They're going to notice the break-ins, notice nothing was stolen, and double down on countermeasures now. You know that, right?"

"Oh, I know," Smalls said, with a note of exasperation in his voice. "But it couldn't be helped. We need the information, so it was worth the risk."

"What's next?"

"I check what's on these drives to see if we have any new leads before tomorrow, when I assume things will get complicated with Garson, and maybe Walterson if he comes back from the Cotswolds early. Once they know about the break-ins, there will likely be some scrambling. I'll alert our surveillance to expect increased activity. With any luck, we'll get a lead. Hopefully our luck hasn't run out yet."

"And for me?"

"Nothing you can do right now, mate. This part is on me. May your side lose 2-1 in injury time."

McRae raised his glass. He knew Smalls was right but felt bad. Partly, he wished he'd been able to help more on this. He felt like this was his work now, and Smalls was helping him, so it was jarring to be reminded that it was actually another man's investigation, and he was the one assisting. He also felt an unhelpful reminder of how powerless he was in the face of last year's catastrophe. For the past week it felt like he was actually doing something about it, which for a year he hadn't. Doing something about it helped him process what had happened.

He had lost his family, his whole world, in the blink of an eye. He was left behind, alone, and without the people he depended on to help him through.

This was the second time now that he had lost a family. In high school, he was too young to understand what was happening when his parents died. He was grateful to his aunt and uncle who took him in, but Ontario was a new province, and much as they tried, he always felt alone. Even in the military, when he was surrounded by colleagues and fellow soldiers, he was still on his own in a real sense. He was used to it, and good at it, but nonetheless he keenly felt the absence of contact. He felt closed off to everyone, with an inner monologue that no one else knew or really cared about. There was no one to share good things with or to take the edge off bad things.

Until Lynn. When he met her, for the first time since his childhood, he had someone he could talk to, who wanted to know what he was thinking and feeling, someone with whom he wanted to share everything.

Then, when he most needed someone to share with, to make him feel like he belonged, he was once again alone and even more likely to cut himself off from contact; he did his utmost to interact with as few people as possible, whether colleagues, fellow patrons of the Friend, or anyone from back home. He swam rather than ran; he taught classes but rarely went to seminars; and he read at a table in the pub rather than sitting at the bar.

Something in him changed when Dee took his arm and put her head on his shoulder. At that moment, McRae once again experienced the first warmth of spring coming after a long, cold, hard winter. Somewhere inside him that sense of belonging was beginning to stir. It was desperately fragile, like a seedling of a maple first emerging from frosty soil, but it was there, it was real. Now he just had to protect and nurture it, so it could grow into whatever it was going to be.

When Smalls left, McRae decided to change seats and move into a better position to watch the matches. There were only a few weeks left in the season, and it was now between Liverpool and City for the title, but there were also a batch of teams all trying to avoid relegation to the Championship, one league below but a world of difference in terms of visibility and profitability. Promotion to the Premier League carried with it not just a lot more exposure but a share of the multibillion-pound TV deal. And since the bigger teams were mostly involved in mid-week Champions League matches and played on Sunday as a result, Saturday matches more often than not featured a team fighting to stay up and a team that was safe from the drop—and the twelve-thirty match even more so.

When he started going to the pub for matches, McRae had no interest in football. At that point it was about the people-watching. He was in a new country, and from what he could tell this was an important part of the culture for a lot of people. One of his Scottish friends from the department had given him a ticket to a match in Edinburgh—Hearts versus Inverness Caledonian Thistle—and the atmosphere was like nothing McRae had experienced any other time he'd watched live sports. Fans would cheer, sure, but the singing, the chanting, the constant activity in the stands was entirely different from baseball—which even in a good game, is a long afternoon of drinking beer punctuated by occasional moments of action—or hockey, which was hard enough to follow for people who knew the game. While there was an ebb and flow of the players on the pitch, if anything it was the calmest part of the stadium most of the time, the eye in the middle of a hurricane of human chaos surrounding it.

The atmosphere at the pub was like a miniature version of the stadium, though with added tension, given that supporters of both teams were seated much closer together than they would be in the stadium. Nonetheless, despite that undercurrent and the significantly cheaper alcohol than you'd get at a match, it seemed there was a general understanding that the pub was a demilitarized zone. If you had an issue, you took it outside, and you generally avoided all but the most benign of banter—what he'd have called "smack talk" or "chirping" in Canada. In four years now of watching matches in pubs, McRae had only ever seen violence break out once, and that time, one of the combatants was looking for a fight more than he was looking to watch the match.

His thoughts turned to Dee again. He hadn't heard from her since the night before. He wondered how her evening went and what she was up to today. He decided, unusually for him, to send a text.

— Hope you had a good time last night and
that your day with the girls goes well.

A few minutes later, he had a reply.

— Thanks! Tonight should be fun—
hen party for a uni friend—but I am very
much looking forward to tomorrow. 😊

He decided to keep it simple

— As am I 😊

It was odd to be texting again. At thirty-three, he was a shade too old to have been raised on texting but was still young enough to know the etiquette. It wasn't a part of his life until he was in university, after he met Lynn and realized this was how people communicated now and that it was surprisingly pleasant.

When the match was starting, Smalls was just returning to his office for the day. While plenty of people at MI5 took their weekends, it wasn't unusual to see someone in, so Smalls wasn't surprised when, arriving at the sixth floor, he found Moss working one of the terminals, doing searches on names he didn't recognize and that were none of his business.

Upon seeing him walking toward her, she asked, "Anything to report?" Smalls nodded toward the black room and made his way inside. Moss followed immediately, closing the door behind her.

"We have Walterson's hard drives copied; I'm in to run them now. He's gone to the Cotswolds for the weekend, it seems. I'm also planning to look into Garson and his family. He has four children, three daughters and a son. I've got photos of them and would like to run them through facial recognition at some point. I have a hunch that his family could provide some leads."

"A hunch is not a lot to go on."

"I know it's not. Listen, I've know already asked, but I really need your permission to access Garson's home and whatever devices are there." Smalls felt a slight pang of guilt, asking for permission to do what he had already done, but thought this was a decent enough way of covering his tracks.

Moss took a moment. "Do it. I'm also going to give you whatever you need for surveillance. This is now our official priority. If only Walterson had left me in charge of this six months ago, we'd be done by now."

"I'm not so sure. I've had some help on this that I didn't know I would have."

"Spill it."

"In Afghanistan I worked with a Canadian named McRae. I was the attaché to the British MI lead, he was the attaché to the Canadian equivalent. He's in London now, working at LSE, and he's been quite helpful on this."

Moss took this in. "What have you had him doing?"

"I enlisted McRae to do a bit of surveillance of the Halisburys for me, and that provided the link between Walterson, the Halisburys, and Garson. I was almost derailed by the Guardian report, but since I wasn't the source and the Home Office reacted, McRae and I were able to follow more leads, and now, well, here we are."

"It's good work, no doubt. Do I want to meet this McRae?"

"Likely. He's an academic now but has a good tactical mind. I have a feeling he could probably hold his own in a fight, but he's also pretty good at avoiding them too."

"My kind of operative. Once this is done, set up a meeting."

"Gladly. So for now, we get Garson's files, and wait?"

"Yes. See how he and Walterson react to the break-ins."

"How do you feel about a bug?"

"On a fucking QC? Are you nuts?"

"I think that much is clear, Chief."

"No. Surveillance will have to do. But expand the net to include the Halisburys. If they're involved and we can prove it, it'll be an earthquake like this country hasn't seen since the Profumo scandal fifty years ago. If they're involved and we can't prove it, they'll be a nightmare," Moss added, and left the room. Unless Smalls was mistaken, she had a bit more of a bounce in her step than she had on the way in.

While Garson's files were downloading, Smalls went to the black room and called Eyre. Since there was an expansion of the reconnaissance team coming, he needed to give their leader a heads-up and a chance to pull in the people he wanted. He couldn't call on his cell from the black room—the whole point of that room was its impenetrability—but there was a secure land line in there.

"Eyre here," he said, answering the call.

"It's Smalls. We're going to be expanding your team and your scope of activity."

"Good. I don't think we could keep up with things on twelve-hour shifts for much longer. It's a long time to be in a cab without so much as a piss."

"How about eight hours then? We're upping you to teams of three—you choose your people—and adding two targets."

"Aye, and who are the new marks?"

"That's the thing; we need discretion on these ones."

"As if we're not discreet on all our marks, ya eejit," Eyre barked.

"Fair enough. It's Major Halisbury and Lord Rutherford. You're familiar, I assume?"

"The *Gleaner*'s involved?"

"Could be. For now, we just need to know what they do and who they meet with."

"All right. Send along known addresses, and we'll get started today," Eyre said, then ended the call.

On his own initiative, without running it by Moss or anyone, Smalls decided to take one additional step. This would be a two-man job, and he'd need McRae in on it.

15

Partway through the second half of the Brighton and Watford match, McRae's phone began to buzz on the table in front of him; it was Smalls.

"What's up?"

"Got a job I need your help with. You sober enough?"

"It's Brighton and Watford, nowhere near exciting enough to need a drink."

"And also too boring to watch without one."

"Fair. You coming here?"

"No, meet me at High Street Kensington station. Half-hour okay?"

"Cutting it close but I'll leave now."

"Forty-five minutes then. Still have your jammer?"

"You noticed I kept that, did you?"

"Yes, I did. Bring it."

"If this is about getting your kit back..." McRae started to say, but the triple beep indicated Smalls had already hung up.

He settled up with Owens and walked briskly around the corner to the Russell Square station. He knew his bike would be fine until he could get back for it later. The Piccadilly line would get him most of the way there, but he'd need to change to the Circle line at some point, probably Gloucester Road.

He hadn't spent a lot of time in the Kensington area. Too rich for his blood, generally, but he knew this was Halisbury territory—it was down the road from the gallery he'd been to only four days earlier. He assumed it had something to do with them, and if Smalls needed the jammer, he knew they'd be breaking in again.

Smalls made his way to Kensington knowing he'd arrive first, likely about ten minutes before McRae. Unfortunately, it wasn't enough time to do a preliminary recon of the area, so he'd just have to wait at the station. Or nearby.

There was an M&S next to the station, and Smalls decided to go in and buy himself some cover. He needed to do some grocery shopping anyway but didn't want to burden himself too much with a full load of supplies, so he just picked up a one-litre jug of milk and a packet of chocolate-covered digestives. As a grown man who made his own money and his own decisions, there was no way he was buying the plain ones.

After checkout, Smalls returned to the station with a conspicuous plastic M&S bag—an extra ten pence these days—and waited for McRae to arrive. This time of day, the station was a mix of tourists coming from the gardens and Kensington Palace, shoppers from other parts of town coming for the slightly higher-end goods that you couldn't find on Oxford Street, and locals arriving home after whatever business had taken them out earlier. A typical London crowd, really, all moving in different directions, and yet with a flow that made everything seem far more organized than it really was.

A few minutes later another crowd began to emerge from the staircase to the platforms, and McRae was conspicuously present. Smalls hadn't really grasped how much the slightly taller-than-average ginger stood out until he saw him in a crowd of tourists, few of whom were over five foot six. Not necessarily the best at going unnoticed, really, but McRae knew how to blend in when he had to. Today was too warm for a hoodie, but the T-shirt and jeans read more like tourist than local in this neighbourhood, and that was usually cover enough.

Smalls caught McRae's eye and began to walk toward the eastern exit. McRae caught up to him a few seconds later.

"Well, what's the job now?"

"Oh, you know, just picking up a few essentials on the way home. You? What brings you to this part of town?" Smalls said, refusing to break cover until they were away from the crowd.

"Looking for a present for someone special. Know anywhere around here with any good memorabilia? Some first edition books, or maybe commemorative mugs?" McRae decided to take the piss, a sign that he may have had a pint more than he should have.

"There's a place on Victoria Road, just down the road here, that might have what you're looking for," Smalls said, with a stern glance.

"Is it a major kind of place?" McRae asked.

"It is. Not sure if it'll be open, though," Smalls said.

"Why not?"

"Well, I called to confirm their hours and didn't get an answer. It's not certain, but I think they may be closed."

"Guess we'll just have to see when we get there, won't we?" McRae said brightly, and the two walked in silence until they turned the corner of Victoria Road.

"Major's is number 8," Smalls said with a quick glance behind to ensure no one was following. "Look for a Range Rover, plate starting with LD." The pair walked the full length of the block, turned onto Albert Place, and kept walking.

"No sign of it. Am I lookout, or going in?"

"You're lookout. I go in," Smalls responded.

"Why don't we both go in?" McRae asked. "I might see something you'd miss and can do a bit of snooping while you're downloading his files."

Smalls thought for a moment. He knew McRae was just coming from the pub and had probably had a drink or two that afternoon. He seemed sober enough, but in this sort of thing even the finest of margins could matter.

"We don't know how long we'll have on this one, and I can't get caught inside that building. I need you outside."

"What if I went in?"

"The major knows you; he doesn't know me. You couldn't pass as a burglar. Give me the jammer."

McRae grimaced. "Fine then," he said, handing over the device. "I'll set up across the street, behind that ugly pale blue building."

"It is ugly, isn't it. A blight on an otherwise pristine neighbourhood. Here, take this, would you?" Smalls handed McRae the M&S bag, then stopped at a doorstep to tie his shoe. Groceries in hand, McRae crossed the road and headed back toward Victoria Road. Smalls watched as McRae passed the Vietnamese embassy on the corner and crossed again before turning left, back toward the high street. He saw McRae tuck into a small alley, coming at a tight angle from Victoria Road behind the oddly shaped, oddly coloured house. Smalls wondered how anyone got planning permission for a place like that. McRae took out his phone, as if looking for directions. He'd have Smalls' number pulled up, ready to dial at the first sign of trouble.

Having untied and retied his shoe, Smalls reached into his pocket and turned on the jammer. He then walked quickly back on Victoria to number 8, putting on his gloves as he did so, and went up the stairs to the front door. The major had a standard lock and a deadbolt, but neither would pose much of a problem. Smalls was surprised not to see any sort of door camera. Maybe the major, who from all appearances lived alone, valued his privacy.

On the inside there was no alarm, but there was a cricket bat immediately to the right of the door: the major's security system, then. Smalls wasted no time. This was a three-storey manor house similar to, if one storey smaller than, Garson's, and he assumed that all the activity would take place wherever there was a study. In the major's case, that was the entire second floor, so Smalls located the laptop and plugged in the jump drive, scanning the documents in the room as he waited for the light to turn green. The wall was mostly photographs, many from newspaper clippings, most of which featured the major with someone of influence. Smalls recognized a few cabinet ministers and a couple of PMs, along with a few senior members of the royal family, and there was one of the major and George Best. There were only a few where the major and the viscount were featured; most were older and had the previous Lord Rutherford, the major's brother, in them instead.

As the light on the drive turned green, a text came through. It was McRae.

— Get out.

Smalls grabbed the drive and stuffed it into his trouser pocket before running three at a time down the major's carpeted stairs. As he exited, he saw the major's vehicle parking down the road, back on to him. He didn't have time to lock the deadbolt, so he had to hope the major wouldn't remember whether he'd locked it or not.

Rather than return to Kensington, Smalls went south on Victoria Road and motioned for McRae to follow. With a bit of a zig-zag across Eldon Street, they would end up on Cornwall Gardens. From there, they could double back to Gloucester Road and then down to the station.

"That was too fucking close," Smalls said.

"I texted as soon as I saw that the major was driving; if anything, we're lucky he couldn't get a closer parking spot."

"True, but relying on luck always makes me uncomfortable."

"Fair, but that's all we can do for now. At least you got out before you were spotted," McRae said, looking around the neighbourhood. "Funny, I was planning to end up in this area tomorrow."

"Really? Isn't she a bit old for the Natural History Museum?"

"Sure, but you're never too old for the V&A."

"No, but you can be a bit too young for it," Smalls responded, and they shared a laugh that served to calm their nerves and break the tension.

"I'll keep you posted," McRae said, handing Smalls his grocery bag.

"Please do, and I'll do my best not to need any help breaking in anywhere tomorrow afternoon."

"Or tomorrow morning, if you can help it. I've got some shopping to do."

"Do it now. You know the markets are shite on Sunday morning."

"Good call. Portobello it is," McRae said, as they reached the station. From here, their paths diverged. McRae would take the Circle line north, toward Ladbroke Grove and the Portobello Market. Smalls was heading back to work, where he hoped to be able to sort through the files from four different computers.

McRae had been avoiding the markets since his move to London. Before, every time he and Lynn came south she wanted to check out a different market. They'd done Camden, Spitalfields, Borough, and Liverpool Street, but Portobello was her favourite. She was a museum curator at heart, and the antiques in particular sparked her interest, but they would always end up with a load of fresh fruit, cheese, and bread to take home for an evening picnic. It was that part of their lives that McRae now found himself replicating.

Doing something alone that you'd always done with someone you love is a surreal experience. Memories flood back and you can find yourself asking what the other person would do at the most random of moments, like when choosing strawberries. The market stall had dozens of pint containers, each of which looked as good as the other on top. But McRae remembered a trick Lynn had used of looking at the bottoms of the containers instead, to see how many of them had gotten juicy and were more likely to be rotten.

So as he picked out fruit for his date with Dee the next day, Lynn was ever present. This was her place, and he had come here to get supplies for another woman. Was this wrong, he asked himself. He heard, in the darkest corners of his mind, her answer: "Don't be silly, my love. This is exactly what I want you to do. I know it's hard, but I'm with you and am happy for you."

There was a cheese shop a few hundred metres down the road that he remembered being really good. Again, this wasn't something he was particularly into when they came to the UK, but Lynn was always trying new things, and he didn't want to let her down or make her do any of them alone. When he found the store, memories overwhelmed him. He could see her there, her long red hair flowing over the pale porcelain of her shoulders, a wrecking ball in a summer dress. She looked back and asked if he was coming. Of course he was. He always went with her, on every adventure. And beyond, for she was now with him as he had new adventures. It was what they promised each other; life would always be an adventure, and they would never have to be alone.

Once he had his cheese and his strawberries, the next stop was a pastry shop a little farther along, toward the place where the food part of the market gave way to vintage clothes, comic and band shirts, and knock-off football jerseys. He decided that rather than pick one thing and get it wrong, he'd get an assortment and hedge his bets.

For old times' sake, he kept working his way west through the market, past the clothing and to the section that, on Saturdays and Wednesdays, was full of vendors of various kinds of antiques. The wares ranged from things that could be quite valuable if they were in better condition, to the downright ridiculously nostalgic—far more rotary phones than one would ever expect to find in a twenty-first-century market. He came across a case of old naval officers' medals. Were this two years ago, he would have bought one of these for Lynn as a present. She was always collecting bits and pieces of nautical paraphernalia. They reminded her of her grandfather, the former merchant mariner who moved to Canada and traded frigates in the North Atlantic for a canoe on Fairy Lake in Muskoka. He didn't know Dee well enough to pick something out for her, but he wanted to, and for now, that was okay.

Smalls' afternoon was spent doing the mundane work of an investigation: sorting through records, looking for patterns, trying to see what was out of the ordinary and would point them to where the killer was hiding. *Being* hidden, rather, to give credit and blame where they were due. The killer wasn't hiding himself. There was a network supporting him, whoever he was, keeping him from facing the consequences of killing dozens of people and harming even more.

Smalls had commandeered a corner of the room with multiple vacant workstations, signed in to each, and begun the downloading and decrypting process on all four available computers, one for each drive he and McRae had copied at Walterson's and Garson's homes. The records had all been downloaded now, but as it was Saturday and his investigation was still unofficial until Monday, when Moss intended to seek Home Office sanction for his work, he was on his own in reviewing them. He started with Walterson's emails, judging him to be the least likely to be cautious. Also, since he was an MI5 employee, his emails were subject to review while under investigation, and if there were leads from them, it would be easier to explain in court.

Keyword searches for all the obvious terms—Garson, Halisbury, Rutherford—were generally coming up negative, so he needed to look at sent mail. There were no emails sent to Garson or either Halisbury on this computer. Searches for Banks and Clegg were also blanks. Whatever they used to communicate, it wasn't email. In fact, it was almost conspicuous how few emails there were between Walterson and either Halisbury or Garson.

He knew from surveillance that business was usually done face to face—McRae had seen as much at the auction when Walterson flagged down the major, who then spoke with Garson. It's likely there were phone calls or text messages in some kind of code, but whatever there was, Walterson's computer wasn't any help.

If Walterson was so careful, maybe his wife would be less so. Also, her files were the smallest. Searches of the emails were busts—mostly family contacts or social commitments, with the odd shopping receipt.

The browser history was also fairly innocuous. Searches for online shopping, tickets to Royal Albert Hall. That said, it was hard to narrow down a search like this until you had a baseline, hard to see the anomaly until you knew what normal looked like.

The final set of copied files from Walterson's house was from the phone McRae had found. This was his work phone, as it turned out. While there was one phone call from it to Clegg on the day of the *Guardian* article, it was less than ten seconds long and could be explained away; there were so many reasons an MI5 officer would have for calling a copper on a day when he'd had a leak. Beyond that, no numbers belonging to anyone they believed to be connected to the cover-up. Was that one call enough to make a connection? Nothing that would hold up in court, but for now they weren't concerned with prosecuting this conspiracy but with finding the bomber. Everything else was secondary.

More and more the threads of this investigation unsettled Smalls. He wondered what would become of Garson, the Halisburys, Walterson, Banks, Clegg, and whoever else was caught up in this network. He needed time and space to think this out, look for commonalities and patterns, see what they had in common and who else might be involved. They were all conservative, sure, but so was most of England. All were powerful, but who could say who was helping whom? To get deeper into The Network, as Smalls had begun to think of them, was beyond him right now. And besides, he didn't have much time before Garson reported a break in. What happened then might either make things clearer or much muddier, but he needed to be ready either way.

Garson arrived home after another long day at the office. Not that he minded. Work focused his mind, which he appreciated. If anything, it helped him avoid idleness, and Mary had always said idle hands were the devil's playthings. He'd always been busy—the cost of a successful practice—but in the years since she had passed, his work had come to consume his life. He might have put in a couple of hours at home on a Saturday before, after their morning trip to the market and before evening Mass, but now he'd rather not imagine what he'd be doing if he wasn't busy preparing for some argument or another.

He didn't imagine he would ever retire now. He was a shade too old for a judicial appointment, and never wanted one anyway, but he wouldn't know what to do with himself without work. The girls were all grown, with families of their own, and much as he loved time with his grandchildren, they were beginning to get older too. The youngest would be starting school soon, and then their focus would turn to their friends rather than their old granddad.

It didn't hurt that his job was also the main part of his social life these days too. It was a Saturday, but the chambers were far from empty. At least a third of the tenants, particularly the juniors, were in today and would often pop in and say hello when they saw his office door open. They were his second family; he certainly knew more about parts of their lives than he did his own grandchildren's and spent more time with them too, particularly if they were assisting him on a matter.

Still, as the day wore on and he began to feel his usual tea-time hunger, rather than head to the canteen for a snack he had decided to call up Alan, his driver, and get a ride home. Driving in London was a nightmare, but at his age he found it hard to put up with the dirt and grime of the Tube. He had decided not to keep a housekeeper—he never entertained anyone at home who wasn't family anyway—but couldn't bear to do without his driver. And after fifteen years together, he and Alan were close anyway. Alan and his family were on the Christmas dinner invitation list, though his children had their own families and could never make it.

If the drive in was one of his favourite parts of the day, the drive home was one of the worst. The anticipation of what needed to be done was always more exciting for Garson than the feeling of accomplishment once it was done. As well, the office was a place where he felt alive, but at the end of a long day he was going home alone, to a place full of memories and shadows of a life once loved but which had passed when Mary did.

It was also on his drive home that Garson usually thought about his kids. His daughters and their families were among his main sources of joy now. He wished his son would settle down too. Joseph looked like Mary and had much of her steadfastness, but he didn't have any of her stability. Garson's work had always been demanding, but his children made it worthwhile, and he wanted to see them flourish as much as possible, whatever that meant for each of them.

The first indication that something was wrong was when he put his key in the lock, turned it, and found that it didn't have the familiar opening click. For a few seconds, Garson thought he might have forgotten to lock up, but to be safe he turned to Alan and motioned for him to come inside. The look on his face would make clear that he was concerned about something, and he trusted Alan to understand what his expressions meant.

He waited on the step for Alan to arrive and demurred when he insisted on going in first. The alarm was tripped, but there didn't appear to be anything missing. Garson asked Alan to call the security company to see what had happened, while he went directly upstairs to check on the valuables in his office and in his bedroom. There was no indication of anything missing, and the safe behind the family photo was untouched. Perhaps they saw the alarm and left? Perhaps what they were after wasn't here? Still, he was unnerved, and when he was genuinely worried, he always knew whom to reach out to.

He pulled out his phone, scrolled down the contacts, and sent a text:

— Lunch after Mass? It's urgent.

A few moments later, a response.

— Stavros'. 1.

Garson breathed deeply for the first time since arriving home. The major would know what to do.

16

Sunday was the day McRae usually reserved for rest and exploration. It was a pattern he and Lynn had started when they moved to Edinburgh. Wake late, grab some baked goods from a local café, and then walk to a part of the city they hadn't been to yet or take in some attraction that had caught their eye during the week.

Today would be different, but it still started like Sunday usually did, with a lie-in. That said, lying in bed on your own is a lot less fun than lying in bed with your beautiful wife, so McRae was usually out of bed by eight and took a few minutes to tidy the flat before having a shower.

Showering was a bit awkward these days; the water always felt cold on the burned parts of his arms, where the hair had not grown back. The pain of watching Lynn die was far worse than the pain in his arms, and every time he felt sensations there he was drawn back to that darkness. He finished rinsing out his thick hair—an envy of many of his departmental colleagues—towelled off, and got dressed. He decided to go with a long-sleeved shirt, not wanting to have a conversation about his scars just yet, despite knowing that he'd have to explain them at some point. He didn't want to push another awkward conversation with Dee about his late wife so soon after the first.

He dressed himself in a checkered green dress shirt and his black jeans. This would work, he thought, if they ended up in a decent restaurant later. He also grabbed a tweed jacket that worked with the green, in case it was colder than it seemed. With London in May, you never did know what kind of day it would end up being.

Her text came in about twenty minutes later.

— Leaving for the station now. My sister is being a pain. Can you send me a selfie to appease her before I do?

This was not his forte; he couldn't bring himself to do the extended arm, overhead angle so popular among his fellow millennials. Instead, he went to the back of his bedroom door and took a picture of himself in the full-length mirror, with a smirk rather than a smile.

— How's this?

— She says I need to teach you how to take a proper selfie but otherwise approves. 😜

— Fair. We can work on that. Let me know when you're on the train, and I'll make my way over to the station. It won't take 45 minutes to get there from my place, even if I walk.

— Have I mentioned how much I appreciate your use of proper grammar in text?

After three checks to make sure the commas were in the right places, McRae replied.

— Haha, no, you haven't, but thanks. See you soon. 😉

He decided that since the trains ran every half-hour, even on Sundays, she would likely get here from Cambridge in about an hour. He grabbed the picnic supplies and made his way on foot over to the station, cutting through the side streets of Marylebone, Fitzrovia, and Bloomsbury on the way.

As he watched the posh red and brown brick of Marylebone give way to the concrete and yellow of Fitzrovia, it occurred to McRae that however long he lived here, there would always be more to find. This route was a new one to him, even if the areas he walked through were very familiar. There was little risk of getting lost, but it was always more interesting to walk by new shops and eateries than to see the same old ones. Especially on Sundays.

A text told McRae that Dee had gotten on the 11:10 train and so would arrive in London a few minutes before noon. He was making good time and would be there when she arrived.

King's Cross on Sunday was far from quiet. It was closing in on noon now, and plenty of shoppers, theatregoers, and other visitors would be making their way into London for the day on one or another of the regional train lines, and all the major lines from the Midlands and north ended up here. From Cambridge, Dee had explained, she could take a relatively quick train to King's Cross or a much slower one to Liverpool Street. The quick one cost a shade more, but not having to stop at every hamlet and rural station between East Anglia and London was worth a few extra pounds. McRae decided to take it as a compliment.

He had picked up some fresh bread at his neighbourhood bakery and some flowers at a stall just outside the station and now stood on the platform, with only slightly less anxiety than when he was standing at the bar of the Clerk. Then he saw her, making her way through the crowd. Her eyes lit up when they caught his, and he was reminded of an old song from home: "Have you ever seen a sight as beautiful as a face in a crowd of people that lights up just for you."

He briefly wondered what the Cowboy Junkies were up to these days but filed it away as Dee approached.

She was dressed far more casually than he had expected, wearing blue jeans and a flowing, flowery top, again highlighting her beautiful shoulders, and with her long, wavy hair bouncing behind her as she gleefully walked up to him. He opened his arms to give her a hug, and she went one further, planting a firm kiss on his surprised lips.

"Now that's a welcome," he said, smiling, as she broke contact a second later. He pulled the flowers—an assortment of daisies, mums, and lilies—from the bag. "For you."

"Aww, aren't you sweet. I can't remember the last time someone gave me flowers."

McRae thought for a second. He could remember the last time he gave someone flowers. It was a year and a month ago, on the seventh anniversary of his and Lynn's first date in April. The slight tinge of sadness might have crossed his face, but as Dee's attention was focused on the scent of the flowers, she didn't notice.

"Shall we?" he asked, raising his right arm for her to take.

She put her left hand on the inside of his arm, holding the flowers in her right, and asked, "Where to, Doc?"

"Have you eaten? I was thinking a picnic first."

"As promised, then. I had a light breakfast a few hours ago so could definitely go for that."

They walked through the station and off to the taxi rank beside it. He offered to take the flowers back and put them in the bag, but she declined. "I'd rather hold on to them for a bit, if that's okay."

"Of course, they're yours."

The taxi brought them to the corner of Hyde Park at Marble Arch, so they made their way around the fencing and into the grounds of central London's biggest green space. They didn't have a blanket, but there were lawn chairs for rent throughout the park. The chestnut trees lining the pathways were now in full bloom, and the late morning sun cast only a slight shadow. At his suggestion, they picked a spot at the edge of the shade, where he could avoid the direct sun and she could enjoy it. They put their chairs side by side and sat to watch the world passing around them.

As they ate the first of the bread and strawberries, Dee told Rowan about her evening out with the girls the night before. “A bit of a bummer, if I’m being totally honest. You know what it’s like when you’re out with old friends—sometimes it’s great, and you pick up right where you left off, but other times, it’s like you’re in totally different worlds and don’t really mesh anymore?” She paused, and he nodded with understanding. “This was definitely the latter.”

“What do you think it is?”

“Well, time, I suppose. We were all at uni together, most of us in the same college but different programs. Now, well, it was a hen night, so that’s a wedding I’ll have to go to in a couple of weeks, but otherwise I probably won’t see much of them again until the next one gets married or has a kid. There were twelve of us in total, but three had to head home before eleven because they’ve got young kids. Of the remaining nine, two are pregnant so they’re not drinking, leaving seven of us with low enough inhibitions to get on the dance floor. They were all very curious about you, though, my mysterious new man in London.” She smiled at him.

“Ah, mysterious, am I? What did you tell them about me?”

“Just the basics. Canadian, a professor, handsome but doesn’t act like it. If you’re not tired of me in two weeks’ time, maybe you can meet them at the wedding.”

“Is that an invitation?”

“Yes, but like I said, only if you’re not tired of me by then.”

“Why would I tire of you?”

“I don’t know. I live for my work, really. This is the first time I’ve not been to the office in two days since I got called to the bar.”

“I guess I’m a bad influence.”

"Perhaps," she said, appearing a touch ashamed.

"Don't feel like I don't understand. I do. When I was deployed we worked every day, ten- to twelve-hour shifts, with very rare breaks. When you're doing something important, it's worth the time. But I guess my perspective is that more than one thing can be important."

"But is it important? I mean, arguing cost awards on behalf of giant landlords or media conglomerates?"

"Well, that's a different question, but there are opportunities for barristers to do other kinds of work, aren't there?"

"Yes, there are. But we can't all be Amal Alamuddin. Or I guess it's Clooney now."

"Well, I'm no George Clooney, that much is true, but I don't see why a similar career path couldn't work for you," he said, and she smiled.

"Entirely possible. I need to get a bit more experience first and build up my connections with the social justice world a bit more. Which is hard when you work at a place like Gladstones."

"Why is that? Wouldn't the prestige help?"

"It does in some ways, but we often act against the people or organizations I ultimately want to help."

"Okay, so maybe you move sooner rather than later. Don't worry, I won't tell anyone."

"I know. I trust you." She turned to him and smiled. Then her gaze shifted up, and she reached out and picked a fallen blossom out of his hair. She added it to the bouquet and smiled warmly at him.

That was the exact moment when Rowan McRae fell in love again. It was a subtle gesture, but such a meaningful one. She was touching him, taking care of him, helping him with something he didn't even know had happened. She did it with such gentleness and elegance in her movements that it almost seemed like it was in slow motion, and yet was over in an instant. Then, to keep the blossom rather than simply toss it away showed that she wanted to remember the moment too. He looked in her eyes and smiled, knowing they would both remember it and, as long as their relationship bloomed, remember it fondly.

Guess I won't be going to Newcastle for the final match of the season after all, Rowan thought. *Looks like I have a wedding to go to.*

17

Half a mile to the east of where Rowan and Diksha were falling in love, Major Halisbury was arriving at an old-fashioned Greek restaurant that the Halisburys had been going to for years now. Seasons was largely known for its seafood and for the ridiculous red octopus overlooking the entranceway. It was owned by the same Greek family that opened it a generation earlier, but the food and ambience inside were both subject to significant upgrades. Now, while it still focused on seafood, it had lost all the Greek kitsch and served a combination of Mediterranean and classic French food, in a room that would not look out of place on the right bank of Paris.

Old connections were what brought the major here, more than the food. The owners were long-time contacts of the Halisbury family—the major himself had written a letter of recommendation to get the manager's son into Eton—so his privacy was assured with the use of a small private room on the restaurant's second floor.

It also worked because of its proximity to another key institution for both him and Garson; it was only a few hundred metres from the Church of the Immaculate Conception, just on the other side of Berkeley Square in central Mayfair. Both men attended Mass that morning and made their way on foot to the square, where they met like old friends, shaking hands warmly under the awning at the centre. They then made their way to the north end of the park and along the street to their lunch destination. Before they left the public space, Garson began to speak.

"Hilary," he said, using the first name almost no one knew and fewer said aloud, "I appreciate what you and your family have done for mine."

But the major stopped him from continuing. "Not here. Did you not notice that we're being followed?"

"Are we? Goodness gracious," Garson sputtered. He began looking around him frantically for possible interlopers.

"Be calm, old friend. We'll be perfectly safe once we're at Stavros'." The major never referred to Seasons by name, only ever calling it by the late owner's name.

The major was the younger brother of the third Lord Rutherford—former chairman of the *Daily Gleaner* and the father of the current viscount. While there was a good ten years between them, the major was the late viscount's closest friend and only true confidant; it was a closeness the major had tried to cultivate with the new viscount, his nephew, but that the younger man bristled against it. Still, the major kept trying. He felt he owed it to his older brother's memory to do his best for family, even when that family wasn't terribly grateful for it. It was through his brother that the major came to know Stavros Papadopolis and his establishment, and also the value of a quiet space in a busy restaurant.

The major and Garson made their way to their alternate sanctuary in silence, Garson looking suspiciously at every passerby, while the major ambled with the typical firm gait of a former military man, looking neither left nor right, giving nothing away to the two surveillance teams that had combined at the church to follow the two men.

Smalls was sitting in the George, near his flat halfway between Hampstead Heath and Belsize Park, watching the Arsenal match, when he got the call he was expecting.

"Yes, Eyre, what's new?"

"A fair bit. First, the major and Garson attended the same Mass this morning, at Immaculate Conception."

"Interesting, go on."

"Second, they're now having lunch at a place called Seasons in Mayfair. Bruton Lane. My team is on them."

"Okay, good. No way to monitor while inside, I take it."

"No, and that's the bad news—we think they've made us."

"Keep on nonetheless, maximal distance. We'll see how they react. Anything else?"

"Surely that's enough, boss?"

"Aye," Smalls said, with a faint trace of a dark laugh. "Check in tomorrow morning unless there is something new to report."

"Understood." Eyre ended the call.

Smalls knew this time would come. It was in their suspects' reaction that they would be able to either uncover this conspiracy or at least learn how capable the forces were that they were up against. His instinct told him to call McRae, but this afternoon McRae was unavailable. Smalls didn't even know if he'd have his phone with him. Probably, but disturbing him would require some kind of cover or explanation, and that might risk further compromising the investigation. He swallowed, then scrolled down his phone to Moss' number and dialled.

"You're not in today?" she asked upon answering.

"Wasn't planning on it, but I do have an update."

"Not now. I'll call back," Moss said, before abruptly ending the call.

It was becoming increasingly clear to Smalls that while he trusted her, and she him, there were definitely people at MI5 that Moss did not trust. Sure enough, Smalls got a call about fifteen seconds later from an unidentified number; she was calling from the phone in the black room. "Go ahead," she said.

Smalls debriefed Moss with the details so far, including that the surveillance had been spotted. She took in the information passively. "So what's the plan now? Withdraw?"

"No, continue to monitor and see how they play it. If they try to contact someone else in The Network, we'll know. And maybe find the bomber."

"Okay. Keep me posted and play it careful; we don't need this in the papers."

"Thanks. See you tomorrow," he said, and Moss ended the call without another word.

While Smalls was watching his match, the major was conducting a thorough inquisition of Garson, attempting to determine the nature of the break in, whether anything had been uncovered, and the extent to which the security services were aware of their operations.

The major had noticed his own surveillance on the way to church. While it wasn't that far from his flat in Kensington to Mayfair, it was still farther than most people would walk. So when he noticed the same person walking behind him from Kensington Gate to the steps of the church, he decided to keep track of him. He then saw that person connect with someone else, who seemed to be keeping an eye on Garson.

There were many connections between Garson and the major, not the least of which was a strong and longstanding professional one. It's possible that the people following them were from the *Guardian*, but that wasn't their usual tactic. No, this seemed more like security forces and couldn't be the ordinary police, or Clegg would have alerted them. Must be MI5, which meant Walterson was the likely problem.

The major guessed that, in the wake of the *Guardian* report, someone had become suspicious of Walterson, and the surveillance started there. He thought back on their movements. He and Walterson had spoken at the auction at the gallery, but that was before the story broke, when Walterson was still in his position at MI5.

The major inquired about interactions between Walterson and Garson.

"He called me at the office, but I refused to take the call. He sent his wife in the next day, pleading for me to do something about his dismissal, but I said there was nothing I could do. That's all for me. Far as I know, he's been off golfing or out of town."

"He has, but those two things may have been enough for someone to get the scent of a trail to you. But that doesn't explain how they connect to me. No, the last time we were all in the same place at the same time was at the gallery, and that was before Walterson's dismissal."

"Is it possible that there are two separate investigations, which just happened to meet at our church this morning?"

"Possible but unlikely. We haven't met since Walterson was suspended; our only other meeting included Clegg and Banks. If that meeting was surveilled, then they're probably following Clegg and Banks now too. If they're still in the clear, then maybe it's a coincidence." The major called over their attending waiter, who was positioned on the opposite side of the room from their table so that he couldn't overhear anything. "Any chance you could bring me a phone? No need for anything fancy. Anything that places calls will do."

The waiter took his own phone from his pocket and unlocked it for the major. He knew the importance of these particular diners and that such a reasonable request should be accommodated if at all possible.

The major accepted the phone and took out his own. He scrolled through for Clegg's number and then tapped it into the waiter's device.

"Clegg, Hilary here. Tell me, any surveillance on you? Check and then get back to me at this number. Don't call mine. Yes or no will do."

The major thanked the waiter for the kindness and returned his phone with the instruction to let him know the answer once it came through. The waiter nodded then headed down to check on their food. He returned a couple minutes later, bearing two steaming pots of mussels in a lemon cream sauce, and an answer.

"Sir, he says, 'yes' and asks that you call him back."

"Then could I please borrow your phone once again?"

"Of course, sir."

It was the most recent number, so he was able to call back quickly.

"Call Banks. We'll need to take more drastic steps. Keep to your normal routine for at least two days, then I'll be in touch again." He ended the call and handed the phone back to the waiter, who retreated to his position. The major turned to Garson.

"Looks like this is no coincidence. You heard what I said to Clegg: for the next day or two, keep to your usual routine. I'll be in touch again on Tuesday evening, if not before."

"How on earth do I do that knowing that MI5 is following me?"

"Simply. What would you usually do today after meeting with me?"

"I'd probably go for a walk around the gardens, then head home, picking up supper on the way."

"Do exactly that. Then tomorrow morning get up at your usual time and go to the office. Assume your phone is bugged, so face-to-face meetings only, and use other phones to call when necessary.

Follow your routine religiously, and don't think about it more than necessary."

"Fine, but I'm definitely not going to be able to finish my mussels. My stomach is already in knots."

"Understandable. Just go about your business as best as you can. Leave it with me. You know how seriously I take my vows."

Following conspicuously friendly goodbyes outside the restaurant, the major and Garson went different ways. The major knew Garson was uncomfortable and that it would probably show.

It's not that the major didn't feel such discomfort; he did, but he had also long ago learned how to suppress any hint of an emotion. Feelings at a time like this, when there was a crisis to deal with, would only get in the way. So he made his way home more directly, stopping only into a newsagent to get a sense of whether his tail was still on. They were much farther back now—Garson may have given the game away—but it was a conspicuously inconspicuous young man, tall, with blond hair and no reason to be looking into the furniture store a block back.

He needed a clean phone, but there was still one person he could call without raising any suspicion.

He opened his phone and hit the second number down in his recent call list. "Paul, would you mind coming in today? I know it's Sunday, but I think I'm going to need a little help this evening."

He would send Paul to pick up a burner phone for him. Someone might see his driver come but wouldn't know what he had with him, and then the major could do what he needed to.

18

Across town, Dee and Rowan were enjoying the sunshine. Their food gone and with it the last of the sparkling wine, they decided to walk on from their perch and enjoy the warm spring day. Rowan suggested taking "the long way to the V&A," and Dee was happy with that plan. She was surprised at herself, realizing how quickly she was falling for this man whom she'd only known now for a total of five days.

As at the pub, the conversation on their second date continued largely unbroken. They talked about her evenings with co-workers and friends, the hen party and the upcoming wedding. It would be in Cambridge, but she said she'd meet him at the station and show him around a bit as they made their way to the chapel for the two o'clock ceremony. After that, it was likely a bunch of the friends would gather in one of the pubs they used to frequent as students while waiting for the reception. Their dates would also likely be there, all wishing they were watching the match.

This turned the conversation to football. She understood it was important to so many people but couldn't really understand why, so

Rowan told his story of how he got into football in the first place. It was endearing, but even more so was that he told it matter-of-factly rather than as any sort of proselytizing. He wasn't trying to convert her, just to explain how he ended up feeling how he felt. It was perfectly fine with him if she didn't want to watch football, as long as she didn't judge him when he did.

When there were occasional lulls in the conversation, they amused themselves with people-watching. Hyde Park drew a fascinating menagerie of humanity, and warm Sunday afternoons were particularly good viewing opportunities. They noticed someone in what appeared to be a Jedi costume, complete with plastic lightsaber, handing out leaflets; a small group of schoolgirls who seemed to be wearing wings; and many, many couples and families, the sight of which pushed Dee to ask a difficult question.

"Do you miss them?"

Rowan didn't need to ask who she meant. "Yes, of course. There isn't much I do when I don't wish I could hear Lynn's voice, and not a day passes without wondering what Harris would be like now. They were my world, really, far more than anything else. Like, I miss the army, and I miss Canada, but the gap left by Lynn and Harris is much deeper than those other losses. And in a real way, I carry them with me," he said, pulling his wedding ring out from underneath the buttons of his shirt. "I only took this off last week, just before we met." He then reached into his pocket. "And this," he said, showing her a chess piece, "is my little totem of Harris. But after a year I've become used to it, in a way. It's like glasses. When you're wearing them for long enough you don't even know they're there, and it just becomes how you see the world. Even six months ago, it was pretty all-consuming, but it's just a part of life now. She'd have loved you, by the way."

This caught Dee off guard. "Really? Why do you say that?" She could feel herself blushing, in addition to the sunshine already warming her cheeks.

"There's a line from an old Joni Mitchell song: 'You don't like weak women, you get bored so quick.' That was me. I've only ever been interested in strong women. She was one and respected it in others."

"You know, I've never really had anyone call me a strong woman before. Bossy, bitchy, a bit of a cow, but never just strong in a complimentary sense."

"It's true. To accomplish what you've done in your life so far, you'd have to be. Lucky too, sure, but also strong. Which isn't to say that you don't have weaknesses or soft spots—who doesn't?—but that all in all you're the mistress of your own destiny as much as anyone can be."

"And what are my soft spots, do you think?"

"Now that's a dangerous question," he winked, "because some of them seem very lovely, and I'd like to get to know them better." She laughed and rolled her eyes. "Others, well, likely your parents, and being a first-generation barrister at a prestigious chambers. That's bound to be stressful."

"Definitely."

"You know mine, of course. So what do you think yours are?"

"This. This right now. Dating. Being romantic. I've never been very good at it."

"Gotta say, from where I'm standing," he reached out his hand, "you're doing swimmingly."

"Thanks." She placed her hand in his and allowed him to squeeze it for a moment before withdrawing. "Maybe you're a good teacher."

"We've only had a date and a half, so far. If that's the reason, you're a very quick student."

She stopped walking to kiss him. Again, their kiss seemed to go on far longer than either initially intended. Her lips, on finding his, realized that they did not want to leave. His responded by pressing and puckering, turning one kiss into many. They became more and more passionate, deeper, until after what was, in actual fact, only about twenty seconds, they came up for air.

"We could go to my place instead," he said, smiling.

"Yes, let's."

Instead of continuing south, toward the open fields and the museums of Kensington, they turned north, toward Rowan's place, only a five-minute walk away. The walk to his empty and recently cleaned apartment had the first moments of nervous tension in their brief relationship, so McRae decided to adopt a mature stance and check in.

"Anything I should know before we get there?"

"What do you mean?"

"I mean things you like, don't like, preferences? Not asking if you've got a third nipple, not that I'd mind."

He could feel her relax. "Well, I will say that it's been a while since I've been in a man's flat. I like that you've asked the question and will let you know if something comes up. Otherwise, let's just see what happens."

"That can work."

"And for you?" she asked, somewhat awkwardly.

"Well, it's also been a while. I don't like pain, but that's about it. Do you prefer to lead or follow?"

"For now, let's say follow, and we'll see if I change my mind later on. How about that?"

"Suits me fine. My place is just up ahead on the left."

As the door to his flat was swinging closed behind Rowan, Dee turned around and kissed him and began tugging his shirt from his trousers. He took this as permission to do the same and pulled her top off over her head, forcing a pause between their kisses as he did. By now, his shirt was freed from his belt. He paused and said, "Here, let me help" and pulled the shirt over his head.

Dee recognized that what she saw before her was very different from the boys of Cambridge. This former soldier, a regular swimmer, descended from generations of fishermen, had very broad shoulders and a wide, muscular chest. She let her hands run over the hair on his torso as he let the shirt fall to the side. He pressed a finger under her chin and lifted her face to meet his, then kissed her again.

Her arms wrapped around him and pulled him close while his hands turned to the clasp of her bra. He deftly flicked the two links open, but it stayed in place while they were pressed together, kissing. He didn't care. He'd been waiting to touch this back and these shoulders since he watched her ordering at the Clerk. The skin was softer than he'd hoped, making silk feel rough.

She broke their embrace and let her bra fall to the floor as she reached down and began to undo his belt. She wasn't wearing one, so he just undid her jeans' button and pulled the zipper tab, letting it fall open while she was still working the clasp of his belt. He pulled her in again and kissed her. Then abruptly stopped. He took her hand and walked her toward his bedroom.

Once there, he picked her up and laid her on his bed, with her knees right at the end and her feet hanging off it, almost to the floor. He reached under her and said, "May I?," waiting for a clear, affirmative "Mm-hmm" before he pulled her jeans and her underwear off together in one motion.

Dee had never experienced anything like this. She'd never been with a man who not only knew how to make a woman feel good, but who seemed to enjoy doing it. Which he did. For Rowan, the feeling that he was making his partner feel pleasure made him comfortable with the pleasure he also took from the experience. He always felt like he had to earn it, but he also enjoyed what he was doing along the way. The unfortunate consequence of male physiology meant that when he was done, he was done for a while. Dee had no such limitations, and so he made a point of ensuring she experienced as much pleasure as possible before his instincts took over and he let himself lose control.

Hours later, both of them thoroughly sated and spent, Dee, her head resting on his chest with his arm underneath, said, "Well, that was unexpected."

"But not unwelcome, I hope," he replied, and he tilted his head forward to kiss her hair.

"Most definitely not." She raised her head and kissed his lips.

"Like I said, it had been a while."

"For both of us. Let's do this again sometime."

"Whenever you can fit me in your schedule. And it doesn't always have to be quite the marathon."

A moment of silence passed between them. It was no longer the awkward silence of two people who didn't really know each other, but the contented silence of two people who felt safe in each other's presence.

As she pulled his arm closer around her, Dee noticed his scarring for the first time.

"Do you mind if I ask?"

"Ask what?" He was lost in thoughts of how beautiful she was and how amazing it was that she was there with him.

"About your arms?"

"Oh, yeah. Burn scars, my only physical injuries from Beltane."

She was silent for a moment, so he asked the obvious question for her. "Did you want to know how?"

She nodded.

"When the explosion happened, I was halfway across the field. Well outside of the damage area. But Lynn and Harris were in it. I ran in to find them. She was holding him, but he was already gone. There was nothing I could do to help her. All I could do was hold her. So I did, and these are what happened."

She looked at him for a moment, tears welling in her eyes, and then lifted his arm to her mouth and kissed it. "I am so sorry."

"Thanks. Me too, for what it's worth."

"What do you have to be sorry for?"

"I don't know, really. I just feel like I've been sorry for a long time now, and it has become more of a habit than anything."

"You've done me no wrong, Rowan. You owe me no apologies."

"Okay then. I'll try and keep it that way," he said before kissing her head once again. "Welcome to my place, by the way," he added. "Hope it meets with your approval."

Dee took her first look around. The walls were a relatively spartan white, with a few pieces of art here and there, mementoes of trips, it seemed to her, though she couldn't always place where they were from. So she asked, and he explained, letting her in on parts of his prior life without anywhere near as much pain as he used to experience when he thought about it. The black-and-white of a couple walking under an umbrella was from Paris, of course—the Eiffel Tower in the background gave that away. Dee said she'd never been.

"Really? You live here, so close, and haven't been to Paris?" She shook her head, slightly ashamed of how little she'd travelled relative to him. "That's okay," he said, noting her embarrassment, "we'll do something about that soon." She looked up at him and smiled before they kissed once again. She'd never had anyone to make plans with before.

"And that one?" She pointed toward an abstract picture of a woman dancing.

"Prague. Doesn't say anything about the city, but I got it in a market there. I really loved the guy's work but couldn't afford much more than a small print."

"Another place to add to our list."

And they lay there in bed, making plans, until the light from the window began to change from the bright of daytime to the rose gold of early evening. They talked about places they wanted to visit, with Paris on top of the list, how they'd split the cheque (he'd pay for rail or flights, she'd pay for accommodations, and they'd go back and forth on meals), and how to spend their days.

"I don't want to go back to Cambridge."

"Fair, but I don't know if we're ready to live together just yet. Let's see how our second week goes, and we'll come back to it next weekend." And they both laughed at the absurdity of it all.

Rowan continued, "Do you want some supper first?"

"Now that you mention it, I'm famished."

"There are a few places on the way back to the station, if you're up for a bit of a walk."

"What time is it anyway?" she asked. Rowan found his trousers in a pile of clothes at the foot of the bed, and reached in to the pocket for his phone.

"Eight forty-five. Shit, they'll be closing any minute."

"I know a good curry that's open until midnight. Will that work?"

"Always. Love a good curry."

"Brilliant then." She rose from bed, not bothering to hide her naked body. He had already explored virtually every inch of it anyway, and she wanted him to enjoy it even more if possible. She thought to herself that it was only fair, as she had certainly enjoyed his.

19

When Paul came by with his new mobile, the major thanked him and got down to work right away. His first call was to the editor of the *Daily Gleaner.* The Monday edition would already be almost put to bed, but he could still get to work planting a seed for Tuesday, which he would leak Monday evening to the television news services.

"Tim. Time to let a cat out of a bag. Would you like to know which minister I have photos of with a young woman he isn't married to, photos I'll be passing along to you on Monday for publication Tuesday?" He paused, knowing that Tim Melanson would be sitting on the edge of his chair now, salivating at the prospect. "Well, you're going to have to wait until tomorrow morning to find out, aren't you. Still, be ready, and hold Tuesday's front page for it."

A good start. Since the Home Secretary was someone who was now refusing to play ball with him, the major needed him out. Now, to secure his replacement, someone more friendly. There were three likely candidates: two men and one woman. The major decided that, in the current political climate, it was more likely the woman would be more effective. Furthermore, as she was a former columnist for the *Gleaner* and her campaign had been heavily supported by the Halisbury organizations, she was more likely to be loyal.

His next call was to Banks. "Hilary here. Did you hear from Clegg?"

"Yes, what a fucking disaster," Banks said, with more anger than tension in his youthful voice.

"Yes, but stay calm. We're doing what we need to now to clear up the damage caused by Walterson. In thirty-six hours, you're going to need to help the PM find a new Home Secretary, got it? I'd take a good long look at Cassandra Atkins."

"Atkins, from Greenwich? Bit junior still, isn't she?"

"Maybe, but you need to even out gender balance, and she's been Minister of State for Immigration for a few months now, hasn't she? Besides, she's an ally, if not exactly on the team."

"Understood. I'll make sure it happens. In the meantime, what do we do about MI5?"

"Nothing. Keep to your routines. We would know if they have taps, so it must just be surveillance for now. I'll handle damage control from my end."

"Okay. Call at this number now?"

"If you must. Try not to call at all." With that, the major ended the call. He kept all his key documents at the office rather than his home. The building was more secure, and he usually spent more time there anyway. His home was functional rather than familiar. While he slept here most nights, particularly when he wasn't at his country house, he rarely ate here and never entertained. Even his nephew had only been here two or three times in the fifteen years he'd owned it. Only Paul was here regularly, and usually only on the outside.

He had one more call to make, this one much more uncomfortable than the previous two.

"Walterson," he said, "Hilary here. Forgive me, but due to your lapse in security we've had to make some major changes. Are you still at your country place?" The major couldn't remember exactly where

Walterson had his out-of-town property and didn't really care anyway. Not that Walterson was entirely responsible for what had happened here—he didn't give the story to the bloody *Guardian* as far as the major knew—but he was a weak link, and the major couldn't afford any breaks in his chain.

"Yes, I am," Walterson replied, "but I can come back to London if needed."

"Do. Not my office, though. Do you know the *Cutty Sark* in Greenwich?"

"I do."

"Good. Meet me there at eight tomorrow morning."

"I will. And I am truly sorry for—"

The major hung up on him. He had no tolerance for blathering. Or mistakes. Everything had its price, of course, but the wise man didn't pay any tolls he didn't need to. And Walterson was getting expensive.

About ten years ago, the *Gleaner* had moved its offices to five floors of a relatively anonymous office tower in Canary Wharf, the development in East London where two generations earlier the major's grandfather had imported paper from Canada and established the family fortune. The money wasn't really from the paper but the printing presses, which printed not only the *Gleaner*, at a discount, but several other London papers. It increased the profit margin on their own paper and reduced those on their competition, but even then their printers were still the cheapest game in town. Time and technology might have changed the news business, but the move back to this area, revitalized in the '80s and '90s after decades of postwar gloom and decline, felt right to Major Halisbury. A homecoming, in a sense.

What no one noticed was that on the floor above the *Gleaner*'s headquarters was the deliberately innocuous office of the Halisbury Management Company and the family trust that owned it. His nephew had one corner office but seldom used it, as he was rarely in the country and preferred to work at home or his peerage office. Nonetheless, for the sake of appearances his name remained on that door. The major, who in fact ran the family business, had the opposite, southeast-facing corner. In the centre, off the lifts, was a bit of a reception area showing photographs of their ancestors and a few of the current viscount doing good works, cutting ribbons and kissing babies. There were no photographs of the major, and he insisted it remain that way. There were also two desks in the lobby area, one outside each of the offices. The viscount's was ostensibly occupied by Ms. Flaggs, his assistant, while the major's was actually occupied by Mrs. Vivian Elders, his own assistant.

If Ms. Flaggs gave an appearance of socially acceptable frivolity, Mrs. Elders was her diametrical opposite. Serious to the point of dour, she was the perfect guard for the major's business interests. She managed his network, his calendar, and was typically in before him in the morning, prepared for whatever business presented itself. This Monday morning, however, when she arrived she found a note for herself, in the major's stark handwriting.

Need files on Home Secretary. Vault material. Back at 9:30.

Elders needed no further prompting. This must be serious. She returned to the lift and immediately clicked the down button. Once it arrived, empty on the descent at this hour of the morning, she clicked L5, indicating the fifth level below the ground and where there was a small car park and vaults for various tenants of the building, including the Halisbury Management Company. Usually, if something was to be removed from the vault, the major handled it himself, so she was rather chuffed that the great man felt comfortable leaving her this delicate task. She also realized that there must be some urgency to the request, since he had been in and already left before eight in the morning and left her with this particular piece of business.

She was not surprised to find a relatively thick file in a cabinet bearing the name of the Home Secretary. She did not pry—she would never—but was nonetheless curious as to what kind of business this would be. She assumed she'd find out in the *Gleaner* tomorrow, like everyone else.

Across the river from the Canary Wharf area, and in view of the major's office, was the formerly independent town of Greenwich, a royal borough from which the British Empire was truly grown. It was the home of the Royal Observatory and the Royal Navy for most of the Victorian era. While commercial ships came and went from the dockyards now underneath the development on the north bank, this was the area the navy that controlled the seas for two hundred years called home.

On the bank was a recreation of one of that era's most famous vessels, the *Cutty Sark*. It was a trading ship that regularly made the trip from China to England laden with tea, then returned with all manner of merchandise to sell in Shanghai or Kowloon. Now, it was a well-maintained tourist attraction.

The major had chosen this place for the proximity to his office and because the nearby gardens of the Royal Observatory were vast and, this early in the day, sparsely populated. He had been driven here by Paul, as usual, but in a different car, arranged specifically for this purpose and parked in the adjacent building with an exit on the opposite side of the peninsula. The only way he could think of to properly lose his tail was to make it look like he hadn't left the building. He carried with him two teas from the Costa next door and found to his surprise that Walterson had already arrived.

"I brought you tea," said the major, emerging from the car without Paul's assistance.

"Thank you, sir, you needn't have."

"Nonetheless, I did." He handed the cup in his left hand to Walterson, taking a sip from the one in his right. "Let's walk."

They ambled in silence until the major was out of earshot of Paul, who had stayed with the vehicle. "I need you to tell me everything about the Edinburgh investigation."

"There really isn't much to tell. While I hate to admit it, the *Guardian* got most of the facts right. Once I learned that there were Department for Transportation duplicates of the CCTV footage we'd removed, I slowed down the investigation as best I could. Moss was the lead. She was starting to get suspicious of the gap in the footage," he said, before taking a sip of tea. "Fortunately, that stabbing in Southend-on-Sea gave me the excuse I needed to reprioritize her and most of the investigative units to that case. Smalls, her deputy, was left in charge of the Edinburgh inquiry. I made sure he had very limited resources, and so it took him forever to get an image of the suspect and of the driver, and by then, as you know, any other images of them had been removed from all the databases. He wouldn't be able to get an ID even if I'd given him access—which I didn't."

"Tell me about Moss."

"Straight shooter, not so much ambitious as aware of her quality and its rarity. She spent a long time in Northern Ireland at the end of the Troubles and helped cool it down. That bought her a lot of credibility at a time when women didn't get much respect in the security services." He took another sip and thought for a second before continuing. "I do genuinely respect her, for what that's worth. She's also by-the-book, for the most part. No enhanced interrogation techniques, no offsites or dark ops for her."

"And Smalls?"

"Former military. Served in Afghanistan, I believe, and a rising star in his own right. Wasn't terribly happy about everyone being reassigned—had some remote personal connection to one of the victims, I believe—but did his job as well as he could with me making it impossible. I thought he was the *Guardian* leak, but the info was too dated and all his devices were clean."

"Who else was involved?"

Walterson went into detail about how the investigative team was broken down, who was moved over to the Southend investigation from the Edinburgh case, and his own take on their various merits. Most were the products of good schools—not Eton, but still good—and Oxbridge. A couple of Mancunians, but by and large southerners. A few with military backgrounds, a couple who were originally seconded from Scotland Yard, but no one who struck the major's interest. He made a note to look more into Moss and Smalls but left things there.

After a half-hour or so of walking, the major and Walterson had made their way around the gardens and were now nearing a pool on the far side of the area. At this point, Walterson was beginning to appear faint and sweaty. He spoke up.

"My apologies, Major, but I don't think I'm quite well."

"No, Walterson, I suppose not. You see, there was a great deal of ricin in that tea. I'm impressed you made it as long as you did, but we cannot afford any weak links in this organization, and I cannot trust you to remain silent should this investigation into you go further. Too many people, both above and below me, depend on our secrecy. I doubt you leaked this to the *Guardian*—that would have been colossally stupid, and you don't strike me as a moron—but it all happened under your watch. So what I can assure you is that if you do try to scream, I will also make sure that your wife and children join you sooner rather than later. But if you keep your tongue, I will ensure they are taken care of far more pleasantly."

The major watched as a combination of nausea and shock washed over Walterson's face. Indeed, he wasn't sure if Walterson could scream if he wanted to. Two seconds later, once the shock began to fade, he grabbed at his chest, as if trying to tear out his heart, and the pain left him unable to stand. He collapsed, falling—with the gentlest of nudges from the major—head-first into the water.

That's better, thought the major. *Now they won't know if he died from the heart attack or drowning, but it'll look more like an accident.* He picked up the cup Walterson had dropped, took off the cap, and turned it into a sleeve for his own. He'd drop them in the bin once he was back to the *Sark*.

Moss and Smalls. Two leads. Hopefully they would be enough.

Smalls' morning began with a call from Eyre.

"The major must've had an early meeting. He left at seven and headed straight to the office. We have no eyes on him there, but from what we can tell the car is still in the garage. The others, no changes. Garson is on his way to work now by driver. Clegg too, in a marked car, and Banks walked in as usual."

"Okay, good. Keep an eye on the major if you can. He caught our scent yesterday, so we need to know if anything changes."

What could the major have been up to that early? What was coming? Smalls felt a tinge of fear in the pit of his stomach like he hadn't since he was on active duty. What would the major do? What wouldn't he do?

Once he arrived at the office, he checked in with Moss. "I'm going to run Garson's son through facial recognition now for good measure. Knowing that he met with the major again privately makes me want to delve a little deeper there."

"Alright, go ahead," Moss said, then returned to her work.

Smalls copied a family photo from the Facebook page of one of Garson's daughters and ran a comparison between her brother and the images of the suspect from Waverley and King's Cross. It took about three seconds before returning a 98 percent match. Smalls caught himself. This was it, they finally had a suspect, and it was Joseph Garson, the barrister's son.

It took Smalls a moment to process what had happened here. After months and months of stonewalling, followed by break-ins and surveillance no one had sanctioned and involving several civilians, they finally had a suspect, a suspect whose photo someone had removed from the various government databases. The surprise passed through relief and into anger, and with it a desire to tell McRae. He wasn't sure how his friend would react, but he knew he wanted to be the one to break the news to him, news that wouldn't have been possible without his assistance and that couldn't help but further salt the wounds this investigation had made raw again.

As the anger gave way to concern for his friend, he remembered that he had a job to do. To back up his suspicion, Smalls uploaded the photo of Garson's driver from his phone and checked it against the driver from the traffic cameras. This time he wasn't in luck. No match.

Smalls called Moss' name and walked into the black room.

"That was quick."

"Aye, and I don't think we'll need to be meeting in here much longer. We now have confirmation: the suspect is Charles Garson's son, Joseph. His image matches the surveillance footage of the suspect from Waverley and King's Cross. No ID on the driver yet though."

Moss took a second to process this, sitting as she did. "Okay, so we've got Garson's son but not the driver. Now, how do we find the kid?"

"I'd say the smart money is that daddy is hiding him somewhere. We could bring in Garson senior for questioning, but he wouldn't give us anything. He knows better than to talk with us."

"How wide a net would you need to cast?"

"No idea. The kid is in the country, I'm fairly certain. I checked his travel records, and it seems he hasn't left the country since March of last year. Other than that, no idea."

"What about properties? Anything out of London belonging to any of the conspirators?"

"Lots. Garson has a place in Buckinghamshire. Lord Rutherford owns a decent chunk of land in a lot of different spots, and the Halisbury family trust has even more. To check them all we'd need a dozen surveillance teams."

"Or a smaller team that goes from place to place. Do up your list. Find the options. We're going to be running out of time now that they've got the scent. Any idea what the countermeasures will be?"

"No, and that's what keeps me up at night."

She looked him square in the eye. "That makes two of us, Marty."

20

Following one of the best curries he'd had in London, at Punjab on Neil Street—leave it to his new girlfriend of Pakistani extraction to find the good stuff—and a walk through Bloomsbury to the station, McRae again felt more alive than he had for a year now.

It was perverse, but there was something familiar in falling in love with Dee. It reminded him of when he and Lynn started to see each other. He didn't particularly want to compare the two women, but it wasn't so much them that he was comparing as the way he felt. He was comparing current him with past him and finding the similarities both unnerving and comforting. If this was what it was like to fall in love with someone, then he knew what to expect. But this was also falling in love with someone different and so would be full of surprises too.

As he walked back to his flat that night, following an extended goodbye at the station drawing stares from other late-night passengers, he had a talk with the Lynn in his mind about everything, once again asking himself what she would say. Would she be okay with this? Would she be glad with how he was handling things?

She would say they were moving fast, but that was also what happened to them once they removed the constraints of their professional tutor–student relationship. What's more, they also slept together on the second date. He'd forgotten that detail until the Lynn in his mind reminded him.

He couldn't quite hear her, but he felt comforted by her presence nonetheless. He knew she would be glad that he was good company and a gentleman. It was okay that they both wanted each other, since he treated her with respect.

Dee texted from Cambridge.

— Back in Cantab. Now that was a date.
What's your week shaping up like?

— Teaching tomorrow and Wednesday,
but it's revision sessions and they're prepped
already. Tuesday and Thursday are research
days, far as I know. What about you?

—Going to be busy until Wednesday.
Drinks and a bite then? Think I might
stay in town overnight too. 😉

Ah, the winky emoji, the most basic of flirting.

— You're welcome to stay at
my place, of course.

A smile in response—trying to show that he was happy to have her in his life in whatever form that took.

— I'll keep that in mind. Usually if
I'm stuck in town overnight I just
get a room at the Clerk.

— So we'll have a "your place or mine" moment.

— I'll see what kind of day it is. Thanks again for today. You were magnificent.

— Thanks. You are magnificent. In every way.

— Now I'm blushing again. OK, gotta go deal with my sister's inquisition.

— Good luck. Text at will.

Before heading off for his Monday morning swim, Rowan decided that things between them now were sufficiently formal—they'd agreed to exclusivity, after all—that he could send her a good-morning text without it being too much.

— Good morning; hope your sister didn't give you too hard a time after last night.

Her reply came while he was in the pool, not long after his initial message.

— She was a little mortified, but nothing I can't handle.

He wrote back before getting showered, shaved, and dressed.

— Mortified? That doesn't sound good. What happened?

Her response came once he got back from his shower.

— Oh, she was just surprised at how fast things have moved, that's all. As am I, to be completely fair. Not that I'm complaining. I am, however, very glad to hear from you this morning. How are you?

— Grand, thanks. Just finished my morning swim and now off to get breakfast and bike to the office. You're on the train now, I presume?

— I still can't believe you bike around London. Yes, just left the station. Now to deal with my emails from the weekend before I actually get to work.

— Good luck with them. Talk to you later.

This was new to Rowan and yet at the same time very familiar. Texting was just another form of conversation, and more than anything else he enjoyed talking with Dee. Sitting there talking was even better than lying there not talking, which was saying a lot.

By the time he arrived at the office, a text had come in from Smalls as well. In the rush of adrenalin and emotion over the last day, their business had become secondary for McRae, and he felt a sting of guilt that he had been so distracted.

— Lots of news. Surveillance compromised. Friend at 5?

McRae took a minute to let this sink in. Compromised how badly? And how? Was he implicated? Was Smalls? Was Dee? As much as he wanted answers to these questions and others, he knew there was no point in making Smalls hash out these details right now. Smalls had a job to do, and managing McRae would be—and should be, he knew—a low priority for him.

— Long as you think it's still safe.

— If it's not, I'll let you know. For now, lie low.

— Understood. Thanks.

Somehow, he was going to have to teach a class summarizing two hundred years of colonial history in an hour's time. To do that, he had to push this from his mind. Thoughts of Dee wouldn't work; too invasive and too likely to prevent him from doing any prep.

He needed music and so went back to his roots. McRae had long held the opinion that the greatest contribution Canada ever made to the world—including peacekeeping and insulin—was Joni Mitchell. *Blue* was too sad for him this morning, but *Court and Spark* would do just right. Upbeat and jazzy enough to keep him moving forward, but interesting enough to occupy enough tracks of his mind that he could get some work done on the other ones. *Blue* was the soundtrack to heartbreak, and he had spent months a year ago bawling his eyes out every time he heard "A Case of You." *Court and Spark* was music to fall in love to, more hopeful and optimistic, even in its bleaker moments where the singer is waiting for her lover to come pick her up for the evening. In fact, he decided to make "Car on a Hill," with its brisk intro horn riff, his new alarm, having tired of "Elephant" after all these years.

As a junior faculty member, a lecturer in the British system, he wasn't working with many graduate students, which left him with a lot more research time than the senior faculty. Which he needed. If he was to get tenure and promotion, either to a readership or a senior lecturer post, he'd need to prove an ability to publish. His dissertation was not long behind him and had provided substance for a couple of articles, but he needed new projects and issues to delve into if he was going to succeed in the academic game.

That said, this morning, as he reviewed his lecture notes from the previous weeks of the course—today's class was a revision class, so anything they had discussed was fair game—his mind kept drifting in two directions. On the one hand, he was pulled into the past, wondering what Smalls was doing now and whether they would be able to track down the monster who had haunted his dreams for a little over a year. On the other hand, he caught himself planning trips with Dee, wondering what kind of hotel she would pick out for them in Paris and when they would get a chance to make the trip.

The contrast made him feel a pang of guilt. His whole life in Edinburgh had been taken from him. He had a career, sure, but he also had a mission: to find the bastard and make him face justice. But now, he was also at what felt like the beginning of a new life.

Once again, he almost heard Lynn's voice. It was muffled, but there was a feeling nonetheless, a feeling of rebirth, or growth, and of joy that comes along with both. One part of his life had ended with the bonfire at Beltane, but another was now being born. He would always carry the scars, but he didn't have to be consumed by them.

At the same time, Rowan felt a strange mixture of comfort and sorrow in this thought. It was possible that a time would come when he would no longer need to hear Lynn's voice, though that time had clearly not yet come. He was allowed to move on—encouraged, in fact. He did not owe it to Lynn or Harris to remain in stasis his whole life. He owed them remembrance, and if he could find it, he wanted to give them justice. Loving Dee did not mean he stopped loving them.

And he had fallen in love with her. It was foolish to deny it, and what's more, he didn't want to. He was glad to be feeling alive again, having dreams and making plans.

Smalls' day was more about waiting than anything else. Starting from the date after the bombing, he began checking every security feed he could get access to from the London neighbourhoods near the Garson family home, looking for a match with the photograph of Joseph Garson. As searches were unsuccessful he broadened the parameters, but each search took longer than the last. When they came up unsuccessful, it was more and more frustrating, not just because of the lost time, but also because it meant that the next search would take even longer. By lunchtime the search covered most of West London for two weeks after the bombing and was going to take a few hours.

He knew he needed a break, but even more than that he needed to clear his mind so he could try and figure out what kind of countermeasures he could expect. The major or someone from his network would by now have spoken to Walterson and might know that Smalls was in charge of the investigation. They might also be concerned about Moss, but she wasn't in on anything until after Walterson was out, so she was probably safe. No, if they wanted information, it would have to come from Smalls himself, and he wasn't about to give them anything. Not if he could help it.

As he sat in Trafalgar Square eating a packet of crisps from a nearby newsagent, Smalls got a call. It was Eyre.

"News, boss, from the police radio. Walterson is dead. Found face-down in a pond in Greenwich. Heart attack the likely cause, apparently."

It took Smalls a second to process this news. Walterson was a relatively young, healthy man, who had no reason to be anywhere near Greenwich. For that matter, Smalls hadn't realized he'd returned to the city; so much for their surveillance. "When did he get back to London?"

"No idea. Since he was out of town, he was off our priority list. Everything else normal. All targets in their offices. Banks slipped out for lunch but didn't seem to meet with anyone."

"Any indication if he was taking countermeasures?"

"None. But he was very efficient about it, so hard to say. Didn't take any detours or stop to talk with anyone. My agent said he didn't seem as jovial as usual today."

"That could be anything, but thanks anyway. Let me know if anything changes."

Now back at his office, the major was once again making calls on the burner phone. First on his list was a contact at Government Communications Headquarters, the agency that oversaw all the UK security services.

"James, Hilary here. A temporary number. I need personnel files on two people, both MI5. Come on now, I know you've got access, and I know your price. I'll send my driver by with the envelope, you send him back with copies. Two hours enough time? Smalls, Martin, and Moss, Sandra. No, not for publication. Background only. Thanks."

James Altricham was a mid-level HR manager with the security institution, so he had access to background files on any security employees. He had been a minor clerk with the less glamorous and less interesting Coal Authority until the major had intervened. Altricham might object a little, but when they needed information—strictly for background, of course, until his intel could be proven from other sources—he was reliable. Four hundred pounds per was a decent deal.

The next call was to Clegg. Pretty soon news of Walterson's death would get to his desk, and the major needed to know when the family would be told, so he could be right behind in wishing them well. Clegg didn't pick up, so the major left a brief voice message, asking him to call ASAP.

This was a lot of trouble Garson's son was causing them all. Admittedly, the major sympathized with the young man's motives. They shared a version of the One True Faith that was highly unfashionable, but that only made its adherents even more convinced of their righteousness. Would the major have bombed a pagan orgy himself? No, but he wasn't going to let anyone hang for it if he could prevent it. Even less so when it was his godson, the child of one of his oldest friends, whose career he and his brother had fostered for decades now. Short of endangering his own life, or the larger network, there was little he wouldn't do for Joseph Garson.

His next call was to the editorial desk downstairs. This early he should be able to get a face-to-face, even as the newsroom was starting to pick up its daily buzz.

Only five minutes later, the editor-in-chief of the *Daily Gleaner* waltzed through his door.

"Tim, have a seat. How would you like to bring down the Home Secretary?"

Tim Melanson was a lean and hungry type. While he'd attended Eton and Oxford, in both cases he had been a scholarship student, and most of the other kids never let him forget it. The Home Secretary would have been one of those boys, so Melanson was loath to miss the chance to get a little revenge on his former tormenters and their type.

"I can think of worse ways to spend a Monday. What do you have?"

"How about this?" The major slid a folder across the table.

Melanson opened the folder. Inside was a photograph of the Home Secretary sitting at an expensive restaurant with a very young woman who was clearly not his wife. There were further photos of the two walking together, standing together in the lobby of a ritzy Mayfair hotel, and one of him apparently kissing her neck in a corner of a bar.

"Well, his wife isn't going to like these."

"Nope, and neither is the PM, I'd imagine."

"Certainly not, and coming on the heels of the recent leaks, I'd imagine it'll have extra impact."

"Feel free to mention that in a sidebar, but please keep the focus on the indecency of our good Mr. Secretary."

"Who's the girl, anyway?"

"Call girl, apparently. This will have cost him a couple thousand quid up front, and an awful lot more once we print it."

"Even better, he's on record against legalization of prostitution."

"Naturally. So I trust these will find their way to AI?"

"Of course. Thanks for the heads-up." Melanson rose to leave. "How long have you been sitting on these, anyway?"

"That, Tim, is a question I'm not going to answer."

An hour or so later, the major received a return call from Clegg, who confirmed that word of Walterson's death would be breaking soon. He was off to tell Mrs. Walterson now. As the major was still waiting for Paul to return from GCHQ with the requested files, he couldn't go pay his respects yet. It wouldn't be a hard act anyway. He did genuinely like Sarah Walterson, more than her husband, really. She was a good woman from a good family with a large estate on the Welsh borders. She'd do okay for herself now that her husband was gone. As he thought about this, he recalled that she was also a good friend of Lady Rutherford. Hilary decided to give his niece-in-law a call to let her know.

"Emmie, dear, I have unfortunate news."

"Hilary? Good lord, what's happened?"

"You remember Sarah Walterson—Sinclair-Lyons she was—her husband has turned up dead. I heard from a contact with the MPP and thought you should know."

"Denis is dead? He's only fifty-two. What happened?"

"No idea of the details, dear, I'm just passing it along. I'm told Sarah will know herself within the hour."

"I was supposed to have tennis with her later this week," she said. "Thanks for letting me know, Hilary. Does William know?"

"He may, but you were my first call."

"That's kind of you. I'll give it an hour or so and then head over."

"Of course. Was planning to drop by myself later on."

"No need, uncle. I'll pass along your respects."

This was a pleasant turn, would allow him to wait a few days before dropping in and promising to take care of the family. He'd have to help with tuition for the kids, of course, but her family trust would likely be enough to keep everyone in comfort for the rest of their days. Walterson had married quite a few steps above his station and never really understood how everything worked. If he had, and had known to be more discreet and keep control, he'd likely still be alive.

21

It did not take long for news of Walterson's death to reach his former coworkers at MI5. By the time Clegg was on his way to inform Sarah Walterson that she was now a widow, Smalls had told Moss what he had heard from Eyre. Moss felt it her responsibility to inform everyone.

"Can I have your attention, please. We've just got word that our former director, Denis Walterson, has been found deceased this morning. The circumstances remain under investigation by the Metropolitan Police, but for now there is no reason to believe that they are suspicious. Once funeral arrangements are known, there will be a general post. Some of you will wish to attend, and we can make that happen but not for everyone. In the end, Walterson would have understood that we have a job to do. So mourn in your own way, but attend to your duties. It's what he would have wanted."

Once her speech was finished, she motioned for Smalls to follow her into the black room. "That was harder than I expected."

"I didn't realize you and Walterson were close."

"No, the opposite. Pretending to mourn him. I couldn't stand the pretentious prig. But there is no way this death was accidental or natural causes."

"How healthy was he really?"

"Far as anyone knew, very. No issues with his physicals over the years, which for a director is unusual enough. Your surveillance didn't have him?"

"Didn't know he was back in London. We were on the major, Clegg, Banks, and Garson."

"Fucking hell. Okay, not your fault, just unfortunate. Keep an eye on them; especially Clegg and the major. Clegg will try to make sure there's no autopsy and that the investigation gets buried as quickly as possible. The major, well, he's a man with limitless resources and no public scrutiny; who knows what he'll do."

"Do you think we're at risk?"

"Maybe, but any move against you or me would raise far more suspicions than with Walterson, particularly as he was out on his ass after the *Guardian*. Still, I'd keep your side arm with you at home."

"Will do."

Moss opened the door and left. Smalls sat for a moment, collecting his thoughts. If Walterson was killed because The Network thought he was a weak link, that would turn their attention to MI5. It's likely they'd be investigating Smalls and Moss next, and if they got too far into Smalls' background, they might make the connection to McRae. Rowan needed to be warned.

Paul gave a polite knock at the major's office, then opened the door. He brought an oversized, sealed envelope over to the desk and without speaking turned around and left. Paul knew better than to ask questions.

The major opened the envelope with the sharp edge of a small dirk, a present from a fellow officer from his enlisted days.

Inside were two batches of papers, clipped together. Based on the cover pages, one was Moss' personnel file and the other was Smalls'.

The major unclipped Moss' file and began to study it in detail. He pulled a pad of paper from the desk drawer and occasionally made small notes to himself, to remember particular details. She was a Scouser, it seemed, and from an Irish-Catholic background, but began her service in Northern Ireland, working against her fellows. More British than Catholic, then. She'd received commendations for meritorious service several times in those years, mostly for defusing situations. Her big break came when her intel led to the discovery of one of the IRA's main weapons caches in the north. Perhaps her diplomatic streak earned her the respect of some possible turncoats and led to the intel. Either way, she knew the value of a good source.

Once things wound down in Ireland and the War on Terror began ramping up, she was moved to HQ and given command of a detachment looking into Islamist networks in the North until the 7/7 attacks. Because of her prior reputation, and some decent work with a couple of Leeds cells, and because of the abject failure of the London divisions, she was put in charge of that side. When Walterson was appointed, her evaluations became more humdrum. Not a fan of his, then, or perhaps resentful that he got the director's post ahead of her.

As for pressure points, there didn't seem to be many in her file. Divorced, no kids, lived to work. Physicals were acceptable, despite her relatively advanced age for the position. Still, if she couldn't be turned, she could still be replaced by a more amenable Home Secretary.

He set Moss' file aside and turned to Smalls'. Despite his shorter career, it was a thicker file, largely due to the recent investigation into the *Guardian* leak. His background was fairly straightforward.

Military man, from a Midlands family. No wife or kids, but since he was in his thirties, that wasn't terribly unusual. Enlisted out of uni, served in an infantry unit but got noticed by his CO and brought in as an attaché. Served with the joint task force in Kandahar for the balance of his term and an extra six months to keep things going until he could be replaced. Came back and went to work for the Security Service. Had been leading a group of surveillance officers in Birmingham before getting sent to Edinburgh to assist with the initial stages of the investigation. Came to be Moss' deputy after a few weeks there.

In the back of his mind, something was bothering the major about this file. He read it again, focusing more on the military time. This wasn't the first time recently he'd heard about Afghanistan. He went back over the events of the previous week until it clicked: the young Dr. McRae was also in Kandahar and had also worked with military intelligence. The two men may have known one another.

The major didn't believe in coincidence. He believed in surveillance. Time for another call.

The *Gleaner*, and the major himself, had made regular use of various PIs in London over the years, but his favourite was a former MPP officer named Terrence Parsons. He was a shade more discreet than the average, and more observant too.

"Terrence. Hilary Halisbury here. Yes, it's a new number. Got a job for you. Usual rates, of course. I need you to track an LSE prof named Rowan McRae. History department, I believe. In particular, looking to see if he has any connection with an MI5 officer named Smalls. I'll send a photo of the latter in a moment. The former I'll trust you can find on the department website. Sooner the better. If you have anything, please let me know immediately. Top priority."

A good efficient conversation. Nothing he liked better.

It wasn't McRae's best day in class. On a good day, things flowed nicely, as one part of a lecture led naturally into the next. Today, however, whether it was because he was distracted or whether it was the nature of a revision class, the lecture felt all over the place. Still, whatever his students had asked about—whether it was differences in trading relationships between Asia, India, Africa, or the Americas, imperial policy and the world wars, or social relations among Anglican and Methodist missionary groups—he was able to answer.

When he returned to his office, he checked his phone. No message from Dee this time. Her work was busier than his, he knew, so he tried to set his mild disappointment to one side. He had brought a sandwich from the bakery for lunch and decided to walk the two blocks to Lincoln's Inn Fields to eat it.

In the week since he had last been there, his life had changed so drastically. At that point, he'd just reconnected with Smalls and had yet to meet Dee, both of whom were now the most important people in his life. As he sat there, a text came through.

— Two new briefs make for a good but very busy day. I'll be in court tomorrow and Wednesday but now also have a hearing on Friday and next week that I'll be prepping for one on Thursday. How was your morning?

— Congrats, that's great news. You'll have to tell me about them when you next have a gap in the schedule. My day has been routine so far, with an afternoon of student drafts ahead of me.

— Trade?

— Haha, no way you want me trying to fit one of those wigs on my head.

— No, though I suspect the robes would suit you.

— Feel free to bring them on Wednesday and you can find out. 😊

— Well played. Now back to work;
I'll write again tonight.

— No worries, I appreciate that you're busy.

— You're the best, have I told you that yet?

— Nope. I'll screenshot it.

And with that, she was gone again. McRae looked up and around the gardens. They seemed brighter, somehow, than they did last week and in a way that an extra seven days of May sunshine couldn't explain.

McRae busied himself with reviewing drafts and responding to increasingly panicked student emails until around three. He then printed off a new paper to review and packed up his laptop, paper, and phone charger to head off to the Friend. There had been no new messages from either Martin or Dee since lunchtime, so he assumed his meeting was still on.

He left his building, carrying his bike, and started his way north by cutting through campus. Houghton Street was pedestrian-only from the entrance to his building, but no one really treated bicycles like cars. Everyone knew how dangerous London roads were for cyclists, and pedestrians usually gave way without complaint.

As he made his way to the Friend, McRae realized for the first time that the route he took, which involved as many side streets as possible and a cut through the Red Lion Square Gardens, was almost impossible to follow. He only realized this when he noticed a cab pull out behind him as he made his way north on Southampton Row past Holborn. He pedalled hard and made it through the light at Theobalds Road. The cab didn't, and as Rowan looked in his side mirror, it seemed like the driver was watching him far more intently than he should be. After that, McRae stayed deep in the side streets and brought his bike into the Friend when he arrived. He'd have to discuss this with Smalls.

McRae tucked his bike into their usual corner and was attempting to read from a stack of paper when Smalls arrived around four.

"What's the subject today, professor?"

"Avoiding Surveillance 101."

"Really, what happened?"

McRae gave him a rundown of picking up the cab at Holborn and then losing him at Theobalds. "I can't tell if I'm being paranoid about this or not right now. And they genuinely might be out to get me, so it seems like a moot distinction."

"No, you're right to be worried. The surveillance has been blown, and Walterson is dead."

Rowan paused, considering the implications of this. Walterson was the only sure connection they had to the major and the rest of his network.

"How?"

"The police are ruling it as natural causes at the moment. Appears that his heart stopped in Greenwich Park, and he fell into a pond at the same time."

"I take it you don't buy that any more than I do."

"Not in the slightest. He wasn't that old, had been through plenty of stress without showing it, and was in solid physical shape. While we had surveillance on the major's building, he's a wily one, and I wouldn't put it past him to have found a way out. His building isn't that far from Greenwich."

"Okay, so what do we do now?"

"I don't think there is much 'we' can do now. I appreciate the help you've been so far but can't risk putting you in any more danger. I had to cover my tracks on the way here just to make sure

I wasn't followed. If the major talked to Walterson, myself and Moss will be their main focus. You know as well as I do how far their reach extends; any more contact and I'll be putting you at risk, if I haven't already. Best thing you can do right now is lie low and watch your back."

"Yeah, but I won't be doing that, so what can I do to help?"

"I'm not kidding, Rowan. I'm worried they're already aware of you and you're already in danger. From my end, we've now got a positive ID on the bomber's identity. We're planning to take it public tomorrow."

"Sorry, what? You've got a positive ID? Who is it?"

"Oh, fuck, yes. I've been meaning to tell you. Joseph Garson, the barrister's son."

Rowan was silent while he processed this. Charles Garson's son had killed his wife and son. The image of Garson senior, laughing and smiling with the Rutherfords a week earlier, flooded his mind. Unconsciously, his hand went to his pocket and clutched the chess piece so tightly that an impression of the etching was left on his skin for hours afterward.

Before he could ask if they knew where Joseph was, Smalls said, "We're bringing Garson senior in for questioning tomorrow."

"Is there any way I could watch that questioning?"

"I doubt it. If you're compromised, might be better for us to keep you under tabs. But I'll take it up with Moss."

"Thanks. It's not like I'll be able to do anything else, knowing what's happening."

"Not going to be spending a relaxing afternoon with your new lady friend?"

McRae understood that Smalls was trying to end the conversation by changing the subject. There was no point in nagging his friend. Smalls would speak to Moss, and it was up to her as to whether he would be involved more. In the meantime, might as well talk about other things and try and take his mind off the tingling in his arms.

His hand finally unclenched the chess piece it had been holding so firmly all this time.

"I did tell you she's a barrister, right? What do you think the odds are she'll be taking a random Tuesday off to play hooky with me?"

"It's playing truant over here. And slim. Good date, though?"

"Yes, it was." It was McRae's turn to make Smalls wait now. He wasn't about to provide a play-by-play of the afternoon and evening, but he figured one salient tidbit would be fine. "We're going to meet up for drinks again Wednesday evening, work permitting."

"Lovely. So she wasn't too disappointed with your museum plan?"

"Hardly." McRae wasn't going to share details. No need to get Smalls' imagination working on anything but the case. "You don't suppose she's in any danger, do you? Makes me very uncomfortable how close she is with Garson."

"I doubt it. He and the major didn't make the surveillance until Sunday. If they have connected you to me, they can only have done that today, by reviewing my files. They shouldn't have access, but this is the *Gleaner* we're talking about. Still, let's see how things are before you confirm anything with her on Wednesday."

"Fair enough. And in the meantime, please try and get me in to at least watch Garson. I may even be able to help."

"I'll do what I can, but I'm not about to cross Moss on it at this point."

"I get that. Still, I've interacted with him more than you have now. And I get the feeling Walterson's death will shake him up. The major is one thing, but I didn't take Garson for the bloodless type."

"It is his son we're looking for. People will do a lot when it comes to their children."

McRae looked at Smalls, a stark, stern look that said his friend had come very close to crossing a line.

Smalls apologized. "There was nothing you could do, Rowan."

"No, Martin, and that's exactly the problem. So let me do what I can now. I don't need to be in the room, but I should be there."

"I'll try."

Both men took long pulls of their respective pints and turned their attention to the TV. It was too early in the day for any football, and there were not always matches on Monday anyway. For now, it was the news. Something was up with the Home Secretary, but the closed captioning left much to be desired. For now, they simply left the issue alone, and once he'd finished his drink, Smalls left to catch the Tube home.

McRae had already decided he didn't want to go home just yet. It was a hard day, really. The killer was out there, the authorities now knew who he was, but the people that had been hiding him were operating with impunity. Garson and the major were clever; they would figure out the connection between McRae and Smalls eventually, if they hadn't already. And Walterson's death, if indeed it was at the major's hands, proved that there were no limits to what Halisbury would do.

McRae had spent a year now wishing he could have done something to save Lynn, Harris, or both. He had accepted, for the most part, that he couldn't. Now, to learn that the father of their killer was protecting him, providing him the security that McRae couldn't give to his own son, burned deep and dark. He didn't know if confronting Garson would make a difference, but he knew he had to try. He owed it to Harris.

As he sat there, wondering what he could do to get in that room—particularly without getting Dee involved—he heard Lynn's voice again, more strongly than before. "All you owe us is to live, my love. Live, and remember us."

In his mind, Rowan answered, "I could never forget you, but is that really enough? If there is more I can do?"

The voice responded, "I can't stop you, but be safe, my love. If something were to happen to you, we would truly be gone."

22

Everything was falling into place. At around four in the afternoon, the major got an update from Banks confirming that the PM was aware that the story of the Home Secretary's indiscretions was about to break, and contingency plans were already in the works to appoint the Honourable Member for Greenwich as the new Home Secretary. Tomorrow was already set up; what the major had to worry about now was what happened next.

Control would still have to be reasserted at MI5. Moss was a problem, as was Smalls, but it would be difficult to get rid of them entirely. What was needed instead was a new director who could keep a lid on them and prevent any further investigation into any of the threads that might point in their direction. Clegg would be ideal, but he was needed at Scotland Yard. Still, Clegg might have a good idea of who could be appointed to clean up shop at the Security Service.

The Widow Walterson also had to be dealt with. While he was confident she wouldn't seek to push any sort of inquest into her husband's death, it would not do well for his network to see her left out in the cold. It might make people worry about what would happen to them and their families if something were to go wrong. He would pay a call on the way home; likely Emmie would be there anyway.

Parsons' first day on the job had been somewhat fruitful, if not perfect. He'd caught sight of McRae at least and had managed to access the university system and find his home address too. The major considered just bringing McRae in then, but if he wasn't involved, the exposure would be unnecessarily large. Walterson had been under a lot of stress and wasn't unfathomably young for a heart attack. McRae, on the other hand, was fit and in his early thirties. Not so likely to go down without a fight.

The major was just about to pack up his briefcase and make his way to the Cornwallis for a drink and a leisurely dinner, when the phone rang. It was Garson.

"Hilary here."

"They've made an ID on Joseph. They think I organized his escape. I'm being brought in for questioning."

"When?"

"Tomorrow morning."

"Alright, thanks for letting me know. I'll do what I can. Just sit tight," the major said, and ended the call.

Now this was unexpectedly aggressive, and worrisome. Garson was a barrister. He was paid to talk but also knew well enough when not to. This would also knock the sex scandal off the front page of every other paper tomorrow. It still wouldn't save the Home Secretary, but it would make his departure far lower profile.

In the meantime, Joseph Garson was out there, ticking like the bomb that had started this whole bloody mess in the first place. As long as his father stayed loyal, they would have time enough to ferry him out of the country before he could be found. If not, then the major would need someone to eliminate the elder Garson while the son could be moved safely abroad. It was a drastic and dangerous step but one he needed to take in order to ensure no further damage came to his operation.

It pained him. Garson had been a faithful ally for a long time, but the major could not take the chance that MI5 would get to the father and use his deeply rooted sense of guilt against him. Garson had to be eliminated. As the major approached his car in the garage, he motioned for Paul to lower the window.

"There's a text I need to send first, Paul," he said, before reaching out for his burner to text Parsons with a new assignment.

The phones at MI5 were ringing off the hook with tips and leads. Reports were coming in from all across the country of people who had seen Britain's Most Wanted Man. He was a wedding photographer in York, a custodian of a sixth form school in Lincoln, a season ticket holder at Norwich, and a student at the University of Sheffield. It would have taken every police officer throughout the country a year to follow up on all the leads, so for now they had to wait and take it all in. Eventually, there would be a pattern, multiple hits with a decent measure of credibility in a similar area that they could actually investigate. Garson's daughters were brought in, but none of them had had any contact with their brother for at least two years, so there were no leads there.

Still, Smalls thought as he watched the news from his flat in Hampstead, this had been a good day. They were finally closer to actually catching the bomber. His identity was now public, and if he had not already been running scared, he would be now. Maybe, just maybe, he would make a mistake and they'd be able to capitalize on it. It was, after all, how most criminals came to be caught: not through the good work of the security forces but through their own incompetence.

His job tomorrow would be to interrogate Garson, the bomber's father. If anyone would know where he was, it would be his father. Of course, the corollary of that was that if the father didn't know where he was, no one would.

Which reminded Smalls of the one call he needed to make. "Rowan? You're in. Moss says you can be there when we question Garson."

"Thanks, brother. I owe you one."

"Pretty sure we're even from that time you stopped my patrol from getting blown up outside of Maghreb."

"Even, then. When and where?"

Smalls gave him the address and suggested he be there by nine, as the questioning was to start at ten. For the barrister, they agreed to lawyer's hours.

"Again, thanks."

"See you tomorrow," Smalls said.

Smalls didn't even notice that the broadcasters were now talking about the allegations against the Home Secretary and his inevitable sacking in the morning.

Neither did McRae, who was still at the Friend, now eating the last of his chips and waiting for a Championships match to come on for the evening after the news was done.

Tomorrow he would see the father of the man who killed his family. He may not get to say anything, but then again, he had no idea what he would say if he could.

As he mulled over and dismissed myriad different possibilities, his phone dinged. It was Dee.

— Now that was a long one.

— Unusually long, or just the usual kind of long?

— Hard to say. Something is definitely going on around here.

He thought to himself, *She doesn't know.*

— Did you hear about your boss's son?

— Who? I have too many bosses.

— Garson. His son was identified as the suspect in the Edinburgh bombing.

Her reply took a moment; she was evidently taken aback.

— No, but that does explain why things have been weird. Also explains why they called an emergency chambers meeting tomorrow morning. How'd you find out?

McRae decided a white lie was warranted.

— Just saw it on the news. Joseph Garson wanted for questioning. Father, Charles Garson, QC

— Bloody hell. Where are you? Up for a drink?

— Not sure I'm in the best place to have a drink right now, but I'm definitely up for company. Do you know the Friend at Hand?

— No, where is it?

— On second thought, this place is about to turn into a football match, so not a great place for a quiet chat. How about the Clerk?

— Works for me. I'll meet you there.

McRae packed up his belongings and made his way through the increasingly crowded bar toward his bike, chained up outside.

Theobalds Road turned into Clerkenwell after a few hundred metres, so it shouldn't be too hard a ride. It also wasn't dark yet, which helped. When he arrived at the Clerk twenty minutes later, he found Dee already at the bar, chatting with the same bartender from their first drinks there, last Thursday.

"Ah, guess it was a good first date," she said, on seeing McRae walk through the door and approach.

"And a good second," he responded, with a smile, as Dee turned. He wasn't sure whether they should kiss or not at this point, but she helped him out by kissing him.

"Definitely worth a third," she added. "What would you like?"

"Just a Coke tonight. Diet, with a wedge of lemon."

"Not drinking?"

"I had one with supper and don't think it would be a good idea to have too many more tonight. Have you eaten?"

"God no, and I'm famished. Some of those chips too, would you, Deirdre?"

They looked around the pub for an empty table, ideally with a bit of privacy. As they scanned the bar, a group of four people—office workers, judging by by their light blue Oxford shirts and navy suits—rose to leave, so Rowan moved in to take their table. It was in the corner, which allowed them to cuddle together on the bench and maximize the distance between them and any eavesdropping neighbours.

Dee brought the drinks and took a seat next to him on the bench, and he let his arm slide across the top of the bench as she did.

"So a long day for you too, huh?" he asked.

"Definitely, and tomorrow's going to be a lot longer, apparently."

"So tell me, from your end, what happened?"

"Our office usually gets a little busier around three thirty, four in the afternoon, as we start to get back from court appearances that end a little early. People are often milling about, swapping war stories, the usual. But today, there was none of that. I remember Tommy Dillon was at my door—he'd had a hearing before a particularly nasty judge earlier—and was immediately pulled into a meeting by one of the senior members. After that, everything got unusually quiet, and then twenty minutes later I got a chambers-wide email telling us all that there was a meeting tomorrow at eight, attendance mandatory, and that was it. Whoever knew wasn't talking, or at least wasn't talking to me. It only made sense once I heard from you about Garson."

"Did you see him at all?"

"No, but that's not unusual. It's a big office, and while his door is usually open, it's on a different floor from mine, so I wouldn't have cause to see him."

She took a sip of her pint, letting the moment breathe, before she asked, "And how are you doing with all this? I imagine it's quite different from where you're sitting."

"Very much so. On the one hand, I'm glad they have a suspect, finally. On the other, it's weird that I met the father of the man who killed my family and didn't know it. I mean, why should I have? But it's still a strange thing."

She looked at him, sitting beside her, facing her, and with such emotion on his face. One of the things she liked about Rowan was that he had such an open face, expressive, not appearing to hide anything, but this was different. He was sad, but there was also an anger there, a tenseness to his movements when he spoke about Garson.

Which was fair. He didn't know Garson like she did. He only met Garson briefly, and now there was this connection between them that neither had known about. But the man she had known as a mentor didn't feel to her like the father of a murderer. He was too kind, too gentle for that.

She reached up and stroked the side of Rowan's face, the tips of her fingernails just penetrating the beard on his right cheek. Her look said "I'm sorry" without any words needing to pass between them.

In response, his gaze, which had drifted off to the empty space between them, became focused again on her and her eyes. He registered the sadness in them, sadness for him and what he had lost. It softened him again in that way that being cared for by someone who loves you does.

"Thank you."

"For what?" she asked.

"For taking time to comfort me when you've got plenty to worry about on your own."

"You're too sweet," she said. "I will be fine. Garson will probably have to take a leave of absence. His briefs will be redistributed. The chambers will need to do a lot of hand-holding, particularly with the media clients that were his bread and butter, but I'll likely get more work out of that."

"Still, when you've got so much on, I appreciate that you can take the time to care about me," he said, and bent forward to kiss her. She returned the affection, and it took a few seconds before they both needed air, and, apparently, another sip of their drinks. "I know how important your work is to you. While I'm happy to be a distraction from time to time, I don't want you to later regret spending time with me."

"I certainly have no regrets so far," she said, looking him square in the eye. They both knew she was talking about Sunday.

"I'm glad for that, and I'm glad to be here with you now, for as long as you'll have me."

At that, she shifted her body toward him and rested her head against his shoulder. "I'm done focusing on work tonight. I just want to rest. Can we do that?"

"Absolutely." He pulled her closer, and she felt the kind of safety that comes from being held by someone you love.

They sat in silence for the next few minutes, watching the bar around them, drinking in peace. Then Dee spoke up. "I do need to go back to Cambridge tonight."

"I understand. I'll walk you to the station."

"No, that was me trying to convince myself. It didn't work. I really don't." She moved away and looked at him. "I'm not sure I'm up for anything like the other day—which was great, by the way—but I would very much like to not be alone tonight."

"You're welcome to stay at my place, of course, if that works for you."

"Why don't we stay here instead? My treat. As I mentioned, if I have a very long day and can't make it home, this is where I usually stay. The rooms are quite nice."

"If you think my bike will be safe outside, I certainly don't mind."

"Let me check," she said, then stood and headed to the counter. After a quick word with Deirdre, she returned with a key.

"Room six. Shall we?"

"I get the feeling I'm going to have a very hard time saying no to you, Diksha Jamil," Rowan said with a smile.

"That feeling is mutual, Rowan McRae." She led him to the stairwell and up to the third floor where they would spend their first night together.

It was a very different experience than their afternoon at his place. While that had been a very physical experience—as if they both had something to prove, whether to themselves or each other—this was about feeling safe. They each undressed and crawled under the sheets. Rowan rested on his back, and Dee curled her body toward his, resting her head on his torso rather than the pillow, mindlessly letting her fingers brush the hair of his chest while she fell asleep in his arms. Once she rolled over to the other side, Rowan turned to face her, wrapped his arm around her, and pulled her close again, and she took comfort in the safety of his embrace.

Garson arrived home late that day. After the announcement, and the notice from the Security Service that they wanted to question him in the morning, he had to tell the other senior members of chambers. It wasn't like an American law firm, where there were partners and associates. In theory, all members of chambers were equal and independent of one another, bound only by the contract they all sign to pay a share of the common expenses. But in reality there was, within the firm, a group of senior members who sat on the chambers executive committee and who had authority over the whole of the practice. Garson was a member of this committee, and he knew he had a responsibility—a requirement, in effect—to notify them of what was about to happen.

He had told them only as much as they needed to know. His son was a suspect. It would be in the news. He was being brought in for questioning, presumably as to his son's whereabouts. He had no idea where his son was, and while that was a source of pain for him, it was a blessing at this point. It was also, technically, true.

It was over a year ago now since he had seen his son, very briefly at his house, where he could pack a bag to go into hiding. Joseph had called him from the train shortly after leaving Edinburgh and confessed to him what had happened. He'd asked for a place to hide. Garson had called the only person he could think of who could keep anything quiet, the man who owned the newspaper. Within an hour, the two had made arrangements for Joseph to be met at King's Cross, brought to the Garson household, and then taken to a secret countryside location, which only the major and his driver would know.

Now the whole arrangement was under threat, and he would have to go answer questions. He knew as well as anyone what his rights were when under investigation by the police. He didn't have to say anything, but he knew that silence would only incriminate him. All he would say is that he did not know where his son was and that he refused to answer any other questions. They might already have enough on Joseph to charge him, but Garson wasn't going to give them anything else to work with.

He offered to take a leave of absence for the duration of the investigation into his son, and the committee reluctantly agreed to this. On the one hand, there were those who thought it would be better to stand their ground and fight any scandal head-on. But there was too much risk involved in such a high-profile case. No one wanted the shadow of this hanging over the chambers, particularly as they had no idea how long it could take to sort itself out.

So he went home, essentially starting his retirement sooner than he had ever hoped to and under circumstances he would never have planned. He wasn't hungry anyway, and there was no way he was going to go to any of his usual places tonight. Instead, he opened his door, turned off the alarm, and made his way upstairs.

He wanted to be in his son's room tonight more than his own anyway. His son, fourth-born of their children but always first in his mother's heart. Joseph had his father's drive, it turned out, but his mother's piety. It was a dangerous combination, in the end, but Joseph was still his son and in many ways his strongest remaining connection to his wife.

Garson sat there on the spartan white sheets in a painfully bright, unornamented room. It was, he imagined, more like a monk's cell than the bedroom of the quiet, awkward young boy he thought he knew. As he sat there, weeping gently, he asked himself how piety could turn so wrong and how they could have raised such a person, but he also wished his son was there right now so he could hold him and not feel alone.

As Garson sat sobbing in his son's room, he did not hear the intruder enter by the garden door, nor did he notice the slight creaking of the stairs as the stranger moved upward through the house and slipped quietly into his own bedroom.

The assassin was patient. He would wait until Garson was asleep and then inject him with enough strychnine to kill him. And if confronted, well, he knew how to kill a man in dozens of different ways. His instructions were to make it as painless as possible, but the client would understand if more intense measures became necessary.

So it was that Garson, returning to his room after mourning for his late wife, lost son, and the unceremonious end to his career, did not bother to look behind the bedroom door he never closed anyway. He brushed his teeth, used the loo, hung his clothes, and took to bed, falling asleep with the aid of two small pills prescribed by a friendly doctor not long after Mary's death. He did not notice when the slight man, masked and dressed in black, slipped over and injected him with enough poison to stop his heart, and then stealthily left by the same garden door he had entered through.

23

Major Halisbury awoke to the text he was expecting. From an undisclosed number, it simply said, *Done.* He breathed a sigh of relief and then opened his banking app on his phone. He transferred another £5,000 to the account he had sent the same amount to last night and got up out of bed.

He felt some remorse at Garson's passing. He had been a good friend, and a good barrister, for many years. But the major did not get to his position in life by being kind and indulgent. It was enough to hide Joseph for as long as he had. Now, with the police closing in, he had to make sure any and all connections to him and to his organization were closed off. The father was gone. Now he needed to work on getting Joseph out of the country. His vow to protect his godson was sacred. This was the one person he couldn't just remove permanently, even at the risk of his own life.

The first night spent in an unfamiliar bed, with an unfamiliar partner, is always an awkward experience, and not just because the pillows are too fluffy or not fluffy enough. When you're dating someone casually, it's all too easy to try and present a version of yourself that is beyond human. But when you sleep, there are always sounds and smells that can't be avoided and that will lead even the hardest of facades to fracture.

So when the sun began streaming in through the south-facing windows, and both Dee and Rowan began to stir, he was the first to break the silence with a fart loud enough to shake the bed. As he apologized, she began to giggle and said, "Glad you went first" before letting herself break wind directly onto his thighs.

As they were both laughing, he pulled her closer and kissed her shoulder. Her laugh turned to a slight purr of appreciation, so he kept moving up, kissing closer to her neck, and then on it. Once he got about halfway to her ear, she turned around and kissed him, then smiled.

"Good morning."

"It is, isn't it," he said, and returned the kiss.

"Well, it certainly feels like it now," she said, reaching down to emphasize her point before pushing him onto his back and climbing on top.

This time was different from their Sunday afternoon exploits. They were slower, more measured, more about enjoying each other's company and comfort than just trying to induce as much pleasure in the other person as possible. She took her time with him, letting him enjoy the view while she enjoyed the pressure of his body inside her. After about twenty minutes and several climaxes that eventually started to run into each other, she slid herself beside him and invited him to take her. He took his time as well, letting himself build slowly toward the inevitable conclusion, trying not to rush when it became clear she was going to climax again. After she came, she put her hands beside her head and asked him to take them. He did, and then let himself lose control while he held her there, just as she had asked him to.

Once they'd both finished, she ducked off to get a shower, and he just lay there, thinking about how amazing his life had become in the last week. Then he remembered Smalls and what he had to do today. As he listened to the water pouring onto her, he checked his phone. No messages, which was good. Guess everything was still a go.

McRae arrived at headquarters with his bike around nine thirty, a good half-hour before Garson was scheduled to be there. Smalls met him at the entranceway, got the visitor's tags arranged, got the bike tucked into a security booth, and escorted him to the sixth floor for a meeting with Moss.

There was no small talk this morning, with both men focused on the business at hand. When the lift doors opened, Smalls stepped out and McRae followed, and they made their way directly to the black room. Smalls gestured toward a seat on the far side of the table. Once McRae was seated, Smalls asked if he wanted a coffee, but McRae reminded him with a glance that he didn't drink the stuff.

"Tea?"

"Water will do fine, thanks," he said, and Smalls ducked out to get his boss and a glass of water for his guest.

The ride in had been helpful for McRae's focus. He and Dee both had busy days ahead of them—he didn't disclose to her why—so it was easy enough for them to agree to skip breakfast and to meet again when her schedule permitted. Now that he was at headquarters, he was once again focused on the job at hand: questioning the man whose son had killed his family and trying to find out where the bomber was hiding.

By the time Smalls returned to the room with Moss, McRae was already mentally following possible threads, depending on what

Garson said. When they arrived, he instinctively stood to greet Moss as a superior officer. Smalls conducted the brief introductions and handed McRae a glass of water before Moss spoke.

"You do realize, Dr. McRae, that you're only here at the discretion of Agent Smalls. If he wants you out, I want you out. That said, he has advised me that you've been useful on this investigation of his. So you have some rope; just be sure you don't hang yourself with it, understood?"

"Yes, ma'am," McRae said. He liked Moss immediately. There was no frivolity with her, no wasting of time or words. With her, you knew where you stood, and in a field like espionage, that's an incredibly rare quality.

"Smalls will lead the questioning. You and I will be on the other side of the one-way glass but will be able to communicate with him by earpiece. If you have anything to say, keep it succinct, and avoid any idle chatter. I'm sure you're a lovely chap, but this is not the time to get to know you better."

McRae nodded, his attention fixed. It had been a long time since he'd had a commanding officer, but he remembered that this was what it felt like. At the best of times, anyway.

"Now, tell me what you know about Garson."

"Barrister, with Gladstone Chambers; specializes in media law and represents the *Gleaner* but also other publishers; widowed, father of four, including the suspect; Catholic, apparently, but I've no way of measuring his piety, for what that's worth. Nothing that I haven't heard from Smalls or passed along to him already, frankly."

"And where do you think he hid his son?"

"I don't think he hid his son anywhere."

"What do you mean?"

McRae looked at Smalls, and Smalls nodded back before he spoke. "Smalls and I have been talking about this, and we don't think Garson has the means to do that, and from what we've seen so far, it appears that Major Halisbury is at the centre of the wheel here. Garson is a spoke, connecting Halisbury to his son, but that's about it."

"Interesting. Why do you say that?" Moss asked, turning her attention to Smalls and back to McRae.

After waiting for a moment during which Smalls didn't speak, McRae answered. "Partly from my meetings with both men. Garson seemed privileged, but also soft. And as Smalls observed, he also seems to be mourning his wife, so his children have a special place in his heart right now. While I think he would reach out to someone to try and protect his son, I don't think he'd have known how to do it himself if he wanted to. Also, as a barrister, he'd want to be as arm's-length from this as possible."

"Well, maybe we'll find out soon. He should be here shortly. Smalls," Moss said, "head down to the entrance and greet him. McRae and I will be in position."

Smalls left without speaking, and Moss turned once again to McRae. "Martin really has done a great job here, particularly enlisting your help when he was entirely unsupported from the organization. And the initial infiltration at the charity auction was good work. If you decide academia is getting too boring for you, let me know. You might not be a British national, but we can make an exception for a Commonwealth ex-serviceman."

"I can already vote here, so that's something," McRae said as a joke. He always found it amusing that, as a Canadian, he was entitled to vote in UK elections while his American colleagues couldn't. There weren't many perks to the Commonwealth, but that was one.

"True, you can. I won't ask you how, though. Wouldn't do. Let's head down and make sure the equipment is working. You can never be too sure with that."

Twenty minutes later, at five after ten, Moss called down to the front desk from the observation room and asked to speak with Smalls. When she learned Garson wasn't there, rather than tell the MPP or dispatch a public bulletin, Moss called Eyre and requested a check on Garson. She was told Garson hadn't left the house that morning, so Moss ordered a door check and authorized entry if there was no response. Garson's body was discovered in his bed two minutes later, and Eyre contacted Moss, requesting direction. She authorized the agent to contact Scotland Yard and asked for an update on the major. Eyre had already been in touch with the full team, and the major was believed to be in his office at Canary Wharf. By all appearances, there was no foul play, and the only oddity was that the garden door was unlocked.

Smalls, McRae, and Moss reconvened in the black room, with the door shut this time.

"Guess Garson *was* just a spoke in the wheel," said Moss.

"And someone obviously needed him out of the way," Smalls added.

"Okay, but how can we possibly track this to the major?" McRae asked. "And how does this get us any closer to finding the son?"

"It doesn't," Moss said. "If the major is indeed at the centre, then this is him cleaning house, making sure there are no connections between him and the bomber. Aside from MI5 agents, the only people likely to have known of his connection were Garson and Walterson, and maybe Clegg and Banks. Even the driver might not have known who he was driving and might not remember him anyway."

"There are two more," McRae added. "The bomber and me."

"Does he know you're involved?"

"I was followed the other day, so we think he has put together the connection between Smalls and me. In which case, I'm in danger, as, I suppose, is Smalls."

"He's an MI5 agent; he's going to have protection," she said, looking at Smalls before turning to McRae, "but you, you're now in protective custody."

Rowan shook his head. "That's a waste, keeping me in here. If we're right and the major has taken out Walterson and Garson, he'll be trying to clean up all the possible loose ends. This means the bomber and this means me. We don't know where the bomber is, but we can certainly keep tabs on me. And I'm much better bait if I'm not in custody."

"You really think he's going to come for you?" Smalls asked.

"I do. He can't take the chance."

"So what's the plan, then?"

"Well, I don't think the major has been killing anyone by himself," Rowan replied. "Maybe Walterson, but definitely not Garson. That was a professional job and designed to look like natural causes. So no more biking for me until this is done. Given his resources, I think it's safe to assume the major knows where I work and where I live. He won't hit me at work. He'd try to hit me on the bike if he could, to make it look like an accident, but he may also have a backup plan to get in my flat. The building is secure, but nothing a professional couldn't handle. If we can subtly get a guard in with me, we can perhaps catch the assassin unaware. They may be inclined to deal rather than face charges or time inside."

"Are you sure you're willing to take the risk?" Moss asked.

"As I see it, until the major is taken out of commission, I'm in danger. This is our best hope of catching him. It's not something I want, but I was a soldier before I was a professor. I can handle a bit of peril."

A text from Parsons came into the major's burner shortly after nine thirty.

> — Target from yesterday showed at MI5HQ this morning.

This was it, then. Parsons all but confirmed the connection between McRae and Smalls. Still, to verify, the major put in a call to

Clegg, his best hope for intelligence on what the Security Service did and didn't know. He pulled out the burner and punched in Clegg's private mobile number.

"Yes," said a gruff voice on the other end of the line.

"David, it's Hilary."

"Oh, sorry, Major. I didn't realize."

"The disadvantage of having to use a burner, but it's no mind. I need to know something from inside MI5. Anyone you can call?"

"Sure, discreetly, I assume."

"Naturally," the major said. "I need to know if there's anyone involved in the Edinburgh investigation named McRae. May be connected to an Agent Smalls."

"Let me make a call and see what I can find out."

"Call me back at this number as soon as you can," the major said, then ended the call.

He didn't have to wait long—barely long enough to reorient the telescope in his office to look at the spot in Greenwich Park where he'd had his last chat with Walterson—before Clegg called back.

"An old friend says McRae was there this morning to watch Garson's interrogation."

"Okay, thank you," the major said, and abruptly ended the call; Clegg was a soldier, so no more needed to be said between them. Then he sent a reply to the earlier text.

— I have two more, if you're interested.
One is as usual, one is protection.

— You know the price for the usual;
protection is the same per day.

— Protection is out of town.
I'll pay an extra 1k for expenses.

— Fair. Send details.

The major took a photograph of his godson taken at a church function a few years ago from one of his bookshelves, removed it from the frame, and placed it on a piece of paper. Underneath the photo-graph, he wrote, *Protection: Marbledon Cottage, Alkham Valley Road, Kent.* He then took a photo of the photograph and the handwriting and sent it to the contact. From a folder, he withdrew a photograph of McRae, pulled from the department website. Under it, on another sheet of paper, he wrote, *Eliminate. Home: Unit 608, Brown Street Apartments, Brown and George, London W1. Work: LSE, Old Building, 5th floor.* He again took a picture and sent it to the contact.

— Please confirm receipt.

— Receipt confirmed. Send deposit.

The major went to his account and wired £10,000 to the same contact. He'd been reliable so far, and the extra money would be worth the investment if it cut off the ties the Security Service had to him and bought him enough time to extract Joseph from the country. He deleted the photographs from his phone, deleted the texts, and then took the papers and brought them to the office shredder. He'd have to remember to burn that batch later.

McRae was brought by cab to his office. An agent would bring his bike from headquarters to his flat with one slashed tire; they needed to make his routine look as normal as possible. He'd have to walk now, or take the Tube home, but two agents would be with him at all times. He decided to forego the Friend as long as this was going on, instead heading home after work via the Underground like most Londoners. Keep to populated areas, avoid isolation, and make sure he kept his wits about him.

While he was at the office, trying to concentrate on student drafts, a team was setting up in one of the short-term lets in his building. A group of five agents would stay there off and on in shifts, dressed like tourists. They needed the assassin to try and break in, so for the duration McRae would stay in his bedroom when home, while one agent would be positioned in the closet near the door, and the other would be in the bedroom, each on twelve-hour shifts.

All this change was familiar to McRae, but the memories it brought back were distant and unpleasant. He remembered sitting on that roof in a town in Kandahar, waiting and watching for a sign of traffic. He remembered the tension and the boredom, the terrible food, having to avoid going to the privy, if there was a privy, because you didn't want to miss anything. You can get used to feeling endangered, but the human body isn't designed to not know what's going to happen.

He had two consolations. The first was that things were getting close. He could feel it, just the way he could tell on the night they finally observed the convoy in Kandahar that something was about to happen. It's the way the air smells before a thunderstorm, the way the hills of his hometown loomed closer when it was going to rain, clues so subtle that only a trained observer knows what to look for, but everyone who's paying even the slightest attention notices.

The second was that Dee was both busy and safe. She would not come calling tonight, and to make sure she stayed safe, he decided not to have any more encounters with her until this was over. They'd texted a bit around lunchtime when he was at the office, and she confirmed that the meeting was not a bad one for her; she would be taking on a part of Garson's media practice while he was "out of office" and so would be spending much of the day, into the evening, trying to catch up on what he was leaving behind. When around three that afternoon she found out Garson had died, she again texted.

— You won't believe this; he's dead. Garson.

— Seriously? What happened?

— No one knows yet. In his sleep apparently.

— Damn. I'm so sorry to hear that.
I know he was a good mentor to you.

— He was, and I was hoping he would continue to be. Not that I have time to grieve—these files are now my files, and I'm going to have to get up to speed fast.

— Good luck. You've got this.
He believed in you, and so do I.

— That's sweet. Looks like I won't be able to see you until the weekend, though.

— I understand. We can text when you need a break. In the meantime, keep your focus.
You're brilliant and you've got this.

— Thanks. You're the best.

— Again, screenshotting for future reference. 😌

24

"You're not keeping me in my room," McRae said, point blank, to the senior of the two agents assigned to protect him at his flat.

"But it's the only really safe place in here," said the agent, an old dog named Billings.

"First, it's not an entirely safe place; it has a window. Second, my safety is secondary here. Third, if we're under surveillance, and it's entirely possible we're under surveillance, we need things to look as normal as possible. And I don't normally spend a whole evening in my bedroom."

Despite his visible frustration, and to the slight enjoyment of the junior agent at having his superior taken down a peg, Billings had to accept this logic. "Fine, but I'll be in the bedroom when you're not, and Parker here will have to wait in the closet."

So he had noticed Parker's smirk, then. Sorry, Parker, thought McRae.

After receiving his assignment, the assassin went back to his own flat—a South Bank penthouse in a nondescript, glass-and-steel structure overlooking much of the old City of London—and had a nap. Overnight assignments required rest afterward, and now he was staring down the barrel of another. He set his alarm for two p.m. and let himself drift into a dreamless sleep. It had been years now that he'd plied his trade assisting various parts of London's criminal underworld—and the occasional foreign government—and had made enough of a name for himself that no one questioned his methods or his fee.

Once he woke, the assassin made his way by motorbike to Edgware Road, parked in an underground lot, and then walked the extra half a dozen blocks to McRae's flat, doing a quick circuit of surveillance. He then buzzed random flats in McRae's building until one simply opened the door without question, then he made his way inside.

He initially stopped on the seventh floor, one above McRae's, to get a sense of the layout of the building. He located the stairwells and noted how far they were—twenty paces—from McRae's flat. He then made his way three floors up to the roof, leaving one of the access doors taped open to ensure he could get back in later. He tucked himself into a corner behind the maintenance shed and watched the night fall.

His calling card was that his work was typically undetectable. He usually used fairly high concentrations of toxins or poisons that, unless someone did an autopsy, simply looked like a heart attack or some other natural cause of death. And if someone did do a toxicology report, he left so few traces of how it was administered that it took even longer to figure out that this was a homicide. By then any trace evidence, which he was careful about not leaving, would be long gone. If you wanted a statement death, or someone blown up, go to someone else.

As one a.m. approached, the assassin quickly prefilled a syringe with his preferred poison, cyanide, and placed it into a cigar tube.

This allowed him to carry it unnoticed in trouser pockets without any danger to himself.

He rose, making sure there was no trace of his presence on the rooftop, and returned to the stairwell, taking his tape off the door and closing it quietly behind him. He swiftly made his way down four flights of stairs to the sixth floor and walked to McRae's south-facing flat.

As with most flats, the door lock was a relatively rudimentary spring and pin one that only took him about ten seconds to pick. Once done, he allowed the door to fall open naturally, making sure not to force it or trip any alarms. He was silent and entered the carpeted apartment wearing soft-soled shoes that ensured his footsteps would not be heard. A small light was on outside the bathroom; otherwise, the room was dark. There was a small closet beside him on the right and a floor mat with McRae's shoes on it.

The assassin stepped into the apartment, leaving the door open behind him. The kitchen area was to his immediate right behind the closet, with a living room ahead of him. The bedroom was evidently behind the closed door on the opposite side of the room. His nose told him that the kitchen was seldom used but that the apartment was frequently cleaned. His ears told him that McRae didn't snore, which was fairly common for a healthy young man. He could, nonetheless, hear breathing, so someone was home and seemed calm, if not positively asleep.

As he walked across the living room he took a quick glance into the bathroom. It appeared as spartan as the rest of the apartment, with one toothbrush sitting beside the sink. Good, he lived alone. He withdrew the cigar tube from his right pocket, not looking down at it as he used his thumb and forefinger to separate the two halves of the tube. He placed the top half in his right pocket before withdrawing the syringe. He slipped the other half into his left pocket then reached out to open the bedroom door.

Before he could turn the knob, the assassin was startled by a sound behind him. Instinctively, he turned and prepared to attack with the syringe. A man stood just outside the closet, holding a firearm pointed at him. Without thinking, the assassin stepped to the side and then charged directly at the man. The shot missed, and the assassin pushed the man back into the wall, winding him and knocking the gun from his hand before he could fire again.

Hearing the shot, McRae and Billings emerged from the room to find the assassin in the closet, looking for the fallen side arm. McRae leapt on him, knocking the syringe to the side in the process and preventing the assassin from getting the gun. Pinned, the assassin struggled beneath McRae's frame. He attempted to push McRae off but found him both too heavy and too strong to make easy work of. So he slammed the back of his head into McRae's nose. McRae's physical reaction to the pain allowed the assassin to roll out from under him.

The assassin was heading to the door when another shot rang out, from Billings, standing in the doorway of the bedroom. This one hit the assassin in the back, and he fell to the floor. He let out a weak laugh, which soon turned to a blood-spurting cough. McRae yelled "Fuck!" and rolled him over as life drained from his eyes.

Blood dripping from his nose, McRae began patting the assassin's pockets. He found the two halves of the cigar tube in his front pockets, and a phone tucked into a pouch sewn into the front of his trousers. Meanwhile, Billings checked in on Parker, who was struggling to his feet, then called in to command as the agents in the nearby flat came through the door.

McRae pulled the assassin's phone from its secure compartment. "Maybe this will tell us who sent him."

It was a recent iPhone, one with facial recognition. McRae yelled to Parker to turn on the light. Once the room was illuminated, he held the phone up to the face of the assassin, and it unlocked. McRae opened the messages and saw a series of numbers. He clicked on the most recent and found two photographs; his own and that of Joseph Garson. Whoever sent these had ordered his death. He scrolled further and found a photo of Charles Garson with his address and confirmation of hit and payment.

He clicked on the photo of Joseph Garson and read: *Marbledon Cottage, Alkham Valley Road, Kent*. He passed the phone to Billings.

"Here, take this," McRae said. "It's evidence and needs to be in your hands, not mine."

Within an hour, during which time a number of the agents knocked on doors, explaining to terrified residents that they were perfectly safe now and that they should, if possible, go back to sleep, Smalls, Moss, and a battalion of police officers had descended on the building.

Smalls and Moss conducted their inquiry of McRae, Billings, and Parker. Once Moss had reviewed the phone, taking the phone number of the assassin's employer from it and the details of Joseph Garson's location, she handed it off to an agent in an evidence control vest, noting that it needed to be processed immediately. She got on the phone and ordered Eyre and his team to head to Arkham Valley Road and arrest Joseph Garson at Marbledon Cottage, preferably before morning.

Having questioned the trio about the assassin's last minutes, Moss dismissed the two agents then turned to McRae. "I can't exactly dismiss you from your own bedroom, and there's not much about this case you don't know anyway, so I hope you don't mind if this becomes our command centre for a few more minutes."

"Not like I was going to get any sleep tonight. Might need to cancel my classes tomorrow, though."

"I can provide you a note, if you like. Class cancelled on account of national security," she said, with a rare smile.

McRae laughed but didn't feel it. His thoughts were still on the life leaving the eyes of the man sent to kill him and on the last time he'd watched someone die, a little over a year ago.

"That would be nice, thanks. It's been a rough night," he said.

A phone call came through on Moss' mobile.

"That was the tech department. They've tracked the number to a burner purchased by a Paul Samuels. Know that name?"

"Not off the top of my head," Smalls said. "Where was the burner used?"

Moss asked the contact on the other end of the phone. "Canary Wharf and Kensington, mostly. The major's office is in Canary Wharf, right? Can we pin down the locations of the major at the times the calls were placed?"

"Cross-reference with Eyre's patrols, and I'd say so," Smalls replied. "Is it enough for a warrant for the major's phone?"

"Should be," said Moss.

"Okay, that's a daylight problem. For now, let's get this man's apartment back to him."

"I can't possibly stay here tonight," said Rowan, his nose now stuffed with two tissues and with a bruise blooming around his eyes. "With the blood spatter in my living room, I'm going to need at least a couple of days to get this cleaned up."

"Quite right," Moss said. "We usually put people up in the Hilton. Will that do?"

McRae thought this was insane. The Hilton was hundreds of pounds a night. But who was he to argue?

"Of course, thanks."

"And Smalls will arrange cleanup, won't you, Smalls?" Moss said.

Smalls rolled his eyes, smirked, and walked out of the room to place a call.

"I do have one other favour to ask," McRae said. "I'd like to talk with the bomber, once you've got him in custody."

Moss became serious again. "I'm not sure that's wise. You've been very helpful, but I won't have you interfering with this operation."

"I just want to show him this," McRae said and turned his arms so Moss could see the scarring.

Moss thought for a moment before noncommittally saying, "I'll see what I can do."

McRae packed a bag with enough clothing for a week, including two pairs of trunks, and met the agency driver at the door of his apartment building. He checked into the Hilton and, a half-hour later, was standing on the balcony of his room, looking westward over Hyde Park from the eighth floor. Dawn was breaking behind him, leaving a rosy glow over the fresh leaves on all the trees, the tallest of which were just below his eye level.

He thought to himself, *I wish Dee could see this*, followed quickly by two other thoughts. The first, a sense of guilt, that it was Dee and not Lynn or Harris that he thought of sharing this with. And second, the realization that since he wanted to share a sunrise with Dee, he must be in love with her. For McRae, the surest sign that you love someone is that you want to share things with them. For bad things, sharing is a balm. For the good, it enhances the experience. Either way, he was most definitely falling in love.

But the guilt would not go away so easily. He had done what he could to help bring their killer to justice, but was that enough?

He looked out over the park, watching the details emerge as the glow grew stronger, and Lynn's voice came to him again, this time clear: "This is what you are supposed to do, my love. The sun rises whether you want it to or not. You fall in love again, whether you want to or not. Let it happen. Don't sacrifice your future for your past. We will always be with you, but you must let yourself live. You don't deserve to be alone."

McRae took his phone and sent a text.

— Good morning.
Hope you had a good night.

A few minutes later, a response.

— Good morning to you. A short night—
was up late digesting Garson's old files. And
now up early to get ready for court. You?

— Eventful to say the least. Guess where I am?

He took a photo of the view to show her. To share with her, if he was being honest.

— Is that Hyde Park? Are you
at the Dorchester or something?

— Close, the Hilton. Long story.
Can I tell you over drinks tonight?

— Oh probably. I'm going to need
one after work today. Usual place?

— How about you come to me tonight?
I'm told they have a great bar here.

— Sure, for a change. Now I'm curious.
How'd you end up in the Hilton overnight?

— Like I said, long story. Text me when
you're on your way, and I'll meet you here.

— All right, keep your secrets. Talk more later.

Eyre's team arrived at Marbledon Cottage just as McRae was looking at the sunrise. They found no evidence of activity and decided to storm the entrances. Three agents, including Eyre, waited at the front door while two teams of two went around back to the garden and garage entrances. At precisely 6:20, when they all barged in, Joseph Garson was upstairs, pulling on some pants and reaching for a cricket bat kept beside the bed. When Agent Jenson emerged through the bedroom door, Garson took a swing and missed. Jenson jumped on him while Eyre grabbed the bat and a third agent reached for her cuffs. They escorted one of the most dangerous men in Britain, dressed only in pyjama pants, to the patrol car, cuffed and cautioned against saying anything that might be used in court against him.

Meanwhile, in London, the night judge was meeting with a lawyer from Her Majesty's Security Service, domestic branch, and hearing an application for a warrant to examine a telephone believed to be on the person of Major Hilary Halisbury of 8 Victoria Road, Kensington, London. The judge immediately knew whom the counsel was talking about and looked carefully at the evidence presented to her. The number had been used to provide contact information for Mr. Charles Garson, QC, who had died the previous evening under suspicious circumstances, and then two more individuals, one of whom had been attacked by the bearer of the phone while under police protection. Her ass covered, the justice granted the application. The warrant was issued immediately, and the lawyer called Moss with the news.

By this point, Moss was waiting in a patrol car on High Street. Once the word came through that the warrant was issued, she went immediately to the door of 8 Victoria Road and knocked.

"Good morning, Major. I'm Acting Director Moss, MI5, and I'm enforcing a warrant that's just been issued to seize your telephone."

"Where is your warrant, then, Ms. Moss?" the major asked, maintaining his usual calm expression.

"If you require the physical, signed warrant, I can advise that it will be here in about fifteen minutes. Until then, I am required to detain you in the name of Her Majesty to ensure that there is no tampering with any evidence. We can do that here, or inside, as you wish."

"I'll wait here," he said, and stepped out onto the landing, allowing the door to close behind him.

As they stood in silence on the doorstep, the major let scenarios run through his mind. Clearly the assassin had failed. Was he dead or just captured? He had already deleted the texts, so there was no worry about that, but if they had the assassin's phone, he would be incriminated anyway. Still, incriminated he could work with. His reputation would be hurt, at first, but if he were exonerated, he could come back from this. He almost smiled at the thought that he would need to call Garson, before realizing that he couldn't. Joseph couldn't compromise him, as he did not know that his godfather was behind his safeguarding. On that side, intermediaries were always used to avoid exactly this problem. Still, the phone was problematic.

After fifteen minutes, the physical warrant arrived, and the major allowed Moss to enter his home. He told her the phone was on his bedside table, so she retrieved it, checked the number to confirm it was the same, then bagged it. When she returned to the front steps, she placed the major under arrest for ordering the murders of Charles Garson and Rowan McRae. He remained stoic and silent as he was placed in the patrol car and whisked off to headquarters for processing and questioning.

25

A call came in at ten o'clock as McRae was making his way down to the Hyde Park Corner station and the Piccadilly line to head to his eleven o'clock class.

"McRae, Moss here. Have you decided to cancel your class? There's someone here you want to meet. A couple of people, in fact."

"Joseph Garson and the major, I presume?"

"Aye," she said. "When can we expect you?"

"I'm on my way to class now. Should be there by quarter past twelve."

"Okay, we'll hold them until then."

"Much appreciated."

McRae sat down across from the major.

"So, you made the connection between Smalls and me, did you?"

The major said nothing, but he had looked with curiosity at McRae when he walked in and then checked himself, adopting a deliberate, studied neutral expression.

"That's fine. You're not who I want to see anyway. He's in the next room, and I doubt he'll be as quiet. Particularly once he sees these." McRae turned his arms over to show the major.

For a brief instant, McRae saw a flash of pain swipe across the major's face. It would do. The man knew who he had been harbouring and who had now bested him. McRae stood up and walked out of the room, knowing any discussion would be pointless.

Moss was waiting for him outside. "Well, not much more out of him for you than for us so far. Doesn't matter, really. It was his phone. He deleted the numbers. He'll try and claim evidence tampering or planting. He may give up the driver and say it was he who ordered it, though I doubt it. It's as good a case as we have.

"This guy, on the other hand. He's only too happy to talk. So far, he's said that he's a prophet, a messiah, a messenger, an avenging angel, and so on. Clearly a religious motive. And he confessed freely, after caution. So whatever he says to you won't be necessary for prosecution anyway. Still, please don't say anything that would undermine a conviction. No threats and no violence."

"I understand," McRae said, thinking, *Lynn wouldn't have wanted that.*

He entered the room and took stock of Joseph Garson. He was a slight man, with thick dark hair and a heavy beard, but not unkempt. He did not smell of anything in particular, despite a long time in the countryside and away from human contact. His eyes were exceptional, though: dark, small, and quick. As McRae took him in, Garson was doing the same thing.

Garson spoke first. "Another infidel to question my works?"

"No, no questions. I just wanted to show you something," Rowan said, pulling up his sleeves to expose his forearms. "I was there, and so were my wife and three-month-old son. These scars are all that is left of them. I'm Rowan McRae. My wife was Lynn and my son was Harris. You killed them. All I could do was hold her while she burned, until now. Because I helped bring you in. I'm not going to harm you; Lynn wouldn't have wanted that, and I wouldn't have wanted Harris to do that if he were in my shoes. But I want you to know that the father of a child you murdered helped catch you. And I want you to remember these scars when you're burning in whatever hell you believe in."

Garson was momentarily speechless, and Rowan took advantage of the silence to leave. He didn't expect to get the last word but was glad of it anyway. He waited until the door closed before he pulled his sleeves back down and buttoned them up. Moss met him outside the interrogation room.

"That was fine. Probably can't be interpreted as a threat of any kind, and I certainly can't blame you for wanting a private word with him."

"I figured it'd be okay. Not sure it'll get me the closure I was hoping for, but it's a start."

"A start few people in your position ever get, really. But let me tell you this: I've known a lot of people who've lost loved ones in tragic circumstances. Closure doesn't come from finding justice or seeking revenge. It doesn't even come from being able to confront the person who has wronged you. Closure comes from within, McRae, so if you're going to find it, it won't be in an interrogation chamber or a courtroom. If you find it, it'll be by reconciling your past and what you've lost with your future and what you have yet to find. Live your life in a way that would make them proud but that isn't committed to trying to bring the dead back to life."

She spoke like someone who knew what she was talking about, as if she had experienced a similar loss as Rowan had and that she too knew how hard it was to move on from it.

While Moss was speaking, Smalls had emerged from the control room.

"Show you out?" he said.

"Should we need your help again, we'll be in touch," Moss added, reaching out her hand.

McRae took her hand firmly. "In the meantime, I'll try not to run up too much of a tab at the Hilton," he said, laughing softly.

"How much damage can one academic do in a week, really? We'll be in touch once your flat is available again."

"Lift is here," Smalls said, and McRae let go of Moss' hand and followed his friend. Once they were on the way down, Smalls broke the silence.

"Drinks at the Friend?"

"Not today. Got a date."

"Look at you go. Good man. Tomorrow, then?"

"Aye, would be great. And thanks."

"Thank you, Rowan. Without you, we wouldn't have gotten this done."

"Sure, but I've been thinking about it, and what really broke this wide open wasn't just me being at the art auction and meeting Garson. It was the *Guardian* article. Whoever was the leak is who we really need to thank."

"I've been thinking about that too. Any idea who it could have been?"

"One. We just left her on the fourth floor."

Smalls was momentarily stunned. He'd never considered the possibility that Moss was the leak, but he had to admit, now that McRae had planted the suggestion, it made sense.

"Best not ask, then."

"Best not," McRae agreed.

When the bell told them they'd reached the ground floor, he turned to shake Smalls' hand. "Tomorrow at five. Should be a match on."

"Deal."

Rowan was waiting for Dee in the lobby of the Hilton when she arrived at twenty after six.

"You've been mysterious today," she said, coming over and kissing him while taking in his injuries. "What happened to your face?"

"It's been a hell of a day. Can I buy you a drink?"

"Absolutely. Been a hell of one for me too."

They made their way to the hotel bar and took up two seats in the window. He ordered a double measure of Caol Ila 15 for himself and an Aperol spritz for her, putting both on the room.

"So what happened to your apartment?"

He began his story, telling her about Smalls and their work together in Afghanistan, how Smalls had reached out to him a little over a week ago now, how they'd been working together to catch the bomber and the people who had been hiding him.

"In fact, it's how we met."

"What do you mean?"

"While I was indeed a Rutherford Fellow and had good reason to be at that charity art auction, Smalls already had suspicions that the Halisbury family was involved somehow in undermining his investigation. So he sent me there to see who else the major and Lord Rutherford met with. I certainly didn't expect to meet you there."

"Was I a suspect?"

"Never at any point. When Walterson came in—he was the MI5 director that died a couple days ago—he went and spoke to the major, who then spoke with Garson. That was how we connected the three. But you were never under any investigation, and no one else you work with was either. Far as I know, it was just Garson."

"So who killed Garson? And you still haven't told me what happened to your flat."

"We had surveillance on the major after the art auction and the *Guardian* leak. He caught on to it and started cleaning house. He may have killed Walterson, and he hired someone to kill Garson. He then hired the same person to kill me." Dee, riveted by his story, looked aghast. "When Garson died before he was supposed to come in for questioning, we figured I might be in danger, so security from MI5 stayed at my place last night. There was no danger when you were there on Sunday, and there won't be any more danger now. The assassin came and gave me a broken nose, but one of the agents took him out. My apartment has a big blood stain in the carpet and a bullet hole in the wall but should be back to normal—with new carpet and a repaired wall—by Monday of next week. In the meantime, I stay here, on Her Majesty's dime."

Dee took a long, deep breath, looked him in the eye, and raised her glass. "To Her Majesty, then."

"Indeed," said Rowan and raised his, before he continued. "The killer had a phone on him with my contact info and the bomber's location. By morning, the major and the bomber were both under arrest. I went to MI5 today to confront the bomber. I showed him my scars."

"Rowan, my God. You've had all this going on for the last week and didn't say anything?"

"Yeah, and I'm sorry about that. It was something I needed to do. It's not that I didn't want to tell you, it's that until now I wasn't allowed to tell you. Still, two good things came from it. My family's killer is now behind bars and is likely to stay there for the rest of his life."

"And the second?"

"I met you."

Dee smiled and reached out her hand. "I am glad you're safe and that you can tell me all this now. But for the record, in the future if you're ever in mortal peril, please tell me about it."

"Of course. I'm just glad there's a future."

"Of course there's a future."

He looked into her eyes and found they were locked on his. He reached out his hands and held hers between them.

"Come on, let's bring these upstairs. You really should see the view."

EPILOGUE

Rowan and Dee made their way up Calton Hill in silence. It was two years since Rowan had been here, and there was a new monument on top of the hill. It was a bronze sculpture designed to look like a stag, a memorial to those who had died in the massacre, which would be dedicated today by the prime minister and blessed by the local pagan community at the Beltane celebrations that evening. It was morning now, and they had the hill largely to themselves.

The statue was already covered in flowers, and Dee had brought her own to add as well. Rowan, however, had brought with him two chess pieces, a queen and a rook, modelled after the Norse pieces found a century ago on an island near the one after which his son was named.

When they arrived at the sculpture, Dee walked up first and laid her bouquet of sunflowers on the top of the growing pile. Rowan took a moment, then walked up and made room in the flowers so he could kneel before the left foreleg of the stag. He took the two chess pieces and laid them behind the leg, one beside the other and with a small leather string wrapped around them. Tears came and fell softly down his tired, bearded face, but he remained silent. You never really say goodbye to the people you love. You carry them with you. But if Lynn taught him anything, it was that life goes on. As he laid the two pieces there, a totem of what he had lost, he knew he was getting ready to move on.

Dee approached him from behind and laid her hand on his shoulder. He reached up and touched her fingers. Whatever shape his grief took from here, it would no longer be vengeance. There would always be grief, yes, but there would also be love. He had someone to share it with now, and he would no longer be alone.

ACKNOWLEDGEMENTS

A confession: I wrote this book having absolutely no idea what I was doing. Only now, after the editing process, do I think I have the vaguest idea how to write a good crime/spy/mystery novel. I'm indebted to the wisdom and kindness of Brock Peters with Galley Creative and Marianne Ward for their insight and patience. They both walked me through the process and made me a better writer as a result.

Thanks also to the staff at Jack Astor's—especially Jessie, Nick, and Matt—Boston Pizza, Big's, and Terre Cafe in St. John's where this was largely written. You brought me hot chocolate, or Diet Pepsi with a wedge of lemon; chatted with me when I wanted to chat; and left me alone when I didn't—all of which I appreciate. You're all good people and deserve to be tipped better than you are.

My gratitude to Rebecca Rose and all the folks at Breakwater Books for taking a chance on me, these characters, and this book. You've made a dream come true.

Finally, I could not have written this book without the unwavering support, encouragement, and patience of my brilliant wife Heather and my amazing elder son Reid. If this is a dream come true, your love is what makes me able to dream. You both put up with me popping out for a few hours at night, a few times a week, to write. Or really, to play, because that's what writing is to me. Without the two of you, and now also our darling baby Lewis, I'd be adrift. I love you all more than words can properly express.

THE AUTHOR

By day, Ray Critch is a lawyer who has appeared at every level of court in Newfoundland and Labrador and at the Supreme Court of Canada. By night, he is a happily married father of two who, once in a while, manages to carve off some spare time to pop down to a local sports bar and do some writing. In what now feels like a past life, but was actually 2010, he obtained a PhD in philosophy from the University of Edinburgh. Before being called to the bar in 2016, he taught at universities in Edinburgh, Vienna, and St. John's.